HE WAS THE PREACHER OF RIGHTEOUSNESS,
THE TENTH RECORDED PATRIARCH, AND
THE SECOND FOUNDER OF THE HUMAN RACE.
HE WAS AN HEIR OF SALVATION, THE
"REST GIVER," AND A FATHER OF MESSIAH.
NONE OF US WOULD EXIST WITHOUT HIM.

NOAH

ELLEN GUNDERSON TRAYLOR

TYNDALE HOUSE PUBLISHERS, INC.
WHEATON, ILLINOIS

Scripture references are from the King James Version
unless otherwise noted.

Second printing, June 1987
Library of Congress Catalog Card Number 85-51285
ISBN 0-8423-4703-8
Copyright 1985 by Ellen Gunderson Traylor
Printed in the United States of America

TO MY SONS
AARON AND NATHAN

I will say of the Lord,
He is my refuge and my fortress:
My God; in him will I trust.

Psalm 91:2

But as the days of Noah were,
so shall also the coming of the Son of man be.

Matthew 24:37

HIERARCHY OF BEINGS
AND THEIR VARIOUS TITLES

Lucifer
also called: Angel of Light,
Golden Orb, Great Governor of the Skies,
Lightbearer, Master of the Air,
Mentor of the Overseers, Orb of Wisdom,
Oversoul, Prince of the Power of the Air,
Prince of This World, the Serpent,
Son of Morning, Spirit of the Air,
Sun, Universal Spirit

Fallen Angels
also called: Angels of Light,
Angels of Lucifer, Beings, Daemons,
Fallen Ones, Gods, Governors, Great Ones,
Lords, Masters, Olympians (e.g., Poseidon),
Overseers, Princes, Rulers of Darkness,
Sons of God, Watchers

Nephilim
(Offspring of Sons of God and mortal women)
also called: Beings, Fallen Ones, Giants,
Heroes
(e.g., Temple Guard, Artemis Beyond the North),
Meteors,
"Mighty Men of Old, Men of Renown,"
Titans

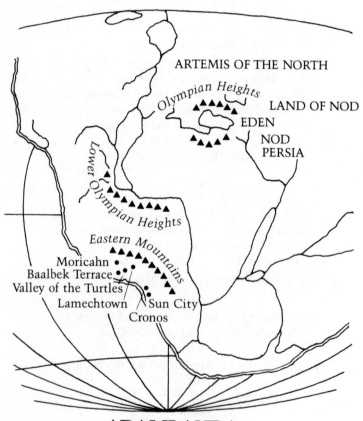

ARTEMIS OF THE NORTH

Olympian Heights

LAND OF NOD

EDEN

NOD

PERSIA

Lower Olympian Heights

Eastern Mountains

Moricahn
Baalbek Terrace
Valley of the Turtles
Lamechtown   Sun City
Cronos

ADAMLANDA
(Adlandia or Atlantis)

A NOTE TO THE READER

WHEN I was asked to write a book on Noah, I had no idea that I would be opening myself up to a world of mystery and adventure such as is found on the following pages.

Many who have read my previous works, *Song of Abraham*, *John—Son of Thunder*, and *Mary Magdalene*, have responded favorably to the fact that I have always endeavored to maintain accuracy in my research and faithfulness to the Scriptures. When it came to recreating the time of Noah—the pre-Flood world—I entered into an arena of investigation which was at once exhilarating and baffling.

Much has been written in recent years by scientists regarding what the earth may have been like before the Deluge, an event to which nearly every culture on the globe testifies in myth and legend, and which the planet itself confirms in its catastrophic evidence. I owe much of *Noah* to the findings and theories of geologists, hydraulic engineers, explorers, archaeologists, and zoologists whose insights I have gleaned.

But scientific questions about the pre-Flood earth are only one aspect of the intrigue which surrounds the period. Far more important for the understanding of human and spiritual history are questions regarding the world system of the day—its government, its technology, its decline. When we investigate this realm we are confronted with a dilemma: should we limit ourselves to the very vague and sketchy clues which are given in Genesis, or should we look to extrabiblical speculations?

The historical novelist does well to use whatever sources are available to shed light on a period. Specifically, I needed to know the identity of the "sons of God" in Genesis 6:1, 2, and of the "giants" of "Nephilim" in Genesis 6:4. My treatment of this much-debated issue would lay the foundation for the entire story, and so I tried to investigate every theory, no matter how bizarre, before I drew my own conclusions. The reader may be surprised at the direction I chose; but my interpretation is based on the best thinking of reputable scholars, historians, and theologians, from Josephus to Unger, from Plato to Albright.

And I did not shy away from writings of more eccentric theorists, such as those which suggest that colossal works of architecture and advanced technology are evidence of a highly advanced ancient society. The legend of Atlantis certainly required my attention, as did extrabiblical Jewish tradition, and the countless folktales and legends of a pre-Flood world in societies across time and around the globe. Many details of my story are the result of these studies, as I tried to include whatever could be consistently meshed with Scripture, to the benefit of the plot.

Whenever one writes about ancient human history, the potential for misunderstanding is always a threat, especially when dealing with the roots of nations and groups of people. A word needs to be said regarding my treatment of the so-called "curse of Ham," an interpretation of a passage which has led to countless injustices and tragedies throughout the history of black/white interaction. In dealing with this very volatile subject, I present the "curse" not as a punishment, but as an admonition applied to the entire human family. I believe that it is not a racial indictment, but a tracing of the consequences of one man's choices on generations of his descendants. I believe this story highlights man's free will—whether or not he will choose God's way—and it is a lesson for people of every color and time.

Also, regarding the genealogy of Noah, I have opted to use the "gap" theory, propounded by many of the best historians and scholars.

Our modern, Western civilization tends to draw a distinct line between the physical and the spiritual. However, one cannot do this and bring an open mind to the story of Noah. To grasp this is to grasp the underlying premise of this book.

In conclusion, if you should find within these pages a discussion of your favorite unsolved mystery, don't be surprised. I encountered several of my favorites as I delved into the time of Noah, and came away amazed at how many unexplained phenomena may well be solved if we ever find a detailed chronicle of the period.

Likewise, if the society presented here, in its manifestation of good and evil, strikes you as familiar, that is because history repeats itself. This is a story, not only of Noah's time, but in many ways of our own.

Meanwhile, until the ark is found (and I believe we *will* find it) this is my version of the captain's log.

May Jesus, the Ark of Salvation, guide your journey.

Ellen Gunderson Traylor
Spokane, Washington

P   A   R   T   I

GIANTS IN THE EARTH

Remember the days of old. . . . When the Most
High gave to the nations their inheritance,
when he separated the sons of men, he fixed
the bounds of the peoples according to the number
of the sons of God [the overseeing Angels].

Deuteronomy 32:7, 8, RSV

And it came to pass, when men began to multiply
on the face of the earth, and daughters were
born unto them, that the sons of God saw the
daughters of men that they were fair; and they took
them wives of all which they chose.

Genesis 6:1, 2, KJV

The Nephilim [or giants] were on the earth in those
days, and also afterward, when the sons of God
came in to the daughters of men, and they
bore children to them. These were the mighty men
that were of old, the men of renown.

Genesis 6:4, RSV

ONE

No breeze had parted the lush bank of undergrowth all morning, and no upstart bird or animal's alarm had revealed the Spectator lurking at the meadow's hem. Even the secluded pond below had seen no activity since early dawn when forest creatures had taken their morning drinks. But now it was full of life, and it was upon this life that the Watcher feasted his gaze.

The four daughters of Moricahn had come to the waters to bathe. There was not one with whom the Watcher could not be pleased. The reports of his hirelings had been quite accurate—indeed, understatements! The damsels rivaled any who had been brought to him in the City of Sun. It had been a wise decision on his part to go forth and spy out the fields himself.

The Watcher took a deep breath and smiled, self-satisfied. City women wearied him with their pallid skin, their insipid wiles. Here was the essence of human vitality, sporting before him. *Female flesh as it was designed to be,* he reasoned, *when the Master of the Air had first brought it forth from Eden.*

The young women were dark, their olive skin deepened to a ruddy glow by outdoor life. Their bare arms and legs glistened, long and sinewy in the water's sheen. *Four fawns,* he mused. *Gazelles!* Such a difficult choice the maidens presented, each with her black-brown hair and supple innocence.

But he need not choose just yet. Let him revel in the moment, if he *never* made a choice. Unexpectedly, however, his attention was drawn to the far bank, against the hill, separating the pond from Moricahn's little farm.

Another young woman was approaching the waters, and the Watcher's breath came in a splinter.

My lady! he groaned, but not so much as to be heard. This one was older than the others, as evidenced by her more graceful carriage and rounded figure. Her legs, too, were long, her arms burnished by the Light of Heaven.

Though a skimming tunic concealed her body, he could see where the fabric was drawn in to her waist that she was a woman, not a girl. And he wondered who she was, what human male might call her his own.

The Watcher raised a hand and carefully pulled back the branches of his bower to get a better view. He thought on the legends of these mountain females. He did not know how much to believe of what he had heard: that they had the senses of wild deer, that they could discern the crack of a twig and see as well as a bird of prey at a hundred cubits, that their ability to flee, their uncanny adeptness in the forest would have them up and gone at an instant's warning. He did not know how much to believe, but he knew he must not risk the loss of this moment.

"*Lady*," he whispered, his heart skipping erratically.

Were she to join her sisters in the bath, were she to disrobe before him as they unwittingly had done, he feared he could not maintain his secret vigil. He was not certain he could remain silent. But his hand, where it grasped the branch, was clammy with the hope that she would do so—and it suddenly slid down the slippery tree limb in an anxious motion.

Had the young girls in the water not been busy greeting the newcomer with giddy laughter at that instant, the Watcher knew she would have perceived his inept rustling in the bushes. His muscles tensed, and he steadied himself.

It soon became clear that the woman would not be joining the swimmers, but was bent on some other purpose. The Spectator's disappointment was mixed with curiosity as to her mood and intentions. She gave only a fleeting response to the greetings of her fellow females and seemed most concerned for the shadows along the bank and the hidden depths of the forest. Frequently she scanned the treetops and the sky just above them, and the Watcher wondered if she knew.

Suddenly, one of the maidens dashed a cold handful of pond water across the lady's bare legs, and then pushed quickly back through the shallows, laughing and teasing, "Come in, Adala! Why do you linger?"

The young woman on the shore smiled obligingly, then knelt down, her light brown hair falling across her torso like the mane of a wild unicorn. She dipped her hand into the sun-flecked waters and returned the gesture, appeasing her antagonist with a half-hearted splash.

"I have not come to play, cousin," she called. "I have come to bring you back."

The pond-sprite was crestfallen. "But Papa said it was a safe day! He said we could stay till noon. Surely he has not changed his mind!"

Adala braced herself on one hand where she knelt and scanned the banks of the pond once again. She pushed back her heavy fall of sun-streaked hair and peered warily over her shoulder. The Watcher across the way studied her perfect features and his eyes traveled down her graceful neck where she had exposed it, and fell down to the round suggestion of her bosom.

Instantly, Adala stood, her quick green eyes flashing on the distant bower with cat-like intuition. Her hand went to her throat and she lightly gathered the slack at the neck of her tunic. "Quick!" she called to her friends in a low but urgent voice. "You must return now!"

The nymph who had baited her for play was most indignant. "*You* go back, Adala!" She shrugged, turning to her sisters. "We do not need to leave till Papa himself sends for us!"

The other bathers had nodded their agreement and turned to further sport, when the branches were parted. On the instant, all five females were poised like alerted does. And when the Watcher stepped forward the ones in the water leaped for the bank on which Adala stood, scrambling for the short linen garments they had stashed among the bushes.

The four daughters of Moricahn need not have been so alarmed, however. Their native beauty had ceased to jeopardize them. For since their cousin had arrived, she alone was the Watcher's focus.

Adala studied the Being on the distant shore with rigid terror. He was, indeed, more than a man. She knew it on the instant and had, in fact, sensed his super-human presence the moment she had entered the little vale. Her father, Lamech, had sent her to stay with Uncle Moricahn to protect her from just such an encounter.

She could scarcely believe than an Overseer would have traveled this far from the cities on such an errand.

Her four cousins were crowded at her back now, their wet skin goose-prickled beneath clinging gowns, and their hair streaming rivulets down their arms as they held tight to her in speechless fear.

At last the eldest whispered, "*Can it be, Adala? Is this one of them?*"

Adala's mouth was dry, but she managed, "*It can be nothing else.*"

He stood nearly seven feet tall, there on the far shore, his wine-red garment contrasting splendidly against the jungle greenery which framed him. The short garb fit the legends told of the magnificent fabric the Overlords were accustomed to donning. It was not of wool or linen. It was soft in appearance, yet glinted like myriad overlapping scales. It shimmered in the morning light, refracting and casting off crimson sparkles when he moved. However, the Daemon which she concluded him to be, hardly moved. The glints off his clothing were cast from the mere rise and fall of his chest as he tried to steady his breathing and his stubbornly racing heart.

For he, too, was afraid. Not with the same fear Adala and her cousins experienced—not fear of danger; rather it was fear of his own emotions, of the beauty of the woman before him, and of her power to reject him.

He knew she could not violate his will if he chose to take her. Her strength could not match his, nor could her fleetness of foot outrun the sky-chariot which even now hummed patiently in the forest depths behind him.

But he did not want her to go with him against her will. He wished for her to feel as he felt—to succumb to his glory as he had already fallen to her primal charms.

How long the two stood in silent confrontation neither could have guessed. It was only when another voice behind her spoke, that Adala shook herself from the Being's riveting gaze. It was the young girl who had splashed her with pond water who gave words to what all the women thought: "It is a god, Adala! A god stands before us!"

The daughter of Lamech turned burning eyes to her cousin. "But what is his nature?" she warned. "Remember our sisters who were deceived!"

There was no time for analysis, however. The Overlord had stepped forward again, this time into the shallow water of the pond. Where the women would have stood knee-deep, the man's calves were not yet wet.

The four daughters of Moricahn clung together and to Adala in breathless awe. But more than wonder filled them, and the youngest held her cousin's hand tightly.

"How grand he is!" she whispered. "The strength of his arms—the breadth of his shoulders!"

"*Quiet!*" Adala insisted. "Do not think such thoughts."

"But, cousin, my sister only marks what is before her," the eldest defended. "No man in our valley was ever so glorious!"

Adala resisted the impetuous observations, but inwardly she struggled with the same stirrings. The Being who had arisen from the dark jungle like the Sun itself, whose ruby sheen shouted against the quiet green of the vale, had not taken his eyes from her since he appeared. And when he once more took a step toward her, her gaze was caught by the iron rippling of his thighs.

The Serpent, too, was beautiful, she told herself. *Lucifer was the Morning Star!*

"Adala. . . ."

His voice stunned her. *How did he know her name? And why had he chosen her?*

But then, as he drew yet nearer, she remembered. Of course—he had heard the cousins call to her. He could not read her soul or her mind, though her heart raced with the fear that he might.

"Lucifer was the Son of Morning," she repeated beneath her breath. "Remember our Mother Eve, and all our sisters who were deceived. . . ."

But, what was this in his dark eyes? The shyness of a boy? The need of a man? And did she see tenderness in his beckoning hand? She had been told that the Watchers took women by force. But this was not force.

The daughter of Lamech drew back, turning her head and trying to recall her father's words and the warnings he had given. But her mind was swimming with the vision of this Prince; and even as she closed her eyes against him, his raven hair—the curls of it—the shine of his beard and the strength of his brow beguiled her.

"No—this is not a good thing . . . ," she whispered.

Now he was at her side. She could hear the waters subside behind him and feel her sisters' silent desire.

"Adala," he said, "whose woman are you?"

The voice was winsome and broke her heart.

At last she looked into his face, so far above her. He could have overwhelmed her, terrified her with his might; but she seemed to see love in his night-dark gaze.

"I am betrothed, my lord," she replied faintly.

"Has the Master told you this?" he questioned.

Adala was shaken. "My father has told me this."

"Whose woman are you, Adala?"

The female was inextricably captivated.

"No man's, lord," she whispered.

The Prince slid his encompassing hand down her slender arm until his fingers entwined her own. She studied the power of his wrist and a tear slipped over her cheek.

As the Being led her from the garden, his lips drew up in a smile. He, among his fellows, was most to be envied. For he had won his lady's heart and not her body alone.

TWO

It was a five-days' journey from the rustic habitat of Moricahn to the industrious hamlet of Lamech, famed for its white oaks and flint-hard cedars. But the time and distance passed much too quickly for Lamech's brother. He had been requested to give his niece, Adala, safekeeping on his remote little farm until the arrival of her betrothed from Cronos, at which time she would have been married. Now it was his sad mission to inform Lamech of the abduction—to tell him that not only had an Overlord gone to the unusual trouble to seek a woman in the outback, but he had done the unthinkable, and had chosen a betrothed damsel, seducing her without thought to her family or to tradition.

Though Moricahn could have taken his manservant with him, he had chosen to make the journey alone, not wishing to expose himself in his sorrow, and hoping in this solitude to find a way to phrase the bitter news—to prepare some consoling word for Lamech.

But the hamlet was now only hours away. The mountain roads were gentle, as were the streams which flowed beside them; and the hills were not difficult to traverse except where they had been specially created for rugged beauty. For the earth's terrain did not speak of cataclysm. It had not been formed by upheaval or eruption, but by sculpture and design. And for the most part, hills and valleys, heights and plains had buckled at the Designer's will and under direct supervision.

Moricahn looked above to the humid white of the low-hung sky and located the great Golden Orb which commanded all life. As he studied its angle and determined that the cool of evening would be fast upon him, he wondered how his brother could question its deity. Surely that great Force on which all existence depended, and which sustained all motive power on earth, had created all life. It was only reasonable to believe so.

But he had debated the issue with his strong-willed kinsman more times than he cared to remember. On this visit he would purpose not to do so. He must be single-minded enough to honor his brother's mourning and to help him plot whatever steps he might take to find his daughter.

It was difficult for Moricahn to view the world without philosophy. It was his supernal weakness never to see anything simply. Even now as he pulled his cloak over his shoulders in preparation for the rising of the dew, he studied the smooth road ahead and marveled at its construction. How many generations ago had it been laid down? Hundreds? And yet it required no upkeep. The seams between its slabs were so fine a man's knife blade could barely fit between. Only where the perpetual encroaching of the broad-leafed forest threatened to overrun it, were work crews ever needed. And the wonder of the roadways was only one of many gifts bestowed by the Overlords.

There seemed to be no accounting for their duplicity, these brilliant Guardians to whom the affairs of the world had been entrusted. Though they were wise, and generous with their wisdom—though they maintained a strict justice, punishing crime and rewarding noble choice—they sometimes used their might to cruel ends, and fell prey to the self-deception of their own pride. And the disparity of their behavior was a continual source of confusion to their subjects—to mankind, the Sons of Adam. For not only was their essential nature unpredictable, but the inhabitants of their various dominions bore fierce loyalty toward them: citizens of each realm claimed that their Lord, their Prince, was the greatest, the most admirable, and the most deserving of worship. That is to say—all citizens but the eccentric sort, of whom Lamech was a type and an example.

Men like Moricahn's brother did not fit the mold. They claimed a truth "higher" and "older" than the wisdom of the gods.

The foot-weary traveler kicked at a pebble in the path. His brow was furrowed and he shook his head. He could agree that the Overlords had not created the world, but had succeeded to the administration of a world already existing. But he could not go so far as Lamech and their own father, Ishna, had gone. He could not believe that the government of the planet was evil at its core, nor could he imagine that the gods were essentially corrupt.

But though he could not imagine it, the very idea troubled him. And so much had it troubled him that he had left home at an early age rather than be exposed daily to the preaching of his kinsmen. The simple life would shield him, he had reasoned. And so he had abandoned the conveniences of the hamlet, and had chosen the rural life. Though he often wished more advanced ways were available, that the tools of the townsmen were at his fingertips —he had found a measure of peace in his valley, freedom from the hum of activity and the drone of conflict.

The Abductor had intruded into his quiet acreage and had not only seduced his favorite niece, ripping at Moricahn's heart, but had badly shaken his mind. He could not accuse the Overlord of trespass, for Prince had the right to go wherever he chose; but the incident had violated Moricahn's property—and had stirred his spirit. It had brought him face to face with the issue from which he had run as a young man—the issue of good and evil, of who could be believed and what could be trusted.

And now it was forcing him back into the world of

other men. For around the next bend lay the Valley of the Turtles, marking the last wild outpost before Lamech's village.

As Moricahn came upon the valley, he was, as always, filled with awe. He knew of no other place on earth where so many different species had taken up abode. It was true that the Prince of Sun City had attempted to stock his gardens with as many animal types as were known to walk the earth; but the Valley of the Turtles was a natural reservoir, not man-made, and none of the varieties present here had been genetically manipulated.

The bend in the road at the entrance to the valley also marked the end of the last steep trek of mountain trail. Moricahn lowered his satchel sleeve. He sat beside the road and removed his cloak, drinking from the skin flask he carried on his belt.

"Eden must have been like this," he marveled, taking in the valley with a sweep of his gray eyes.

There were many such green pockets of wilderness on earth, where a variety of creatures lived in remarkable harmony. While the preserve was not devoid of predators, its meat-eating inhabitants seemed to pick off the weak or the very old, and thus nature was kept in perfect balance.

Even now he watched with a smile as an ostrich and her chick passed fearlessly before the den of the great bear which mastered the vale. He remembered having seen the bruin once when he was a lad. It had shown itself against the far side of the valley's lake early one spring day when Moricahn and his brother had come to fish. It had not been the exaggeration of childish eyes which told the boys it stood three times the height of a man. Though they had no reason to expect danger, they were glad he was on the distant shore and not close by.

But the ostrich had even less reason to fear the bear. Her mighty legs could carry her swiftly from his reach, though it was unlikely he would go after poultry which stood tall as a giraffe.

Moricahn recalled fondly the days spent with his brother. Lamech was the eldest son, but he had taken much interest in his younger brother, and their hours together were a storehouse of priceless memories.

He studied the lazy islands in the little valley lake, the shining, sun-glinted backs of twelve-foot turtles, and he remembered the day Lamech swam between them, climbing aboard the shell of one and hailing Moricahn from atop the patient raft. The brave lad was no more than nine years old at the time, but that day he became a man in his smaller brother's eyes.

"This is my earth!" Lamech had cried, straddling the giant's back. "And this my sea!" he called, looking proudly at the pond.

He had gone on to master a mountainside, and to tame its forests—and thus had never lost his brother's admiration.

But Moricahn had failed him. For Adala was Lamech's chief joy, and now she was gone. Adala had been Moricahn's charge, and he had lost her.

The sound of great whirring roused the man from self-pity. Turning around, he saw that a dragonfly had settled on a branch nearby—its wings, the span of a man's arm, folding like giant fans from its flight.

"Yes," he nodded, reaching up and caressing the huge insect's blue-green body. "Your turn to rest, my friend. As for me, my journey is almost done, but its misery just beginning."

THREE

Lamech's house sat at the far side of the village which bore his name. It commanded a fine view of the little wall-less town, and while not a pretentious home, its sprawl of whitewashed rock was prominent against the green hill which rose behind it. Moricahn and his brother had grown up in a much more modest domicile in another distant hamlet from the Valley of the Turtles. But it had always been Lamech's dream to bring wealth out of the hills. So when he had failed to find ore for mining, he had turned, dauntless, to the wild resource which covered the mountains. He had made the trees his livelihood.

Lamech had put off marriage and family until his business had been established. He had begun with a one-saw shop which had grown to be one of the largest mills in the coast highlands. It now employed 312 workmen, and had been a successful operation since the start, bringing prosperity not only to its founder, but to the little town which quartered it. The cedar and oak lumber of Lamech-town was in demand worldwide, and, indeed, a whole arm of the business was devoted to the export trade.

One product in particular had won Lamech his reputation. He had managed, with the development of a special saw blade, to find a way to mass-produce lumber from the gopher tree—an unusually dense hardwood—which, until he had turned his mind to conquer it, had gone unmastered. While the wood was not so heavy as to lose its buoyancy in water, it was, due to natural oils, incredibly impervious to the penetration of liquid. It was, therefore, extremely popular with shipbuilders as far away as the ports of Nod, around the horn of the continent.

As Moricahn took the last few steps toward the gate of the house, he surveyed the town again. *No wonder Lamech loves it here,* he mused. *This village with its peaceful wealth.* And no wonder the town had adopted his name, for he had made it prosper. Had Moricahn had more tolerance for bustle and business, he might have stayed on himself.

The small garden which flanked the path to the front door had always pleased Moricahn's horticultural instincts. His own farm was bordered and bedded with a profusion of flowering plants. And he had a keen eye for the art of ornamental gardening. But today, as he passed through the welcoming color, he was oblivious to it.

It was not until his nephew, Jaseth, greeted him that he was jerked into the moment. The studious formulizing of just what to say to Lamech was brought short. "I said, 'Welcome, sir!' " the lad repeated.

"Oh—Jaseth!" Moricahn smiled as the young man led him into the parlor. "Forgive my preoccupation. I thought you were the doorman."

"And you are an unexpected surprise!" the youngster laughed. "My father will be most pleased that you have come."

Of Lamech's two sons, Jaseth, the younger, had always been closest to Moricahn. They shared the same philosophical bent, and though it peeved the lad's father, the boy always enjoyed his uncle's questioning nature.

Moricahn sensed that his nephew awaited an explanation of his sudden and unannounced visit. But he chose to keep that for Lamech's ears.

"Your father is home, then?" Moricahn asked, studying the fine furnishings and pristine interior of the elder's domain. He was suddenly more aware of the grime and sweat of his journey and the homespun rudeness of his attire.

"He is." The lad nodded. "He did not go to the mill today, but is working with my brother on the accounts."

"Very well." The uncle smiled, trying to be congenial despite growing uneasiness.

"I will tell them you are here," Jaseth offered, perplexed by Moricahn's stiffness.

He directed the visitor to a divan, but Moricahn shook his head as he eyed the soft white linen of the piece. Running his hand over his dusty cloak, he declined. "I'll just wait here," he said, standing at the edge of the room.

Jaseth deferred kindly and headed for the hallway which led to Lamech's home office. Suddenly, however, Moricahn called him back. "Please!" he interjected. And then, catching himself, he said more softly, "Please, do not bring Noah out. Lamech is the one with whom I need to speak. I cannot bear for your brother to hear my news."

Lamech stood at the balcony door of his parlor watching the traffic on the village streets below. The jubilant greeting he had given Moricahn had been replaced by anger and despair.

When he had first heard the farmer's news, he had wanted to fling him over the balcony rail. But that impulse would have arisen from the old nature he had long ago learned to suppress—the "wild man" aspect of his character which his father had foreseen when he had named him.

"He shall be called 'Lamech,' " Ishna had pronounced at his birth, "for his nature shall be as the wild horse who rules the plain, or the headstrong bull who thunders through the valleys. And it shall be his task to tame himself, before he tames anything else."

How true that prophecy had been! Moricahn could not have known the struggle his brother had endured, pulled by the two sides of his own personality. The elder looked across to the hills where he had years ago watched the younger son of Ishna take his leave. It had been Lamech's oppressiveness which had driven Moricahn away. The younger had never seen it quite that way. His admiration for Lamech had prevented him from laying blame. But the elder had known in his heart that he had made it impossible for Moricahn to stay—that his need to dominate had put the wedge between them. And he knew that Moricahn was blind to his failures, thinking that success had come easily to him.

But their father's words had been true. Lamech had been required to bring himself under control before he had been capable of mastering life, the mountains, the trees—or "anything." And just now, when his impulse had been to vindicate himself on his kinsman, he had been reminded of his weakness.

"My anger should be turned on the Overlords!" he muttered.

"What?" Moricahn asked, stepping up behind him.

Lamech had not meant to speak out loud, and he turned troubled eyes to his brother. "The Overlords," he replied, his fists clenched. "They are the ones who have victimized Adala! Brother, forgive my bitterness toward you."

Moricahn had always felt small next to his brother. Though in their adult height they were nearly even, he had never outgrown that sensation. He studied the beloved face of the one he admired above all others and shook his head.

"No, Lamech. I failed you. And I shall never forgive myself. But surely you cannot hope to go against an Overlord!" Moricahn exclaimed. Joining his host on the balcony he looked in the direction of the coast, four days south. "Besides, Lamech, did you not tell me, when you brought Adala to the farm, that Obad the Sethite would be arriving this week?"

"My daughter's betrothed. . . ."

"Yes."

"They were to be married when he arrived," Lamech

whispered, his heart heavy with regret.

"Indeed," Moricahn reasoned, "should we not wait for him to lend whatever support he can?"

"Support?" Lamech muttered. "What do you think I can tell the man if I have not even attempted to find his betrothed, my own daughter, by myself?"

And with the mention of Obad, the elder brother was caught away in thought.

"A Sethite, Moricahn. Obad is one of us—of the line of Seth. Do you know how hard it was to find a Sethite for Adala? And not only a Sethite, but one whose family has kept the genealogies and the old ways?"

Moricahn sensed a sermon coming and looked sideways, hoping it would be short-lived.

"The Sons of Seth know that the day of the Overlords is drawing to an end!" the elder warned, speaking not so much to Moricahn as to the sky. "Our Father Adam prophesied as much, saying that the world will be destroyed by force of fire and by violence of water!" he exclaimed, his head now thrown back and arms stretched across the balcony rail.

Moricahn grew more uneasy by the moment and reached out apprehensively to tug on Lamech's sleeve.

"Brother," he said softly, "yes—I know. I have heard it all before."

"Indeed!" Lamech cried. "And it cannot hurt any of us to hear it again!"

"Perhaps, but. . . ."

"No 'perhaps'! Even Enoch. . . ."

". . . 'the seventh patriarch from Adam . . . ,' " Moricahn interrupted, picking up the oft-repeated tale as it had been rehearsed again and again by his elders.

"Yes!" Lamech declared, his eyes full of storm, and the wild man within bursting forth in righteous zeal. " '. . . the seventh from Adam prophesied as much, saying, "Woe to them! For they have gone the way of Cain! Behold, the Lord came with many thousands of his holy ones, to execute judgment upon all, and to convict all the ungodly of all their ungodly deeds which they have done in an ungodly way, and of all the harsh things which ungodly sinners have spoken against him." ' "

With these repetitive cadences Lamech's face was radiant with triumph, his chest heaving in spasms of ecstatic emotion. Moricahn had promised himself he would not get into a dispute on this visit. But as he observed his brother's fanatic rapture, he had to take himself firmly in hand.

"Truly, brother," he managed with great control. "So what does all this mean for our present crisis?"

Lamech did not respond immediately. His eyes were full of believer's tears, and he had to calm himself to deal with the emergent issue.

But in the intervening silence another voice gave answer.

"Adala is my sister," it was saying, "and Obad my trusted friend."

It was Lamech's elder son, whom Moricahn had requested Jaseth not to summon. He stood in the shadow of the hallway which led to the accounting room, and he had been there since Moricahn had given his dreadful news.

"Noah!" Lamech called. "So you have overheard?"

"Yes, Father," the young man replied, stepping into the parlor.

A striking figure, he stood well over six feet tall, and his olive skin, coarse black hair, and heavy beard matched his father's when he was young. While the fair-complexioned Jaseth reminded one of Lamech's wife, Noah was the picture of Lamech, Moricahn had always thought. At each stage of Noah's growth, from childhood until now, he had resembled the elder brother, and more so today than ever.

Moricahn went forth and embraced him warmly. "Nephew! I had not wanted you to know just yet."

The young man bristled. "So Jaseth told me! And when would I have been informed?" Then, softening, he returned the embrace. "Good uncle, I am sorry this burden fell to you."

He studied Moricahn's ruddy face. He knew the man had seen 670 years, yet his brow was still smooth, his countenance barely marked by time. Only the hoary streaks at his temples and the fine silver threads of his beard revealed his venerable age. Noah clutched his hand firmly and then, releasing it, turned to Lamech.

"It is I who shall see what can be done," he insisted. "Since Obad is already on his way, I shall meet him between here and the coast, and together we shall find Adala."

"But you cannot go alone," his father objected.

Noah chose his words carefully. He did not wish to threaten his aging father's pride by reference to his own youth and strength for the journey. "It is better that I do so," he reasoned. "You must stay with the mill. It cannot run without you." And then, clasping his kinsmen to him, he swore, "I will return as swiftly as possible, and ask only for your prayers."

FOUR

The terrain which led from the mountain hamlet downward toward the sea became gradually plain-like, Noah discovered, after a day of traveling a winding and sometimes precarious highway. This route was not the same one Moricahn had traveled on his way to Lamechtown, for then he had come across the highlands from the west, and had only entered low land at the Valley of the Turtles.

Since the trail leading from Moricahn's farm was rugged and squeezed through mountain passes, the farmer had been forced to make his journey on foot. But Noah was more fortunate. His trip was on horseback, along the smooth path of the Overlord's Highway, and he was therefore able to cover much more ground in two days than his uncle had managed in five.

So far he had passed few other travelers on this trek. Mountain folk rarely made trips to the coast cities, and city folk hardly ever journeyed inland, making it even more surprising that an Overlord would go to such lengths to procure a wife.

"Wife!" Noah smirked, spitting on the ground. "This is a spurious thing, indeed! That a Son of God should marry a human woman! A *betrothed* woman!"

His dark eyes flashed angrily as he contemplated the horror, and when scenes leaped to mind of his beautiful sister in some fallen monster's embrace, he nudged his horse's flank sharply, and the steed carried him more swiftly over the empty road.

"My friend!" he shouted to the wind as it whistled through his hair. "Obad! Where are you?" His stormy gaze studied the stretch before him, checking out each stop-off, each resting place along the pike. His heart ached for the grief his old companion would feel when he told him—at the rage he would experience at that thought that Adala had been touched . . . had lain . . . with such a Being.

For, indeed, she would have done so by now. Even if she had been taken against her will, she would have been defiled by now.

Noah suppressed his own fury at the images which flashed before him. "*Was* it against your will, Adala?" he cried through clenched teeth. "Or were you easily seduced?"

He slapped his whip rudely against the horse's heaving side and fought the demons of his own imagination.

Stinging tears forced their way through hot lashes, and he bit his tongue. "No—sister . . . not my sister!"

But he wondered. The doubt was strong. Not because Adala was unusually weak, but because the Overlords were so powerful.

Nevertheless, the thought of her succumbing enraged him, and the anger which would best have been directed at the Enemy, he turned on her. "Did you enjoy it, Adala?" he muttered. "Was it delicious—as the apple of Eve?"

He had lost track of time. He wondered how long he had forced his steed to endure his compelling indignation. It was only when the horse suddenly stumbled, nearly throwing him to the ground, that he came to his senses.

"*Whoa!*" he commanded. "Easy!" He reached forth and stroked the horse's mane, until the animal slowed to a canter. "It is I who am driven," he said in a breathless tone. "Yet I inflict my torment on you."

He drew the creature to the side of the road, and dismounted. The cinch of the crimson saddle had loosened from the run, and the horse's flesh beneath the intricate harness tapestry was almost raw. A light foam covered the smooth white coat. Noah took off his own cloak, rubbing the heavy perspiration from the animal's glistening body.

"I am no better than the madmen who experiment with your brothers and sisters," he apologized. "Forgive me, friend."

Noah knelt down and checked the knees and hooves for distress. "At least your legs are long." He smiled, massaging them firmly. "And you stand on hooves, instead of toes!" Then, rising up, he stroked the horse's shoulder. "It is good you are taller than I, and not the size of a sheep." He winked. "At least you have your dignity, and have not been pared to a sliver of God's original design!"

The horse nudged him with its velvet nose and then threw its head back. Noah thought he heard it laugh.

The vegetation had changed from heavy mountain foliage, with its broad-leaved forests—to the denser, spongy growth of low-lying sea-hills, before Noah spied Obad.

The bridegroom had begun his journey a day before the mountain man, but was only now entering the plain which led to the highlands because travel through populated areas had slowed him.

In fact, as Noah had come closer to sea level, traffic had picked up on the highway leading to the coast. He had found it necessary to keep a careful eye on passing clusters of pedestrians and riders so as not to miss his friend.

He had ignored the humming contraptions which occasionally used the road. There were not many of these with which to be concerned. The city travelers usually limited such transports to town use, preferring the sky chariots or land skimmers for longer journeys. Besides, Obad, like Noah, simply preferred the horse.

When the two men came upon one another, no casual onlooker would have seen much else in common between them. While Noah was dressed austerely in garb befitting his mountain home, Obad was clearly a city dweller. Noah's robes were road dirty, and Obad was dressed in shining raiment, embroidered and tooled, gilded and tailored. At some point in the journey, Noah had tied his cloak about his waist like a great bandana, and his tunic was gathered up between his thighs in a knot, revealing sweat and dust-streaked legs. Obad's short-skirted toga met smooth thighs, and his calves sported the crisscross strapping of high-laced sandals, their crafted leather polished and gleaming. Noah's long, dark hair, wild from travel, and his collar-length beard, disheveled by the wind, contrasted crazily with Obad's barbered, blond head and shaven chin.

But Obad's appearance was deceiving. Both men were ruddy, in love with the sky and the earth. Though one dwelt inside city walls, and one on the open side of a hill, they were more alike than not.

"Aha! Obad!" Noah had cried when he first spied him. "Look at you!" Laughing, the mountain man had clapped him on the thigh as their horses drew near.

"Noah!" Obad had responded, surprised and perplexed. "But, what . . . ?"

"I will explain in a moment," Noah had nodded, soberness overtaking him. "Where is the nearest wayside?"

Obad had said no more, but with a shake of the head had turned his company around and bid Noah follow him back toward the city a little way.

The Sethite's companions guarded several wagonloads of gifts which he was taking to Lamech in exchange for his bride. When they drew into a palm grove a few feet down the road, they dismounted and rested gratefully.

As Noah confronted his old friend, he remembered the day Lamech had taken him to the city to find a man for Adala. His sister had been but a girl then, and he a mere adolescent; but he had felt the grave importance of the journey. He remembered how he had watched his father's searching eyes, listened to his inquisitions of men in the market and families in their homes. And he recalled when the young Sethite had been found.

Noah and Obad were the same age. Though one had been raised in Cronos and one in the country, the two had struck up an instant friendship, and as Lamech and Obad's father had counseled together, Obad had shown Noah the wonders of the coast and its mighty ships.

For Obad's father was a merchant, and the lad had enjoyed access to the interiors of his vessels. That day Obad had taken Noah down to the wharves, and from ship to mighty ship, the mountain boy had run his hands wonderingly over the curves and laminates of their water-resistant woods. From that hour, Noah's blood had been deeply stirred for the mysteries of sailing.

The connection between the families had been mutually beneficial ever since. For Obad's father had been the first to contract a boat-building package from Lamech's mill, and Noah's world had been broadened to include the sea.

Over the years, as they had all waited for the consummation of the betrothal, Noah and Obad had visited many times—Obad sharing in the peace of the hills, and Noah in the exhilaration of the sea. But the Obad who stood before him today was a figure of finery, and Noah could not help but contrast him with the carefree, casually groomed lad who had introduced him to sand-filled shoes and salt water.

Obad read the twinkle in Noah's eye. "Wedding garb," was all the Sethite would say. "The women of the house packed my clothes, and not a worthy thread is among them!"

Noah felt for the man who, he knew, would have preferred sailcloth, and the two laughed together.

"But—now—to what do I owe this surprise?" Obad insisted. "Has Lamech sent you to tell me Adala has run off with another man?"

The Sethite's voice was full of merriment at the supposed bit of humor. But Noah's breath caught in his throat. And he wished he had not volunteered for this assignment.

FIVE

The surf had always intrigued Noah. Its churning, its power to break down anything left long in its way, its always-changing yet never-changing form. It amazed him to consider that he would never see the same wave twice, that every one was unique, yet all together formed a pattern, a whole design which was consistent, persistent, reliable.

His upbringing had conditioned him to see all things in relation to the Creator—and so he saw the sea. It was, to him, the Designer's greatest achievement, and was symbolic of Yahweh's orderly mind.

"You are the one thing they can never alter," he whispered toward the water as he followed Obad down the shore.

"What?" the Sethite interrupted.

"Oh, just talking to myself." Noah shrugged. "I was just telling the sea that it is the one thing no man . . . or Overlord . . . can ever change."

Obad studied Noah suspiciously. "As long as I've known you, you've had a habit of letting your thoughts tumble out as though you are in dialogue."

"A sign of a weak mind," Noah said smiling.

"Not a weak mind, friend. Quite the opposite! In fact, a mind so deep it runs in channels I can barely fathom. But, I do wish it could hold its tongue."

Noah laughed. "I am too much like my father. He has the same idiosyncrasy."

"Well," Obad chuckled, "I admire both of you immeasurably, but you know what they say about those who speak to themselves."

"Yes—'lunatic.'"

"Perhaps. But they also say such people speak with the gods. And I know you would not consider that a compliment."

Noah's brow furrowed and he shook his head. "You know me well. But," he grew contemplative, "I do speak *of* the 'gods,' the Overseers of this world. Of their abuses of nature and their desecration of the way things were meant to be."

Obad listened respectfully. He knew that Noah had given such matters much thought and believed fervently in his conclusions.

"Do you see the churning waves? How they grind at the shore, but never destroy it?" Noah directed. "I believe the Almighty's ways are like that. I believe he breaks things down as only one part of his life-giving process. Death, therefore, is not destruction, but ongoing life."

"You speak of very high things."

"Yes—but there are other kinds of breaking down. Such as the Overlords have done. In their manipulations of nature they destroy the divinely established orders of created things."

"You refer to their great exploits?" Obad inquired.

"Not all attempts at betterment are evil," Noah assured him. "Yahweh gave us minds and material things to be used to our advantage. But when man begins to alter the very foundations of the life order—the given arrangement of God's original designs—he authors chaos."

Obad was silent with thought. "I think I have observed such things in the city," he said, reflecting uneasily on the sport which the citizens of his town derived from the hemi-bodies—creatures which had been contrived from genetic gimmickry. The potential variety of such pathetic beings seemed infinite. And the proportionate percentage of creature to creature within any one being was a perpetual game of experimentation.

It had begun with the lust for immortality. "To be like the gods!" had been the cry of the people. And the "gods" had not withheld their assistance to the projects. In their own lust to control Yahweh's creation, they encouraged any move on man's part in that direction. And so from the crudest beginnings—surgical transplantation of body parts from one creature to another, the exchange of limbs, brains, and even whole heads—to the finer reaches of cellular manipulation—they had tampered with restructuring the very stuff of life.

But all of this had involved centuries of trial and error, and in the wake of the progressive push were left countless tragedies of thoughtless accident.

And so minotaurs were sent into the circus ring to do gladiatorial battle with mighty men; centaurs and satyrs became garden spectacles and objects of adornment at the Overlords' parties, or were shunted off into the back-country where they roamed lonely and purposeless in supposed freedom. Numberless were the forms the experiments took, and due to the cleverness of the gods, people were convinced to see the odd beings as "wondrous," "legendary," and "mystical."

"The deception of Lucifer," Noah sighed, his mind running to the same subjects as Obad's.

"Yes," the Sethite nodded, realizing that he had not voiced his thoughts, but accepting Noah's empathy. "You are fortunate you live in the hills where life goes on as it was meant to."

Noah glanced over his shoulder to the distant highlands which marked his home. They were shrouded in the filmy white veil of the low-hanging sky, and his eyes clouded.

"Not so protected, Obad. Adala was victimized in the very depths of hill country."

The young bridegroom, the Sethite who would soon have been Adala's husband, had not forgotten. For a few moments he had been able to set his mind to other things. But with the reminder, anger and vengeance flashed across his face.

With a mighty heave he spurred his brown stallion and the sleek creature responded with a snort. Instantly it was racing down the coast, its hooves kicking up sand and its great head pointed arrowlike toward a just-now-visible skyline. Obad stared straight toward the towers of Sun City, his heartbeat matching the thunder of the chase.

SIX

The City of the Sun stood on the shore of the white-blue sea like a set of gleaming blocks erected by a giant child. It had grown up along the beach, spawning off itself in all directions, carelessly ambling, but strangely appealing in its free form. The town walls had been pushed back numerous times over the generations, and were now, in fact, obsolete. There was no reason to wall a town today. The state of military art had outgrown the necessity of fortresses and gates. A city was protected not by walls, but by higher forms of intelligence.

Private homes, however, were another matter. Rather then forego gates, walls, and bars, citizens of the town had been obliged of late to increase their home protection. Front doors were now several inches thick on new construction, and owners of older residences were remodeling their entryways to accommodate such additions. And the doors were not swung open for guests, but had to be unbarred and then slid into wall pockets through small trenches.

Such was the evidence of growing violence in this city, as Noah and Obad rode wonderingly through the streets. But the mountaineer would never have thought to search this place first.

It was only after Obad reminded him of the rumors concerning its Overlord that Noah had seen the reason for starting here. For word had it that Poseidon, the god of this capital, had been neglecting his duties of late. Lust for human females had begun to distract and preoccupy him.

Appetite for erotic adventure had become common-place among the Overseers of earth. Legends and tales of old were replete with such references. But Poseidon had been especially overcome by the lure as his quest for the perfect female had led him to send out search parties of underlings into distant territories.

Was it not possible, then, that it would have been Poseidon whom Moricahn's daughters had reported seeing at the pond, and who, they swore, had captured Adala's soul? Could he not have taken the search upon himself since he had been frustrated in his pleasures for so long?

It was reasonable to assume so.

And, therefore, Obad had chosen the City of the Sun.

A conspicuous pair they made as they rode through town: Obad in his wedding garments, windblown and perspiration-soaked; Noah in his backcountry habit, wild and disheveled beneath a homespun hood. But the city dwellers, who were used to seeing peculiar folk about the streets, gave them little mind.

And so they were not detained as they made their way straight toward the temple compound, where all affairs of government were managed, and wherein were hid the secret counsels of the Overlords.

For Sun City was the capital of earth, and the halls of the Nephilim home of earth's mightiest men.

Noah had seen a giant only once. He had been just a boy when he and his father had spied one during a hunting trip in the high country behind their village. But that giant had been but a distant and inferior kin to the giant Nephilim who inhabited this city.

In fact it was still a mystery whether that hairy mountain dweller had been more animal or human. Not that the Nephilim were entirely human themselves. Certainly not. While the worshipers of the Overlords called their unnatural offspring "demi-gods," Noah called them "half-breeds." For they were half human and half. . . .

". . . monster," Noah snarled beneath his breath.

Obad followed his friend's gaze to the turret which marked a corner of the temple compound. His eyes traced it to the very pinnacle, where a powerful Being watched them with suspicion. The two newcomers would be free, like any citizen, to enter the outer courts; but the warning stance of the fellow stationed high above reminded them that they would be under scrutiny, and that they could not go further without a pass.

"The people of my country call these Beings 'Meteors,'" Obad commented, as they passed under the guard's searing observation.

"Fitting," said Noah. "'The Fallen Ones.'"

"But they are mighty," Obad replied. "They are the stuff of legends. Are they not redeemable?"

Noah stared at the mammoth walls of the compound and studied the architectural marvels of the great halls. "I do not know, Obad. I do not know how much of the earth is redeemable, and how much is fit only for Yahweh's wrath."

SEVEN

Noah was somewhat in awe of the ways of the Overlords, though his awe was not translated into worship. The Temple to the Sun was one of their most wondrous achievements.

A gigantic cone of rock, it rose up from the court like a mammoth fingertip. Whether its four triangular sides rested their broad bases on the pavement, or sunk far beneath it, one could not easily tell. There seemed to be no fissure about the foundation, but it blended imperceptibly with the floor. And the tips of each triangle met at the top, so that the sides were sloping. But the triangular walls were not, in themselves, a whole. They were the result of colossal blocks resting one atop the other and forming the pyramidal design.

It was said that the building itself possessed power or could capture and store the power of the Sun. It was reported that this solar energy fed all the works of the Overlords, and that they knew how to tap into the bank whenever they chose.

All this Noah could believe. Even now, as they drew near the central grounds of the compound where the granite marvel sat, he could sense its pulsations and perceive the hum of its charge.

But he did not, as did so many, deify the structure or consider it sacred. Neither did Obad. For both men were of an older tradition. Their fathers' fathers had taught each generation that the religion of the Overlords was a lie, and worship of the gods an affront to Yahweh.

The gods had made it attractive to follow the Way of the Sun. "Exchanging worship of the Creator for worship of created things," Lamech had said. And so had his father understood—and his father before him, back to Seth, the son of Adam, father of them all. Always the truth had existed, though men and the Deceivers sought to pervert it.

But the lie was delicious. As the two Sethites walked through the grounds, it was clear how appealing it could be. For the gods had shared their knowledge with mankind, and the court was full of the results. Mankind could have come to wheels and gears on its own. But it never could have raised a pyramid or honed a seamless pavement without the power of the Sun. Mankind could have gone from horse to horseless carriage on his own, but he never could have captured a ray and cauterized a wound without the gift of godly wisdom. Yet upon this floor was laid a seamless path, and in that corner a surgeon mended limbs, and over there the instruments of war were condensed to a bank of flashing lights.

Mankind could not have achieved this without the godly gifts. Not so early on—not without a primitive beginning.

But there was no "primitive" stage, and never had been to that point. This civilization had never known a "dark age." Rather, all was golden with the grace of the Master Star. And all power belonged to the Son of Morning, men were told—to Lucifer, Prince of the Air, for he and the Sun were one, an Angel of Light, an Orb of Wisdom.

How *could* a human being deny such preaching unless he had been taught at his father's knee to think otherwise? When he saw the mighty works of man, and when all his needs were met in an instant—how could he not believe?

And who among men possessed more knowledge than the Nephilim—the offspring of the gods?

He was one of the grandest ever born. He was a youthful thousand years, and he stood nearly eight feet tall in his glittering garb. He was a son of an Overlord and was positioned as gatekeeper of the temple.

Neither Noah nor Obad had ever been so near one of the Nephilim. As they approached his doorway they could not help but be awed by his stature, and by the look in his eyes. With wordless and scornful scrutiny he warned them. Yet they might have been flies for all the heed he gave them.

Each Sethite had his own thoughts as they came upon this giant. For Obad, the Colossus was a dismal reminder of Adala's seducer. If this Being was so grand, what must the god have been like who wooed her away? The young suitor shrank inwardly, and his mind was filled with doubts. What did he think to accomplish here? If he *were* to find the woman, what hope was there that she would turn from such glory?

But for Noah, the significance of the gatekeeper was more far-reaching. Instantly he perceived the spiritual contest between the "Meteor," the "Fallen One," and the Sons of Seth. For Obad and Noah were of untainted lineage, "perfect in their generations," and they were as alien to this monster as he to them.

The millenia of the Overlords' earthy government had allowed sufficient time for their prurient lusts to so corrupt the line of Adam, that it was a rare family indeed which had no blood of the gods in its veins. Especially on the side of Cain, the murderer, had the human family been invaded. And it was a violent strain which emerged, the deceptive spirit of the Overlords mingling with the outcast, wandering, and marked breed of Cain. But the line of Seth had not been above seduction. The Overlords had not preferred the daughters of Cain, but had been indiscriminate in their tastes. The daughters of mankind had so often been vulnerable to seduction, that even among the Sethites, it was extremely rare to find an unblemished line.

Noah sensed the conflict instantly. He knew it was a spiritual thing, but he was only more aware than Obad because his training had been more intense.

"State your mission," the giant demanded, his mighty voice filling the court. As it died out in long echoes, Noah steadied a trembling hand upon his staff.

"We seek the human woman Adala, daughter of Lamech. We are her brothers, Obad and Noah, and we bear her wedding gifts."

The Titan leered at his little visitor. "Wedding? Your weddings, son of Lamech, are a quaint tradition. The gods have no weddings."

Obad turned fleetingly to Noah, a spark of hope flashing in his eyes. But just as soon, it was doused. "When a god takes a wife, he simply *takes* her!" the giant roared, his face full of angry mirth. "If your sister was brought here, it was without a wedding!"

Noah looked uneasily at the ground, and then cleared his throat. "We are ignorant of your ways," he offered. "We only wished to bring to our sister her family's . . . kind wishes."

"And you have brought them. I will relay the message."

Obad's anxiety rushed forward. "But—the gifts . . . ," he repeated.

"I see no gifts," the Titan replied.

"At the front gate," Obad stammered. "We left them there."

"Then go your way. If your sister is here, the gifts will be delivered."

Neither of the Sethites had actually expected to gain entrance without a struggle. Their intent to this point had been simply to gain what knowledge they could of the fortress' layout. Should they be able to do more, they would be far more successful than they had hoped.

But Obad was not about to turn away just yet. "You have a human mother?" he asked.

The Titan studied him suspiciously. "You know I do," he replied. "Or . . . I did."

"Of course, she would have been long dead," Obad acknowledged.

The giant stared away with a wistful silence, and then countered quickly. "Why do you speak of my mother?"

"Because, if you have memory of her, you will understand our feelings. For *our* mother would be greatly saddened if we could not bring her tidings of our sister. We have come a great distance for that purpose," Obad pleaded.

Noah wondered at his friend's gift for melodrama, and stifled the grin which worked at his own lips. And now, as Obad sensed the giant's softening, he proceeded quickly.

"Here," he said, reaching into the pouch of his broad girdle. "My mother sends this. If only you will see to it that my sister receives this directly, we will be satisfied."

The Titan surveyed his outstretched hand carefully. "What do you have?" he asked.

"A flask of perfume, our mother's favorite. It will bring delight to Adala and her Lord . . . and to the linens of his bed."

The gatekeeper grew less wary with Obad's smooth persuasion.

"Well—I suppose no harm will be done," the Titan assented, reaching down and opening the great spread of his palm to receive the little vial.

"Your kindness will be blessed by the Master." Obad smiled, and placing the glass bottle in the giant's hand, he made a sudden thrust, driving the container's tiny but incisive needle into the meaty palm.

The Colossus sunk to his knees, his dazed eyes angry and helpless.

Noah looked on in amazement.

"I never take a journey without a weapon," Obad explained, pulling the slender prick from its fleshy target. "What will kill a road bandit, will at least stun a Nephil."

Noah glanced over his shoulder incredulously as he passed through the gate and followed Obad down the temple hall. The Titan did not stir, but lay limp upon the pavement, his contemptuous eyes now glazed and vacant.

EIGHT

The Hall of the Nephilim was not a place for secrets. Every footstep echoed as Obad and Noah made their way further into the interior of the temple compound. Every whisper was amplified, for this marble corridor had no carpets, no tapestries to muffle a sound. It was in fact an entirely masculine place, a museum of military marvels. And the lack of direction the two felt, the ignorance of just how to get about in a building foreign to them, made every reverberation a fearsome thing.

There were no onlookers—no one around to question them—but they felt surrounded by spectators, for all along the walls were displayed the armor and helmets of a thousand mighty warriors. Men of renown, whose deeds had lived on in legend—their memories were captured here for the wondering eyes of posterity.

And all the armored suits, pillared in rows along the hall, towered above the heads of the Sethites. For these were coats of war which had been worn by the Nephilim, the giant offspring of mortal women and immortal gods— begotten by the Angels of Lucifer.

"Fallen Angels," Lamech had called them, when he had first trained Noah in such matters. "And the Nephilim are fallen from their birth, the offspring of illegitimate union."

Noah could still remember the first talk on the history of the race, when Lamech, his father, and Ishna, his grandfather, had comforted him after his initiation into manhood. The pain of circumcision, inflicted when he had become of age, would have been unbearable, having been given at his father's hand, had the elders not stayed with him for two days following.

He smiled now as he recalled the patience with which the men had answered his elementary questions. It was a night he would never forget, as the three of them had huddled about a low fire in the center of a forest cave behind their home. It was to this retreat that Noah had been taken for this rite of manhood, and it was in that sacred grotto that he had learned his first lessons in the origin of earth and the tale of mankind.

"But, Father," he had inquired, "humanity is fallen as well. Since the Garden we have all been born in a fallen state. If we are redeemable, why not the Fallen Angels—and the Nephilim?"

"The angels were not *deceived*." Ishna had taken over, his old eyes tempered with the wisdom of 800 years. Noah recalled how the firelight had transfigured the elder patriach that night. Always the sage had been an awesome figure to his grandson, but this night the coral glow upon his pale, aged skin, the golden sheen of flame reflected off his fleece-white hair and chest-length beard burned into the young man's heart. Noah would always remember how the leaping tongues of fire reproduced themselves in the pupils of Ishna's eyes.

"They followed the Prince of This World despite full knowledge of the truth," he had explained. "When Lucifer rebelled against the Creator, saying, 'I will raise my throne above the star of God; I will make myself like the Most High,' his denizens rejoiced. And in their foolish pride, they thought to dethrone Yahweh!" At that point Ishna had flung a faggot onto the fire, punctuating his disgust.

"I see, Grandfather," Noah had conceded. "The angels were not deceived, but Adam was—and so Yahweh gives him a second chance."

"Exactly!" Lamech had confirmed, his own zeal rising for the topic.

"But, what of the Nephilim?" Noah had repeated, returning to the question which had been debated among the Sons of Adam for thousands of years.

The two elders glanced at one another, as if to ask which had the courage to tackle this matter. It was appropriate that Ishna should do so, and he cleared his throat as he rubbed the palms of his hands upon his knees.

"We have no scrolls dealing with these traditions," he began. "All our knowledge is passed down as we are handing it to you, Noah—by word of mouth. In this way it is better retained, for our memories are forced to store at great effort. All our sons learn the mysteries we are sharing with you in the depths of forest caves or in the hollows along the rivers at the time of their initiation, where the affairs of life and the troubles of this world cannot interfere." His venerable eyes gazed deep into the night sky beyond the cave's mouth, and he seemed a little wistful. "I recall asking the same question you have asked, when my father and his father waited with me in my soreness, and I find that I will repeat their words as my own."

He leaned toward the fire, prodding the embers with the tip of his walking stick. "It is my opinion that the Nephilim *are* redeemable. Any son of a human mother is a man. But redemption is not easily accepted by such Beings. The blood of rebellion and deception runs thick in their veins. And the pride inherent in their own greatness makes it hard for them to bow the knee."

Lamech nodded his agreement and then turned to Noah. "Such matters are indeed a conundrum, son. They deal with the line between the physical and the spiritual—a line which only Yahweh fully discerns. But your grandfather speaks well. Any degree of humanity necessitates the existence of a soul. And the Nephilim are part human, being a life form conceived in a woman's womb, dependent upon her fertility for its conception, borne by her, delivered by her to the world."

Noah remembered all this as he and Obad passed beneath the hollow gaze of great metal helmets, and as they skirted the iron husks which had protected the lives of giants. He shook his head and a chill went up his back. How could such monstrosities be human? Marvels they were, indeed, and awe-provoking to the offspring of Adam. But redeemable?

Again, Noah envisioned his sister in the arms of her lover-lord and he imagined his father's lineage spoiled by an infant demi-god. His racial spirit sprang up fresh and soon he was running ahead of Obad.

He sensed that the gate at the end of the corridor would lead to Poseidon's chamber.

NINE

The City of the Sun, being a port metropolis, bore a marine flavor throughout. Poseidon, its lord, was known as "god of the sea." His penchant for all things nautical had not been ignored when the temple had been designed. As Noah and Obad drew near the doorway which marked the end of the compound corridor, the sound of water, spilling and splashing, testified that they had reached the heart of Poseidon's lair.

The chambers of the sea god were, in fact, designed to resemble ocean caverns, and it was upon a gigantic aquarium that Obad and Noah came to marvel as they crept through the last gate of the hall.

The two Sethites knew that at any moment temple guards would be seeking them. By now the stunned Titan at the entry to the corridor would have been discovered, and undoubtedly there was already a team of searchers combing the Hall of the Nephilim. The fact that Poseidon had not felt it necessary to station a sentry at the gate of his own quarters only testified to the arrogance of the Overlord. It was apparently presumed that no one could get past that glorious giant who protected the military museum, so there was no reason to erect further barriers.

But even now the intruders could hear the footsteps of their pursuers echoing against the cold marble pavement of the gallery. They scrambled for the shadows of a fabricated cave—one of many which ranged the walls of the "sea chamber." Each cavern, fitted with low benches and floor pillows, provided a different view of the numerous illumined windows of the aquarium, and each window looked onto a different scene of aquarian life, from mollusks to octopuses.

Noah was too preoccupied with his own safety to appreciate the wonders of this nautical world, but as he hid himself against the back wall of the cave, his eyes were caught by the sulphuric light of the window just across the way. He shook his head to be sure his nerves were not betraying him, and yet he still saw what he had feared. There was a woman in the tank across the aisle—half woman, half . . . fish. Yes—the torso, the arms, and the head were that of a human female, and the rest of the body, that of a fish.

Obad, who was also most concerned with survival, noticed his friend's alarm, and he empathized. "Pathetic creature, isn't she?"

Noah studied her with horror. "What is it?" he whispered.

"My people call her a 'seamaid,' or 'mermaid.' It is more often women who are mutated to this form. But the Overlords have played with men to a similar fate."

The creature had seen them enter the chamber and was pressed now directly against the glass of her tank, where she seemed to be pleading with them to help her. Her eyes were round and anxious, and with her hands she beat against the pane, as if begging them to set her free. With the great fin on which she supported herself, she jumped repeatedly, knocking her body vainly against the barrier, and Noah's heart ached for her.

"But," he stammered, "how does she breathe in there? How can she survive at all?"

"The manipulators worked with her life matter to produce gills. They are hidden beneath her hair, so as not to spoil her beauty."

As Noah watched her helpless gyrations, another figure advanced toward the window from the depths of the tank.

"I suppose you call this a . . ."

". . . 'merman,'" Obad agreed.

The handsome fellow had a dignity which belied his state. He cast a quick glance toward the two onlookers and quickly went to the female. Embracing her, he pulled her from the glass and tried to calm her. At first she resisted, but at last he was able to escort her toward the shadows from which he had emerged. As the couple swam away the merman looked at Noah over his shoulder. The expression in his eyes would haunt the Sethite for years to come. Anger and despair were dominant, but beneath was the cold death of resignation.

It was an irony that the god they had come to challenge should save the Sethites' lives.

Noah and Obad had just been blinded by the searchers' flares. They had just been grasped by titanic hands and were being taken to detention when the Overlord intervened.

What proceeded from that point happened so quickly that the Sethites were barely able to comprehend it, but it seemed Poseidon, having heard of their escapade, was intrigued by their daring; that no human had ever before attempted to invade the premises; and that, hence, he must have an interview with these "fools."

However it happened, within the hour of their entrance to the temple, Obad and Noah found themselves at the very throne of Adala's captor. And it was announced that within moments Poseidon himself would stand before them.

TEN

Lamech did not realize the extent to which his elder son was a record keeper. He had hired Noah to keep the books for the family business because from boyhood the lad had shown a bent toward the meticulous. And Noah had never failed to perform admirable service in the capacity of accountant.

But Lamech did not know that his son had kept voluminous journals from the time he was old enough to master literacy. The journals had covered all kinds of subjects—anything which had ever struck Noah as interesting, curious, important, mysterious, or noteworthy had been written down and tucked in the chests and trunks which formed part of the furnishings of his room.

Noah's mother had known about his writing. She had often come across entries on scraps of paper and in little booklets and scrolls left in his small-boy clutter. She had sometimes spoken to him about his diaries, encouraging him in his eccentric activity. But she had never bothered Lamech with it, for she knew her all-business husband would see little of value in such dallyings.

But even Noah's mother had not known that he had written down the oral traditions—the secret knowledge to which only the men of the Sethitic line were privy. The words of Adam and Seth, of Methusaleh and Enoch had been captured on Noah's own parchment, as he had followed his compulsion to record even against the verbal custom of his ancestors.

"If I ever have sons," he had told himself, "they will receive the written word." Much as he saw the logic in the argument for oral transmission, he believed the children of Adam could not be trusted with it. The luciferic power to confuse was becoming far too insidious, however great a man's strength of conviction. And Noah did not wish for his sons to have to rely on word of mouth. "If it is written down," he reasoned, "the power to twist it will not be so strong."

Noah's mother was dead now. She had left him when he was still a boy, giving birth to a twin son and daughter who lived only a few days. No one else knew of his hidden volumes, not even his closest kin, Jaseth.

As he stood now beside Obad on the narrow carpet which led to Poseidon's throne, he thought about the little scroll in which he had recorded his first memories and impressions of the sea and ships—subjects which his friend had first introduced to him.

Someday—if they survived this adventure—he would show the diary to Obad.

As they waited now for the sea deity to enter his chamber, Noah considered the history of Poseidon's deeds. The Overlords and their descendants were as interested in record-keeping as any Sethite. And Poseidon was near the very top of the Adlandian King List. Not far below the Master Lucifer himself, this mighty lord found his slot in the hierarchy of earth's government.

Poseidon was best known for the formulation of the lengthy Adlandian legal code, and for the execution of that basically humane set of regulations. It was taken for granted that all matters nautical, from the protection of sailors to the might of the shipping industry, and all that related to the sea (which tied all the continent together) were in his hands. But his mastery of parliament and justice and his keen mind for government were his greatest praise.

It was no surprise, when Poseidon did finally appear,

that he was a most magnificent Being. Noah had no difficulty understanding how Moricahn's daughters—and, yes, even Adala—could have been overcome by his majesty. The god was not quite so tall as the Nephil who had been at the guard station. But his physical powers were surely equal, and his dark handsomeness, his brooding brow, and penetrating eyes would have cast a spell over the strongest of women.

Noah sensed his friend Obad tense at the sight of him, and peering sideways toward his partner, he read his helpless disgust.

But now the god was speaking and the Sethites could not deny the awe which his voice provoked.

"Two strangers, one of Cronos, I presume, and . . . what is your village?" he inquired, studying Noah carefully.

". . . Lamechtown, sir," Noah replied.

"Ah—yes. The lumber mill."

Noah bit his tongue and looked at the floor.

"Speak, man," the god insisted. "You wish to correct me?"

"Sir," Noah began, "my village is more than a mill. Many human beings call it 'home.' We raise our families there. We eat, work, and marry there."

Poseidon smiled broadly and shook his head. "I meant nothing less than that. But now," he turned to Obad, "let us deal with the matter at hand. You explained your mission to the guard, but then treated him with unnecessary rudeness. Who are you?"

"Obad . . . son . . . Lamech," the Sethite stammered. He was not comfortable with the lie, but had extended himself so far with it he decided to see it through.

"And Noah, son of Lamech," the mountaineer responded as the dark gaze questioned him.

"But you hardly look like brothers," the Great One said with a gimlet eye. "Why have you invaded my halls?"

Obad took the challenge without hesitation, and with courage surprising even to Noah.

"The human woman," Obad began, "is part of our family. We feel *we* were treated rudely by your abduction of her. And, though we realize she is now your . . . wife," the word sticking in his throat, "we feel we have the right, as her brothers, to give her the family's good wishes."

The god, who had taken a seat on his pearly throne, surveyed the Sethite up and down. "For this reason alone you would risk your lives to enter where you do not belong? You, Obad, are strangely attired for such a venture. I perceive more in your impulsive actions than the fondness of a brother." The god's brow bore the shadow of suspicion and he analyzed Noah with similar doubt. "As for you, mountain man, you hardly look like you belong with this dapper fellow. No. I perceive that we have here the anger of a rejected lover and his irate—though helpless—friend. Perhaps, at the most, your tale bears truth when Noah claims to be my lady's kinsman. There is more the familiar horror in his eyes, than in Obad's—just as there is definite jealousy in the lover's clenched fist."

Obad quickly relaxed his grip, and said nothing. But Noah would not remain silent.

"So, great deity, you have deduced the truth. I suppose we should not have expected less from you." The son of Lamech squared himself and took a deep breath. "Poseidon, you have accomplished many wise and wonderful things for your people. But what you are doing—you and the other lords of earth who seduce our women and mingle your blood with theirs—what you are doing is an abomination!"

What could have aroused the ire of lesser beings seemed not to stir Poseidon. He was silent a moment, his only response a benign smile. And, after a kind interlude during which he appeared to consider the challenge patiently, he laughed a little.

"My good man," he nodded, "am I understanding you correctly? Are you seriously implying that the co-mingling of divine and human blood could do anything but strengthen the inferior race? Are you saying—having just now come through the Hall of the Nephilim—that the Overlords do not spawn supermen?"

Noah stood steadily before the Father of Meteors and rode the momentum of his boldness. "I repeat," he asserted, "that what you are doing is an abomination! You have overstepped the bounds appointed you, and have brutally disrupted the established orders."

"Established orders!" the great voice echoed. "All earthly orders have been established by the will of the Master. And his orders are undergirded by flexibility. Nothing his servant's have done has gone against his system!"

Noah tensed angrily. "You speak of the luciferic system! You speak of the Serpent for whom this world was not created!"

Poseidon now leaned forward, the first sign that his own indignation had been aroused.

"What blasphemy is this?" the god demanded. "Is Lucifer not rightly called the 'Prince of This World,' the Serpent being his symbol, and the 'Prince of the Power of the Air,' from whom the Sun shines forth eternally?"

"Prince, indeed!" Noah agreed. "Manager by default! Who through his subtlety won the dominion from our Father Adam, and our Mother Eve, when they abdicated their station to his wiles. Prince, indeed! But not King. The King has always existed and is yet to come!"

Poseidon now leaned back in his great chair, his breath escaping in exasperation. He struck a fist against the arm of his seat and laughed aloud.

"You rave, Noah!" he cried. "How can you deny that all created beings are dependent on the Sun, that all motion and progress are dependent on his great power? Each movement of man and beast is derived directly or indirectly from the energy contained within the fruits and fibers of the fields—from the food which sustains them. And this energy, in turn, is imparted by none other than the rays of light descending from our Master, from the Golden Orb who governs all things!"

Poseidon was filled with zeal as he spoke, each word leading to another with frantic enthusiasm. "Why, consider, Sons of Seth, the gentle breezes of Adlandia. Consider the ocean currents! The smooth-flowing rivers and tumbling cascades of your own mountain land! Are these not all the children of solar heat? All man's works, then, whether empowered by steam, water, wind, or horse, are driven by the Sun!"

Noah and Obad did not take their eyes from the orator, who had risen now and was pacing the wine-red carpet which robed his platform. "Lucifer! His name means Lightbearer!" he cried, throwing his arms wide. "He is the source of energy in all earthly phenomena! Adlandia is *his* realm, Great Governor of the Skies! The heavens, the land, the rocks, and the beasts—man himself—all depend on his conversion and expenditure. All life is sustained by him, and he is the Master of all!"

The Daemon stood still now, his eyes uplifted and his breath heavy. The chamber was filled with silence.

But Noah could not hold his tongue. "Truly, an Angel of Light!" he murmured, looking at Obad out of the corner of his eye.

"Yes!" Poseidon agreed. "Lucifer, Angel of Light!"

"Like lightning, he was cast from heaven!" Noah dared to reply. "And he still uses his brilliance to deceive! To lead the Sons of Adam into darkness! He is Master of the Air for now—Prince of This World—but he is not its Maker! Neither is he the Sun which feeds the earth. The sun is the work of Yahweh's fingers. It is not divine. It is a creature, not the Creator. And it is in keeping with Lucifer's distortions that he should claim the luminary as his throne. He is, after all, the twister of the covenants, the defiler of Yahweh's handiwork!"

Obad, who knew that Noah's logic could bring their

demise, was nonetheless close to applauding. But Poseidon's wrath had been kindled.

"It was daring of you to enter this sanctuary. But you are a fool, Noah, to speak such heresy to my face. Do you not know that I hold your life in my hand?"

Noah raised his chin and faced the dark angel directly. "It is the Lord God, Maker of Heaven and Earth, who holds my life—and yours, Poseidon—in *his* hand! It is only by his mercy that you and your fellow-governors have been allowed to manage this realm as long as you have. But the time is coming when your era will be at an end. For the Great Day of Yahweh draws near!"

As Noah spoke it was more than zeal which prompted his words. He was surprised by his own declaration. And yet—somehow—as he opened his mouth, he knew that it was time to issue these warnings, and he knew that those things he had only suspected were being confirmed within his spirit.

"Great Day of Yahweh? Yahweh is only one deity among many!" Poseidon rebutted. "Is he the god of your hamlet?"

"Yahweh is King of kings and Lord of lords!" Noah replied. "He is *your* Maker, Poseidon, and he shall be your undoing!"

ELEVEN

As a consequence of Noah's daring, the two Sethites would spend the night in the temple dungeon while Poseidon decided what should be done with them.

Few words passed between the prisoners as they sat upon the cold stone floor. At least they were not in chains or shackles. For that they could be grateful. But Noah felt himself a failure, and having no light but that of the torch which flickered through the door grate, it seemed the hours only inched by.

At first the son of Lamech had faced the circumstances undaunted, being borne up by the enthusiasm of his own sermon. But with the deepening of night, and the further gloom of soundlessness, he began to question himself.

"Friend," he broke the silence, "if I had been more cautious, Poseidon might have freed us."

Again there was quiet, augmented only by the sporadic dripping of water down the outer wall. And he began to fear that Obad agreed with him.

"No," the Sethite at last responded. "You said what needed to be said. To do less would have been to go against the prompting of Yahweh."

Noah was incredulous. "Then, you sensed it, too? The leading of our God? Oh, friend, I had hoped it was not my imagination."

The mariner's son leaned toward the mountaineer and pointed to the dim light which filtered in from the corridor. "Do you see that?" he asked. "A mere glimmer—but it testifies to a mighty flame just outside our door. You, Noah, are like that light. In this dark world you may not be appreciated fully. Your message may be only a glimmer now. But the day will come when the door is thrown open wide. And then all men will see the brilliance of your words."

Noah was amazed at this endorsement, and hardly knew how to receive it. But Obad was not finished. "The gods may spawn supermen, but occasionally mankind spawns a prophet. There have been only a few since the world began—like diamonds scattered and nearly buried among the granules of humanity. But I have always known you were a special person, friend," Obad insisted. "I believe Yahweh has greater plans for you than I had imagined."

"You mean. . . ."

"I mean, I feel that you are a prophet. *The* prophet chosen for these days."

Noah pressed his back against the rocky interior and pulled his knees up to his chin. He had never thought of himself in such terms. Since childhood he had wished to be used of Yahweh. But he assumed that all sincere men would have such yearnings. To actually be singled out for some special service—this had never occurred to him.

"I am humbled by your kind thoughts," he said, "but I think you are biased by your feelings for me. Besides," he added, brushing away a spider which had set to web-making on his shoulder, "I really do not relish such a destiny. It would be no pleasure to be the bearer of bad tidings to the world I love. No, friend," he chuckled, "let someone else carry that burden!"

Obad turned his eyes to the ceiling and rested his head against the wall. "I will pray for you, Noah. For with your office the burden *will* be great. And, pray for yourself. For the responsibility is heavier than any man dreams."

Noah was about to make a rebuttal, but could see that Obad was in no mood to argue. The man from Cronos retreated into silence once again, and as Noah studied the solemn face where the dim light touched closed lids, and the shining head where golden hair caught the light, he knew his friend thought on Adala, and that his brooding had been for none but her.

The mountaineer pondered what would become of the man and woman who had been meant to spend their lives together, and he wondered what the future held for him.

The obstinate spider had made her way up Noah's arm again and rested on his shoulder. The son of Lamech drew her gently onto his fingertip and held her to the light.

"Little web-sprite," he whispered. "Do you think on deep things? You are a marvel to me. An architect in silk. If only I could follow Yahweh's designs as easily as you do."

Obad could not sleep. He had managed to close himself away until he knew Noah had drifted into much-needed slumber, before he opened his eyes. And when he did look again on the dark cell it was through the blur of silent tears.

Not since he had been informed of Adala's abduction had he been free to experience his grief, or even to think on it.

Since he had been old enough to have a man's feelings, he had loved the girl. Though the culture of the Sethites did not allow even betrothed men and women to be alone together before marriage, the two families had often spent time in each other's homes, and he had had many occasions to see Adala. Space had been allowed for them to share hours free from direct observation, and over the years he had come to believe the woman felt as he did.

In fact, even now he could not believe those feelings were dead. Surely Adala's heart could not have been utterly lost to him.

But then he recalled the Glorious One who had seduced her. And he looked at himself in the yellow light. "Fool," he whispered. "Scrawny, pale fool! Who am I to think she could even remember me, after being with him!"

He recalled how it had felt when Adala let him hold her hand. He relived the few times when his lips had touched hers. And then he thought of her with Poseidon.

Suddenly Obad was standing. He paced the floor a few times, and pounded his fist against his thigh.

Still, if there were any way under heaven that he could see her, he would attempt it. He must know with certainty that she would not leave this "husband" of hers, that she would not return to the one Yahweh had intended for her.

Just as he was making this resolution, however, he heard soft footfalls in the corridor. Thinking it the guard, he went to the dark corner where he had spent the evening and sat once more, eyes closed, leaning against the wall.

The steps hesitated before the door, and Obad could discern the anxious breathing of some onlooker. He peered carefully through one eye toward the grate, and could see the face in the torchlight before the visitor could make out his presence in the black cell.

"Adala!" he cried.

"Obad?"

"Yes—Adala! It is I! You have come!"

The beautiful girl glanced furtively down the corridor, and then grasped the bars, pressing her face against them.

The Sethite was on his feet instantly and rushed for the grate. His fingers reached up to touch hers where they wrapped the cold iron, and she did not withdraw them.

"Obad," she repeated, her voice throaty. "What have they done to you?"

"Not they," he answered. "He. It is Poseidon who has done this."

Adala studied his expression briefly, then turned her eyes to the floor.

"Oh, no, Adala," Obad hastened, reaching out to stroke her cheek. "We must not speak of this! Tell me how you are. Have you been treated kindly?"

The woman glanced up, her face flushed. "Yes. The Master treats me well."

"So—he is your master, then, and not your husband!" Obad insisted. "Adala—there has been no true marriage here. Your own words betray that!"

Adala drew back, shaking her head. "I do not know. . . ."

"Of course you do not! You have been confused, my lady! Listen to one who loves you greatly."

The woman was torn with the battle of her soul. Truly, she did not understand what had happened to her. For three days she had been the recipient of pleasures beyond description—of love glorious. But her spirit had been confounded. And she no longer knew herself.

"Oh, my lady," Obad repeated, reading her bewilderment. "You are bewitched. Don't you see? This thing is not what it appears!"

Adala searched his eyes, and with the searching came memories of their times together. A large tear rose up and spilled over her lashes. She reached up to wipe it away, but met his finger already there. "It is a tear of cleansing," Obad whispered. "And I will wipe away every one as it comes. Only tell me that you still love me."

The ravaged one smiled a little as he caressed her face. And she fought the shame which challenged her joy.

"Obad," she replied brokenly, "I *do* love you!"

The man's heart surged, and the woman laughed a little.

"*Shhh!*" The Sethite gestured, looking at the sleeping Noah.

Adala glanced into the dank cell and spied the slumberer. "My brother!" she whispered. "Is he well?"

"He is," Obad assured her. "Only let him rest. He has done duty beyond call."

"I heard of his speech before Poseidon," she acknowledged. "And I also know that the god plans to bring you forth tomorrow. When he does, I will plead for your safety, and you shall be set free!"

Obad traced her face in the firelight. "I believe no man could go against your wishes," he said. "Perhaps even the gods must obey you. But I will not leave this place without my lady."

TWELVE

Morning was not brought to the cell by sunlight, but by the clatter of keys in the lock. And the two occupants were not allowed to stretch the kinks from their rudely quartered bodies, but were forced to march instantly toward Poseidon's chamber.

Barely had they found their equilibrium when the mighty Daemon began his inquisition.

"You are an eloquent man," Poseidon opened. "I desire to hear more of your doctrine."

Noah cleared his throat and glanced at Obad, who nodded encouragement, and then the son of Lamech studied his challenger for a moment. "I will be pleased to tell you whatever you wish to know, majesty. Where shall I begin?"

"Tell me of your Father Adam," the Being said, leaning back in his great throne and stretching his powerful legs as if awaiting entertainment.

"Adam was the progenitor of all man and womankind. He was the one for whom we call the earth Adamlanda, Adalandis, or Adlandia."

Poseidon sighed with a flick of the hand. "Elementary, Noah. Who does not know this? Speak of your doctrine."

"Very well, I will," Noah assented. "Adam was made but a little lower than the angels—a little lower than the Sons of God—whether they be good or evil."

"In what way was he created lower?" Poseidon inquired.

At this point Noah became uneasy, for he realized that as a Son of God, though a fallen one, Poseidon already knew these things.

"I perceive," said Noah, "that you are only testing me. You do not seek enlightenment—for, though you have bent the knee to Lucifer, you know the fundamental truths."

Poseidon seemed not to hear this and repeated, "In what way was Adam created lower?"

Noah shuffled but responded squarely, "Physically and intellectually, we are not your equals, Great One. You well know this. Nor do we have the second sight which you possess to read another's heart and mind. We do not shake the earth as we walk, nor do we have the power to leap space and time as you do, nor to levitate great weights or telepathically speak without means. It is said that such abilities may have been latent within us, ready to blossom—for from time to time they have shown themselves in members of our race. But mostly they were shed with the Fall, and we no longer enjoy them. Yet we were Yahweh's special treasure, and in the sons of men he took his delight before the foundation of the world."

Poseidon fidgeted with his braided cuff and Noah wondered if he still dealt with things too fundamental. "You refer to 'the Fall,' Noah? What is this?" he asked.

Noah felt more strongly now that Poseidon was indeed testing him. For some reason the deity wished to know just how much the human knew. But he fought the fear which rose with the examination, and proceeded to supply the answers.

"In creating humankind," he explained, "there was one other way in which Yahweh limited us. While the angelic hosts were created with the knowledge of good and evil, we were created in innocence. While the angelic hosts would choose their paths in full understanding of the consequences, mankind would be governed by conviction, and would respond through faith or doubt. Hence, while God loved all his angels, man would hold a special place in creation—for we would make our choices solely from the heart and not from sight. These are all things which the hosts of God have desired to look into, but have never experienced. And these are things which mystify the Overlords, but which man knows instinctively. And it is because of our special place in Yahweh's heart that we are the objects of loving care on the part of our Holy Guardians—but the targets of jealousy and temptation by the Rulers of Darkness."

Poseidon looked at the ceiling of his chamber as if deep in thought, and Noah seemed to discern a twitch along the side of his face.

The son of Lamech then glanced at his friend, who had stood silently beside him throughout his discourse, and Obad nodded toward the walls of the room. As the mountaineer had been speaking, a small crowd had been gathering, and he noticed them only now. They were a strange collection of people, each attired differently, some in long white garments and others in black, with peculiar emblems adorning them. They appeared not to be servants of the chamber, but specially designated elders of some kind, both men and women.

Here was a group with heavily painted faces, and pendants made to resemble rays. Their eyes seemed to bore through him, and he reasoned that they were the oracles of the chamber. In dark habits, their heads veiled by hoods, stood the witches and warlocks who were said to have great powers. And overseeing them all was one hoary old man, a tall staff in his hand, with a large black bird perched upon its crook.

The mountaineer, because he was a man, could not help but especially notice the female who, with her courtesans, stood in one corner of the room. Her simple white gown, gathered at one shoulder by a sun-shaped pin, and cinched into her waist like an hour glass, revealed one bare breast. "A priestess," he told himself, "—priestess of Lucifer." And he turned his eyes quickly to the floor. He dare not look her way again, but he wondered if he had seen his sister standing not far from her. *Oh, Adala,* he thought to himself. *May Yahweh spare you.*

But now Poseidon spoke again, and Noah was riveted by his voice.

"Once more," he demanded, "you have not explained 'the Fall.' Adam lost his original estate?"

"I was leading to that," Noah assured him. "It was because we were created for a faith walk that we were presented with doubt. The perfect setting of our birth necessitated the presence of its opposite, evil. 'It is good,' Yahweh said of our world, but the light could shine only through the presence of darkness, and the good could exist only in the presence of evil!"

Poseidon laughed now, and so did the members of his congregation. "But Adam was ignorant of this? What pleasure could Yahweh have in ignorance?"

"I did not say 'ignorant,' Daemon. I said 'innocent.' We did not lack wisdom. We lacked knowledge. But not for long. And our knowledge, when we received it, would be from a voice beyond ourselves, not from an inborn sight. Thus, we would have to choose by faith or doubt."

"And from whence did the voice originate?" Poseidon demanded.

"When we listened to the Serpent, we became fools of knowledge, and lost the wisdom of innocence," Noah concluded.

The Daemon did not take his eyes from Noah now. For a long moment he scrutinized the homespun philosopher as if not convinced that one so unassuming could weave such shining logic in the presence of oracles. At last he found the words for one more challenge and spoke forthrightly.

"I fail to see how knowledge of any kind can produce foolishness, Noah. Can you explain this?"

The mountaineer received the query graciously, sensing

that the truth was taking hold. "Our lack of knowledge was not a lack of facts. We knew all the particulars necessary to life, happiness, and wisdom. What we lacked was experience, the experience of failure, the fruit of doubt and disobedience. The Serpent convinced our Mother Eve, and through her, our Father Adam, that such experience would be liberating. And the Serpent, your Lightbearer, your Lucifer, proved himself the minister of death to our souls!"

Poseidon stirred angrily, but did not say a word.

"And so," Noah summed up, "the fundamental difference between men and Lucifer's angels is that the angels fell through choice and man through choice based on deception."

Now the deity's eyes flashed and a nervous laugh escaped his lips. "This hardly seems a radical difference!"

"It is the *most* radical, Great Poseidon. It is the ethical and fundamental difference. And because of it, Yahweh has already prepared a Redeemer for our race, for the race created a little lower than the angels. And the world as we know it shall be obliterated!"

The Daemon's mocking was now unbounded. "Obliterated?"

"Yes, Knowing One. Our Father Adam, in whom you seem to have a great interest, predicted the destruction of all things because of apostasy. This terrible cataclysm will take place alternately by the force of fire and the overwhelming powers of water!"

The crowd was overcome now by hilarity, holding their sides and laughing together. The deity could stand no more. Pointing an enraged finger in Noah's face, he cried, "You are lunatic, son of Lamech! You must leave this place and, for your own good, keep your lunacy to yourself!"

Adala, who had been observing the proceedings fearfully, yet with pride in her brother's eloquence and courage, breathed a sigh of relief at this pronouncement. It appeared that she would not now need to challenge her Master for the freedom of the Sethites.

But Poseidon had noted her happy expression, and was also aware of the fond gaze which passed between Obad and the woman.

"However," he quickly judged, "your companion shall be retained. For he has the spirit of insurrection!"

Adala gasped and turned speechlessly to her lord. Tears welled in her eyes, but the god was not moved. Poseidon only leaned, self-satisfied, into his great chair, as guards laid ruthless hands upon the intruders.

As Obad was taken one way toward the dungeon, and Noah was escorted to the hall, the Sethites had time for only a quick glance at one another.

"This way," some brute demanded, forcing Noah from the room.

As he was ushered through the door and into the corridor, he passed leering and mocking faces—painted, gaudy, obscene. But one in particular would remain with him. The very old man, the sorcerer with the great white beard, studied him ominously as he went by, and Noah sensed a warning in his eyes. At that instant the old fellow was caught by Poseidon's gaze and nodded to him as if in silent communication. But just as quickly he returned his eyes to Noah, and the last impression the Sethite would hold as he walked from the secret chamber was the cawing of the raven on the wizard's staff.

THIRTEEN

Noah's breathing was heavy and tears stung along his lashes as he raced his horse up the shore and away from the City of the Sun. A salty midday wind lashed his hair as he drove the horse faster and faster, and with each drumming hoofbeat his heart thundered.

A great distance from the capital, he stood in the stirrups looking back at the gleaming skyline where it was now tinged pink in the glow of afternoon. He wondered what fate the Daemon plotted for the friend of his childhood, and he wondered if Adala, too, was now more endangered than she had been before their impetuous escapade.

"Yahweh!" he cried, his voice lost in the pounding surf as he pushed the horse to greater speed. "I thought you were with me!"

He wiped the sweat and the tears from his face with a swipe of his sleeve, but not until he reached a rocky protrusion which rose from the sea north of Cronos did he slow his steed and stroke its heaving sides. He dismounted and tied his animal to a weathered root, then climbed the jagged black granite to a niche hollowed out just above the salty spray.

The sky was lit to scarlet where the fiery orb descended, and Noah watched it sink to the horizon. He marveled at the way it seemed to melt and spread into the sea, as if it were dissolving, and he understood why the uneducated might think the earth was flat and that the Sun was reborn anew each morning.

As he rested in the hollow of the stationary granite, his spirit eased with his slowing pulse. He awaited the rising of the pinpoint lights which never failed to adorn the canopy of earth each evening. And he remembered the science of the stars which he had learned in the village school. His master, though a Sethite, never denied that the travels and the position of the luminaries did sometimes portend great and universal events. He explained that they often served as the map by which wise men could read of the plans of Yahweh for their own age. The planets were not equal to Yahweh, but were responders, as was all creation, to the movements of his will and design. From the moment of creation, when the void had taken substance, they had been the instruments of Yahweh's fingers; their music had hummed his praises and they had shouted for joy at his decisions. So had their Overlords. For each pinpoint—not the flickering suns, but the stabler lights—had its government, and its Sons of God in control. Earth was the only dark planet, the only garden to whom the luciferic hosts had been abandoned. But it would one day shine, Noah knew. It would join the celestial choir.

The Rulers of Darkness had sought to wrest the study of the stars to their own advantage, claiming that they could predict and manipulate all things through special insights. "All things have been perverted," Noah muttered, casting a crooked pebble into the frothy waves. "There is no power or gift which they have not distorted!"

But as he spoke he was interrupted. A glistening gray sheen drew his eyes to the surf, out from the spray which dashed against the rocks. It leaped high above the waters in a silver arc, and the setting sun caught its dorsal fin in a red flash.

"Son of man!" the dolphin cried. Noah sat up sharply and rubbed his eyes. He had heard that certain creatures of the sea had retained the gift of speech to a greater degree than land animals. But he had never before witnessed anything like this.

Just as he was about to pass it off as imagination, however, the glistening creature came nearer, leaping within the surf itself, over and over. "Son of man," it repeated, its rigid mouth drawn up in characteristic smile, "do not sorrow!"

Once more it dove beneath the surface and came up again.

"Son of man, rejoice!" it called, and then disappeared in a white curtain of brine.

Noah stood up now and watched for its return, but it did not appear again. He studied the water of its departure, and his eyes were caught by the spraying surf where it had descended.

The long rays of sun were captured in the vapor strangely, bent and prismed in a multicolored bow. He had seen such a thing before, in the steam of waterfalls or in the tumbling cascades where rivers fell down. But the sign had never seemed so important before, and he wondered at its beauty.

As the colored vapor dissipated his heart sang, and he left the rock with renewed courage. His horse waited patiently upon the sand, and as Noah mounted he whispered a *thank you* in its ear.

The road home did not seem so foreboding now. The son of Lamech pointed his horse toward the twilight hills, and did not look back.

If he had he would have seen the steel-eyed raven, the sorcerer's familiar, who tracked him overhead.

FOURTEEN

The hills of earth had always intrigued Noah. While the world's single continent, which spanned nearly one-half of the globe, was broken up by lake-sized rivers and great seas, there was no part isolated, or which could not be reached by foot. There were areas, however, where the terrain ascended to such heights, it became lost in the mists of heaven. And no man traversed those places. Such mountain lands had always been considered mystical and even sacred by the bulk of humanity. Even the Sethites, who limited themselves to the worship of Yahweh, could not help but wonder who might inhabit the shrouded regions, and what power such beings might possess.

Legend had it that in the early history of the planet, when the gods had been established over the various territories of men, and when the human population had begun to push back the wilderness, the "greater" gods had taken up residence in the highlands. The mountains of the gods were known by various names, many of which were corruptions of the name Adamlanda, or Adalandis. "Atlantis," "Alantis," "Alampis," "Olympus," and even, as time passed, distant etymological cousins such as "Shamballa" and "Nirvana."

It was said that from these heights the "greater" Overseers communicated with the "lesser" (such beings as Poseidon) and with the even higher MENTOR, the Prince

95

of the Air, Lucifer. Thus all the high or heavenly bodies, the sun and the moon, the stars and other planets came to be viewed as divine entities with minds and wills to be invoked and worshiped. Progressively, as man lifted his eyes from the plains to the hills, and eventually to space, he deified all creation, forgetting the one true God, to whom alone his eyes should have been lifted.

But it was all part of "The Plan," anchored on earth by the Fallen Ones, and systematically indoctrinated into men's hearts. From the worship of the elemental spirits of nature to the high scheme of universal polytheism, the hearts of men were turned to the "Master."

And why not? The government of the gods was, for the most part, quite humane.

And their works were even greater. No one could doubt the existence of the "Olympians" when they observed the mighty structures whose building the Masters had overseen. And it was a rare man or woman who had not been eye-witness to the comings and goings of their sky-chariots when the ziggurats, the pyramids, and the lofty flight terraces were constructed, or when the giant monolithic faces of Zeus and Baal were lifted along the sea. So many were their works and so close were they to populated regions, that only the blind could fail to realize the involvement of the Great Ones.

This day as Noah rode toward the mountains of Lamechtown, his eyes were drawn, as always, to the foggy heights which towered, no one knew how high, above. He contemplated the countless dynasties and civilizations which had risen and fallen on earth. He thought on the wars which city had played against city, and the ceaseless violence which had become a part of everyday life on the plains below. Yet, progress never faltered, advancement was never delayed, and despite man's successes and Yahweh's generosity, people's hearts were increasingly hardened.

And then he remembered Obad's prediction and raised a trembling hand to his mouth. "Lord," he whispered, "I am a man of unclean lips, and I dwell among a people of unclean lips. Surely I am no fit prophet."

Yet, he thought, how presumptuous that he should even be arguing with a prediction that had no verification. Obad alone had planted the notion of such a calling in his head. There had been no word from Yahweh to this effect. "In fact," he laughed, "I have never had a word from Yahweh to *any* effect. My knowledge of Yahweh is strictly what my father and his father and their fathers before them have handed down!"

Still, even as he made this objection, his heart ached. For he knew Yahweh had been with him since childhood. Though he had never heard the Lord's voice, Noah had known his guidance and companionship more surely than a brother's.

Noah could now see the little hamlet he called home peeking white through its green bower along the hill some five miles ahead. He considered his father, for whom the town was named, and remembered the story of his own weaning party and how Lamech had chosen the name for his son. Names were often considered an endowment among the Sethites. While sometimes they only indicated a personal feature, a life quality, or a hoped-for trait, they were often believed to predict some destiny for the child.

Lamech, according to tradition, had disappeared into the wilderness for three days prior to the celebration, where he would spend his time praying for Yahweh's mind regarding his son. When he returned to the festive garden where his friends waited, he had borne a puzzled expression.

Times had been rich for the people of Lamechtown. Work had been easy and fruitful, and the village basked in leisure and economic security as never before. What Lamech had to say of his son's purpose seemed of little import in light of the prosperity the family and their associates were experiencing. Nevertheless, Lamech was certain Yahweh had impressed him to announce, "His name shall be 'Noah,' for he shall give us rest from our work and from the toil of our hands arising from the ground which the Lord has cursed."

The guests had fallen silent as they awaited the pronouncement, watching the father raise his three-year-old in strong hands to the sky. But with these words, they were as puzzled as he, and a ripple of laughter had moved through the gathering.

Lamech had eyed them sternly, however, and as they read the seriousness with which he took the moment, they had returned to their banquet in a somber mood.

Noah's mother had told him this tale when he was old enough to hear it, and she had embraced his small shoulders with her ample arm. "I know that your purpose shall be great," she had assured him. "We cannot see all things on this plane, and Yahweh's plans are often inscrutable. But one day we shall see his design and you will be surprised at your own destiny."

The mountaineer spurred his horse. Suddenly he was very eager to be with Lamech, and with his only brother, Jaseth. The sure-footed steed sensed his anxiety and made its way over the familiar trail rapidly.

It was peculiar, then, when the horse's foot slipped. He had traveled this route a hundred times. But without warning he was tumbling down the bank and to a rude halt on the graveled flat beside the road.

Noah found his own footing where the horse had thrown him, and helped the creature rise up. He dusted the dirt from his garment and stroked the horse's nose with a gentle "Steady, boy," while he looked for a way up to the trail.

Suddenly, however, the earth along the hill above began to move and a slide of rocky shale plummeted across the road and into the ravine below. Noah and his animal dashed for a hollow along the bank and watched in terror

as the great mountain seemed to heave before them, splitting the road ahead as with a giant cleaver.

The earth did not do such things, not that Noah had
ever heard. The earth was a stable mass, not given to
throes and shaking. The son of Lamech waited for the
tremor to abate, and after some moments, stepped hesi-
tantly out of the cave.

"What is it, boy?" he asked his companion. "Is the
earth angry?"

He quickly determined that there was no way he could
reach home as he had planned. He looked down the ravine
for the nearest way around the slide, and his eyes lit on
a tattered branch wedged between the shale. A black bird,
the raven of Poseidon's chamber, was perched there. And
as it watched him, it let out a laughing caw.

FIFTEEN

A light breeze from Poseidon's bedroom window flirted with Adala's hair, blowing it back from her bare shoulders. She sat beside the opening, leaning her head upon one hand, and watched the white seabirds making arcs high above the pale blue water of the Adlandic, or skimming its surface, foraging for fingerlings.

A tear slipped down her lashes and fell upon the fine coverlet which she had thrown over her torso. She had done nothing all afternoon but think on Obad, and on all that she had witnessed in the court. An hour in the steam caves below the temple and a dip in the mineral waters of the priestess' spa had not served to clear her mind, although she had been told it would.

She had been told many things since coming here: that she would be happy beyond imagining, that in time she would forget her family and her betrothed, that Poseidon truly loved her and wished only happiness to kiss her days.

She gazed at the coverlet, into which such fine embroidery had been worked she felt she could go blind by tracing it. All the fabric of the gods was based upon one weave, she had been told—a weave of 365 filaments per thread, and twelve threads per cord. All designs applied to the cloth were in increments of sevens and fours, representing the days and weeks of the twelve cycles and the 365 revolutions of each year. The extra days of the calendar not covered in the twenty-eight allotted each

month were put to advantage in little assymetrical sur-
prises within the design, so that all together, every garment, blanket, and tapestry was imbued with worship to
the Sun, and protected not only the body, but the soul.

Adala studied the activities of the gulls again and
watched as one headed toward the beach with a flopping
piece of silver wedged within his rigid beak. As he lay it
on the warm sand, it tried desperately to wriggle its way
back to the brine, but with one flick of the gull's head,
it was impaled, the beak serving as a stake to halt its
rebellion.

Adala rose from the window and threw herself across
the gigantic bed upon which Poseidon had made her his
own. Quiet sobs shook her. She dare not let anyone know
that she felt as helpless and as mortally spoiled as that
tiny fish.

At last she sat erect and tried to compose herself. She
held on to the great iron bedstead which framed the
resting place, and felt extremely small, engulfed by the
proportions of everything about her. Intricate dolphins,
mermaids, and heads of gargoyles were the featured decor
of the footboard, and she recoiled at the memory of those
black faces and obsidian eyes which had watched her
virginal initiation.

Suddenly, she was weeping. She drew one of the heavy
pillows from the bed and buried her face in it, as visions
of Obad and the sorrow she had caused him danced gro-
tesquely through her mind.

Her uncontrolled mourning brought the response
which she had tried to avoid. She heard the chamber door
open and knew that her lord had been summoned. "I will
see to it," he was telling someone in the hall. "She will
be fine."

And now she sensed his presence beside her. She was
afraid to take her eyes from the pillow, but she knew he
stood at her shoulder.

When he placed his warm, beseeching hand upon her,

she could contain herself no longer, and wrenched herself away with a low moan.

"My lady," the Being whispered. "You mourn for your brothers, I see. And this is well. It should be so. But in time you will see my wisdom."

Adala still had not faced him and as the deity sat beside her he pulled her around and lifted her face to his. The woman remembered how his gaze had entranced her at the pond of Moricahn, and she resisted with all her strength the beckoning of his eyes.

"You know, my lord, that Noah alone is my brother! You knew it from the start!" she cried.

The Sea Master passed his hand slowly over her shoulder and then reached up to stroke her brow. "Of course, Adala. Your lord knows all about you. But, you will see. In time the memory of your past will fade away, and my love will be all you need."

The daughter of Lamech could have been caught away by his persuasion, but it was no longer her upbringing alone on which she relied for her strength. She had the wisdom of experience now, and she knew that the Halls of Poseidon were the marketplace of lies.

"You and your governors are deceivers!" she insisted, leaping from the bed and turning her eyes to the sea. "I believe my brother is right in all he was preaching when he stood in your hall. And your rule is coming to an end!"

The Fallen One sensed her strength of will, and somehow knew that it was past breaking a second time. He studied her graceful form where it was framed in sunlight and his heart ached. "I see then that you have been mesmerized by this lunatic son of the mountains!"

"Not mesmerized!" Adala cried, flashing an angry countenance. "I have been brought back to myself—a self which you beguiled from me as surely as the Serpent beguiled our Mother! I am Obad's rightful wife, and none of yours!"

The deity did not flinch at this. In fact, he made no

move at all. Suddenly he was sitting upright, his chin lifted and his eyes rolled back in his head. For a long moment he held this position and Adala trembled with the witness. She knew he was "communicating," as he called it. And she turned her eyes to the door.

It was not long before it opened. No one told her where she was being taken. But within a short while she would be joining her Sethite lover in the peace of eternity.

SIXTEEN

Noah had never been to the great elevated plain west of the Valley of the Turtles. But as he sought a way around the fissure which had begun along the Lamechtown ridge, he was taken across the valley and high onto the slopes to the west, which overlooked the mesa in the misty distance. He had often heard strange tales of the place, told by those who traveled in that part of the world. Rumor held that it was a flight strip for the Olympians, and was named Baalbek Terrace for one of the great gods who had helped construct it.

Today, as he finally came to the far end of the cleft which the earthquake had created, and as he was about to make his way around the fissure back toward his home-town, he spied the strange tableland as a flash of silvery light bounced from its summit.

Having come this far out of his way, he reasoned that half a day's journey to spy out the activity of the terrace would not be a sacrifice too great for the knowledge he would gain. If the gods truly were involved in the doings of Baalbek, it would be worth his while to look into the matter.

The slope ascending to the platform was extremely steep, and, after four hours of travel across open plain, could be attempted only after the swamp at its base had been traversed. The motivation to perform this, however, urged Noah past delay, for just as he reached it the ground along the plain began to tremble. Perhaps if he sought higher footing quickly, he would be spared any danger which the heaving ground might pose.

He did not stop to remove his sandals, but only gathered his robes between his legs before he strode knee-deep through the sluggish waters. And as his feet touched ground at the base of the mesa, the earth gave one more wrenching jolt and subsided.

At that instant, a roar as of many waters filled the air overhead, and Noah looked up to see a dozen sky-chariots leaping from the mountaintop and darting across the plain. They rose and dove repeatedly as if inspecting the ground for damage, and finding none returned to their port on the tableland.

Now curiosity spurred the Sethite to even greater effort. This sign, along with the laughing raven, made him fear that the gods themselves were responsible for the strange tremors in the land, and he inched his way up the precarious mountain wall determined to know the meaning of it all.

What he found when he reached the top chilled his very soul. Bracing his feet against a dry root, he pulled himself up so that his chin rested on the table top and cautiously turned his head this way and that until he was convinced it was safe to proceed. He had not gone far across the mesa before he heard the sounds of drumbeats and strange chanting. From the vantage point of a concealing bush he saw the participants, some of whom he recognized from Poseidon's court.

They were performing a ritual. He need not be told what it would lead to. He had heard of such meetings being held in the temple courts of most Adlandian cities, between the pillars of law and upon the orichalchum altars. This was the ritual of sacrifice and would climax, he knew, in the death of some human being.

The members of several city courts apparently were represented here. In fact, as Noah made a hasty calculation, he reasoned that the terrace held representatives of every Adlandian state, the governors of all the earth.

An awesome vibration rose from the chorus of chanting voices. Over and over they repeated a single syllable in a great hum, and Noah knew they were invoking the Oversoul, the Spirit of the Air—the Prince of This World. The teaching was common among all people of earth, save the Sethites, that the Higher Good and Universal Spirit could be petitioned by this method. For it was believed that the sound was in synchrony with the hum of the stars and the music of the spheres, the vibration of "universal energy." Noah and his kin would not have quarreled with such a practice had the rite not been so often mixed with worship of the gods. Hence they suspected that the "Universal Spirit" being invoked was Lucifer himself. Had Noah ever doubted, his doubts were put aside today. For the ritualists were none other than Lucifer's own. And with the monosyllabic chorus he now heard the rising chant of one number, repeated three times, over and over. This number repeated thrice was, he knew, symbolic of a trinity, the principalities, powers, and unseen agencies of the world system, and it was one number below the number of perfection—below the number of Yahweh himself.

Just as this symbol began to be chanted, however, the ground at the base of the mesa heaved again, and the mountain shook dreadfully. The response of the petitioners was unexpected. Noah would have thought the rumblings an answer to their prayers—that the strange behavior of the earth had been at their instigation. But this appeared not to be.

For the worshipers were clearly terrified, falling to their knees and chanting yet more vehemently. Here and there members of the throng threw dust over their own heads and rent their garments.

Suddenly the chant changed from the symbolic to the literal. *"Lucifer—Lucifer—Lucifer!"* they cried, pleading that he intervene with the trauma of the landscape.

And when yet more rumblings followed, and the mountain itself threatened to divide, a great cry was heard from the platform at the head of the congregation, upon which, to this point, no one had taken a stand.

The figure who ascended the stage was familiar to Noah. He recognized him instantly. Eight feet tall he stood—his mighty legs spread in a straddle. He was the keeper of the Hall of the Nephilim—a son of Poseidon. Noah drew back behind the bush, though he knew the giant's eyes would not be upon him.

"Sacrifice!" the Being cried. "The ground will not be appeased without sacrifice!"

Noah trembled and followed the gaze of the throng. Someone was being escorted down a wide aisle from the back of the tableland. For a moment the crowd was hushed, but at the sound of the victim's cry, they went wild, screaming and raising their fists to the setting sun.

It was not until the human scapegoat was brought to the platform that Noah was able to catch a glimpse of her. And as he did, his heart stopped.

"Adala!" he groaned, the word escaping past his fear.

Dressed in white linen, she stood pale and helpless before the Nephil, her head bent beneath his cruel gaze. But she would not die alone. Apparently Poseidon's jealousy had convinced him—or would convince the crowd—that the circumstances called for more than one atonement. Beside her stood the golden-haired Sethite of Cronos, Noah's dearest friend.

The mountaineer would not witness the execution of Obad and Adala. He would hear their final cries and then the abrupt silence which followed. But the rumbling of the earth which began again along the plain reached his place on the mesa before it reached the others, and he was thrown from his footing just as the sword of death descended.

Nor would the throng along the tableland have time

to celebrate the sacrifice. They would know only that it had not satisfied the ground.

Like a knife, in synchrony with the death sword, the quake rent the mountain, casting hundreds into its abyss.

The son of Lamech, bruised and torn, slid feet first to firmer ground. And when he had reached a cleft which seemed secure, he observed the ravaged mesa.

The rumbling had ceased and the sound of weeping could be heard coming from the scattered few left alone on the mount above. Noah clung to the hillside and buried his face in the yellow earth. Convulsions of sorrow and fear wracked him. For a long while he lay thus, until darkness overtook the land and the vapors of night ascended from the broken ground.

He could not see the mountains of home. They were lost in the blackness; but he descended the place of destruction and turned instinctively to the east.

When the caw of the raven haunted his steps, he raised his fist to the air. "I know, devil bird! You thought your master's Master ruled the earth, and that these things were wrought by him. But you see now the warning of Yahweh, and that he holds this planet in *his* hand!"

P A R T   I I
ONLY EVIL CONTINUALLY

*The Lord saw that the wickedness of man was
great in the earth, and that every imagination of
the thoughts of his heart was only evil continually.*

*Now the earth was corrupt in God's sight, and
the earth was filled with violence.*

*And the Lord was sorry that he had made man on the
earth, and it grieved him to his heart.*

Genesis 6:5, 11, and 6, RSV

ONE

The ships of Adlandia were not sailing vessels. They were equipped with small riggings which could be raised to capture the fleeting breezes that occasionally dappled the salty deep. But since there was no strong wind, there was no use for the great sheets which would propel the ships of later generations.

The ships of Adlandia, however, were speedy vessels. They took advantage of the currents and tidal forces of the network sea, but they also ploughed the waters with the force of unearthly power.

The harbors of earth, therefore, were not quiet places. The shooting of steam from mammoth boilers, the chug of great cranks and wheels and gears, the whistle and sleek whirring of engines driven by the splitting of atoms and the fission of neutrons made harbors the scene of dynamic commerce and unceasing activity.

Noah was enamored with such places. Though a large part of him would always need the solitude of mountains and the restorative peace of trees, though he preferred the horse to a ride in a sky-machine, he loved the sea and all the industry of man which encompassed it, traversed it, and used it.

Noah was not a simple person. His father had always wished he were. But the accounting desk could not appease his sense of life or his call to adventure. He was many-faceted, taking delight in the varied world of his nativity. To sit beside a quiet stream pleasured him, but to sit upon a metropolitan dock fed another part of his soul.

Lamech, who was content with the mountains, and who wished Noah were more pleased to serve there alone, had actually bred into his son a love for the wider world by teaching him of Yahweh. For God, he had told the boy, holds it all, and is to be found in all things.

What *was* simple about Noah was that he thrived on the challenge of change.

Change had been a long time coming of late. Noah had been staying in Cronos for several months, and today, as he sat upon one of the pilings of a harbor pier, his eyes did not linger on the fleet ships of trade so much as on the great floating barges which slowly passed the mouth of the sound.

One of these, apparently constructed of gopher wood and bitumen, was likely a product of his father's own export business. He followed its patient passage as it set its rudders to float north.

"Toward home . . . ," he whispered.

He wondered what its cargo might be. Something which could abide long storage, he reasoned. Dry goods of some kind. Likely fabrics and bulk grains from the cotton-woolen mills and wheat fields of the interior, up behind the Cronos peninsula. There was a steady demand for such products in the mountains, and the merchants who specialized in them could afford the more time-consuming travel of the barges, especially as such transportation was vastly cheaper than the quick passage of powered ships.

He thought about his father and the quiet existence he could be sharing with him now. He thought of his years with Jaseth, and how he was losing touch with him. But nothing had been the same since the deaths of Adala and Obad. Though five years had elapsed since the grisly spectacle at Baalbek, the son of Lamech had never shaken it. His life had been in perpetual tension between the love of home and the urgency to pace the cities—to observe, to record, to watch the increasing evidence of man's depravity.

Why this must be, he feared to contemplate. Yet, since the night Obad had predicted it, Noah had sensed a quiet call. He still resisted, but found his steps more and more leading to a climax of surrender.

After the night at Baalbek and after making his way through the devastated landscape, back to Lamechtown, he had tried to forget. He had tried to be content with ledgers and figures. But his sleep was never easy. His waking thoughts were obsessed with what he had seen, and his dreams at night were repetitions of horror.

And so he had left home to stay with Obad's father, Shubag, in the coast city. He had maintained himself by working for the old Sethite, helping to keep his mercantile books in the large office which housed several accountants. But his spare time—all of it—was devoted to the streets, where he lingered like a shadow, evening upon evening.

It seemed that Yahweh propelled him there. It seemed, though he had never heard the voice of the Lord, that Yahweh was saying, *"See, Noah; observe. See what my people have come to. Watch and learn what sinfulness stalks the byways. Understand why my heart breaks, and why my anger is kindled."*

What he witnessed was repugnant to him, not as blatant or blood-chilling as the Baalbek scene had been, but in some ways more ominous. For the violent immorality of the people was no longer secret rite, nor was it veiled by any religious pretense. It was not only without rationale, but without conscience. It had grown past defiance of God, to utter godlessness. Sorry as conditions had been five years before, they had deteriorated so rapidly he hardly recognized the culture as the same one he had preached against at Poseidon's throne.

Therefore, today, as he watched the harbor, his eyes were more often drawn to the great barges than to the speedier vessels. His heart was carried toward their destination, the north country. And he longed for home.

An evening breeze wafted inland from the sea, and the orange sun began to settle upon the Adlandian horizon, sending its glow fanlike through the sky's white veil. Noah pulled his cloak close to his chest and stepped down from the piling. The mists which watered the earth each day were always heaviest near great bodies of water, and always began to condense there first. Noah knew that if he did not seek shelter soon, he would return home damp to the skin.

Already he had turned toward Shubag's too late to avoid the thick fog which would quickly fill the streets nearest the shore. The old man had warned him of the dense blanket which the coast city donned each night. "You will have trouble knowing one foot from the other if you are down by the water," he had said. "Folks who have lived here all their lives are sometimes confused. Be sure you memorize the landmarks if you would find your way home!"

Surely Shubag exaggerated, Noah chuckled as he went the first few blocks without difficulty. He had spent so many evenings in the city without incident, he could not believe the proximity to shore would make so much difference. But the fog was growing soupy, the way less familiar. If he could only find the road to the market square he knew he would be all right.

The flashing lights of the tavern rows were no help. He did not recognize this part of town, and the brilliant signs served only to add an eeriness to the already vague pathway.

Only as he actually passed the doorways where the interiors of fogless cabarets beckoned, could he discern one building from another. And the raucous laughter, the

118

obscene fellowship which met his eyes and ears forced him on.

At last, when he could not even see his own hand before him, and when he did not know which way to turn, he stopped and, reaching forth, found a low wall beside him. He reasoned that it must be the fence bordering some establishment; but no one would see him stopping there, so he sat down to rest.

He had heard voices as he had come upon this place. But voices had been everywhere along the way, shouting from the brothels, laughing in the gutters. He had taken little heed of the sounds behind the wall. Now as he sat still, reasoning how to proceed, they became more clear, and Noah feared to listen.

Several of the utterances were those of grown men, and the men seemed to grapple with one another for some coveted object. "I found it first!" one cried. And then another, "No—it was mine from the start. I saw it walk into the place!"

"*It?*" Noah wondered. Did they speak of a thing or of a living being?

The answer was quick in coming, as he discerned a muffled cry. It seemed they had a victim in tow, who now struggled to be heard.

"Quiet!" one of the brawlers demanded.

"Don't let him go!" yet another cried. "We'll never find him in this fog!"

So the helpless one was another male. Noah scooted quietly down from the wall and hid himself beside it. Perhaps they meant to rob this poor fellow—or—Noah feared to consider the ways in which they would ensure their quarry's silence.

But their crime would not even be that common. As their prey managed a loud outcry, the Sethite jolted. It was the plea of a young boy, and suddenly he knew the intentions of the captors.

Had there not been so many of them, Noah would have leaped the wall to the lad's defense. But he had discerned at least half a dozen different voices besides the boy's, and he slumped down weakly, reliving the agony of Baalbek.

"Where are the children of Seth?" he whispered. "Do the Sons of Cain rule the earth? Yahweh!" he whispered. "Is there nothing you can do!"

But all the answer he received was a momentary silence, as the assailants beyond the wall wrestled their little subject to the ground. And as this was followed by the brutal groans of sexual assault, the Sethite staggered to his feet.

He managed to make the next corner before his stomach revolted and oblivion overtook him. It would not be until morning had burned away the night and the sun had dispelled the fog that he would be forced to remember the cries and accept his impotence to change what had happened.

TWO

Shubag would have sent servants to find the son of Lamech, but something prevented him. As he stood at evening on the veranda which gave his home a commanding view of the wharves and docks, he had feared for Noah's safety, wondering why he had not returned. With descending dark, his anxiety had grown. But he had waited, even through the night, sensing that the delay was in Yahweh's hands, and would work for good.

The old Sethite could not sleep. He rose from his bed and paced his chamber over and over. "He was meant to be your prophet, Lord," he muttered. "He has resisted but must ultimately yield." His eyes lingered over the fireplace in the center of the room where he and his son, Obad, had often spoken of deep things. The two had agreed early on, when they had become involved with the family of Lamech, that there was something very special about Noah. What Obad had predicted in the dungeon of Poseidon was not original with him. Shubag had believed it years before, and experience with the son of Lamech had only confirmed it time and again.

Therefore, tonight, he claimed that assurance, just as he had been forced to do on several occasions since Noah had come to stay in his home. Had any of his other employees frequented the streets, or taken to lingering around the dark corners of town, he would have upbraided them severely. But—with Noah, things were different. He had known, from the moment the young man had arrived, that he was on a mission. And, indeed, it seemed Shubag understood that more clearly than Noah himself.

He recalled how bewildered the young Sethite had been at the strange compulsions which led him to the evening vigils, to the treks through town at odd hours. He recalled the first times when Noah had returned from those journeys only to sit for hours in his room, jotting notes in his diary.

Shubag knew that Noah did not comprehend his own destiny, but he also knew that in time he would. And he sensed that this evening the understanding had taken hold.

It was therefore no great surprise to Shubag when word came of Noah's whereabouts. The news was brought by an elderly female housekeeper, known for her nervous reactions to things. She pummeled the door with anxious knocking, and when Shubag admitted her, she burst in with a flurry, rubbing her hands together and pointing toward the street. "Young Master Noah is in the marketplace!" she cried. "It's barely dawn and he's causing a ruckus in the square!"

Shubag stood up from his couch and nodded to her patiently. "Well, then, so he has been found."

"Found? Who could miss him? He's wakened the whole city! Oh, my lord, I told you this one was a troublemaker. I warned you he belonged in the hills!"

"Now, Matrina," Shubag said smiling, "you have been with us for years and I can entrust you with many things about this house. But there is no need for you to worry over my guests."

The old servant snapped her dark eyes toward the veranda. "But, you should hear him!" she insisted.

"What is he saying?" Shubag deferred.

"He's . . . he's . . . preaching!"

The elder Sethite studied her carefully. "Are you certain?" he inquired.

"Hear for yourself, sir!" she pleaded. "Lean your head out the window and listen!"

Shubag did as she suggested, his heart almost afraid of the fulfillment. He walked to the veranda and peered up the street. He could not see the square, for it was around the corner from the wharves which fronted his home. But, indeed, he could hear someone's vehement cries, and though he could not make out the words, the voice was certainly Noah's.

As he stepped back into the chamber his eyes were misty, and his gaze faraway.

"Didn't I tell you?" the housekeeper insisted. "First his strange wandering and lurking about town, his hours of isolation—and now this! I tell you, the son of Lamech is not well!" With these words she pointed to her temple, making a circular motion with her finger.

Shubag chuckled and led her to the door. "Oh, Matrina —dear friend, the young man is sane enough." And then, glancing toward the veranda, he said, "Very unusual he is—but sane."

The man from the mountains had never looked more the part than he did today. His night in the street and his agony of soul at what he had witnessed had made him haggard, but he had the strength of vengeance in his stance. And the disheveled hair, the flashing eyes only enhanced the impression that he was a wild man from the north country.

He stood at dawn upon a crate unloaded from some ship at a merchant's booth and ready to be opened for the day's bartering. When the wizened old barker who owned the box had crept from his tent at the first sounds of Noah's preaching, he had tried to wrest the crate from beneath the stranger's feet. But after delivering many curses and much threatening, he had given up and had hidden within the sanctuary of his tarp, hoping no one would associate him with the "lunatic."

The marketplace was a common resort for peculiar thinkers. Daily amid the traders, and between the little shops where the haggling and hawking took place, strange folk with philosophies to sell and politics to peddle could be heard. They were often marked by odd appearance and eccentric behavior. Inevitably they were loud and competed valiantly for their audience. The town square was therefore a circus, not only of commerce, but of intellect, religion, and entertainment.

Such people vied for a hearing from atop any elevated spot available. Quick-thinking merchants had to be on guard lest their bundled goods become the podiums or the stages for self-appointed orators. But the old fellow whose crate had been commandeered today could not have known anyone would overtake it so early in the morning. He peered from behind the flap of his tent, rubbing his chin nervously as his neighbors were roused from sleep and clustered angrily about his booth. *What hope is there for a profit today?* he wondered.

But Noah was not concerned for any of this. The memory of last night's ordeal had joined with the Baalbek witness to hound his soul to submission. Yes, Yahweh, he would preach. Oh, how he would preach!

"The sin of Cain has fallen upon us!" he began, his head thrown back and his arms spread. His words filled the marketplace like a trumpet, and he repeated them over and over, until a great crowd had gathered. "The sin of Cain has fallen upon us! The sin of Cain! Sin of Cain!"

At first the audience watched him in bewilderment, wondering at his strange message, and inquiring of one another who he might be. But as he continued, their bewilderment changed to ripples of laughter.

"The whole earth is corrupt in the sight of God," he cried, "and filled with violence! All flesh has corrupted its way upon the earth! And—indeed—every intent of the thoughts of man's heart is *only evil continually!*"

The manager of the marketplace sat with his paramour in a corner of the square. Though intrigued by the spectacle, he fidgeted nervously. The market was not only a forum for goods, products, and philosophy. It was a trading place for fleshly indulgence. He glanced to the far wall where the tents of the prostitutes stood in scarlet rows, their colorful banners a brazen summons. He saw the painted faces of the harlots peeking from behind the tarpaulins, and he saw the oiled bodies of their male consorts as they emerged from the parlors of seduction to observe the preacher. He had never heard such words as this mountain man was speaking, but he sensed that they were not good for business.

"This was a great planet once," Noah went on, "created for our Father Adam and his descendants. But our traffic with Lucifer has corrupted it—and the children of Cain, who slew our brother Abel, have overcome the righteous line of Seth!"

Now the manager glanced to the far wall of the square and saw the town guard—a brutal fellow known to have killed a dozen men in his time. The guard was watching Noah with a cruel gleam in his eye, and the market chief became still more uneasy.

What was this crazy talk? the people wondered. They had heard of Cain. He was one of the most prominent progenitors of the race. They had certainly heard of Adam. But what "god" did he refer to who was not pleased with planet earth? And who could judge that the thoughts of men's hearts were evil? Was not the whole world system designed to follow the will of the Sun? Perhaps there was too much violence. Perhaps the enticements of the flesh did not always satisfy. But wasn't the human race improving all the time? Wouldn't their devotion to the gods bring them to perfection?

"You blaspheme the Sun!" someone challenged him, lifting a fist to his face. "Who is this god of whom you speak? If our Father Cain did sin, he has surely been redeemed—for his mighty works are evident through his children!"

"Mighty works, indeed!" Noah responded. "Truly the advances are marvelous. The skills of the Creator are our inheritance, and we work wonders with our hands. But Yahweh's Spirit shall not always strive with man. There shall come a day when the God of heaven will be grieved in his heart that he has made us!"

One of the tents against the far wall housed the trained creatures of bestiality. Their keeper's business was a great financial asset to the square. At the sound of Noah's warning he had stepped out of the shadows near his establishment and had cast a menacing glance at the market's proprietor. Obviously he was calling for some type of interception, and the manager knew he was expected to take action or face rude consequences. The market chief cleared his throat and stood up on shaky legs.

"Good sir!" he called, beckoning to Noah. "We are entranced by your fluency and your able preaching. But you must have patience with such folk as myself, for while many of my brethren here are highly educated, I am ill informed regarding the lofty things of which you speak."

The manager cast a furtive look at the gathering. The people were not displeased, and so he proceeded. "I deduce, from your words, that you are a Sethite. Is this true?" he began.

"I am."

"Then if the Sethites are especially approved by this god of yours, why are they a dwindling race? It seems to me that when the Sun blesses, it is with life-giving power, and it produces growth. Your race is not growing but diminishing, and Cain's race is the powerful one!"

The crowd liked this fellow's reasoning, and applauded as he drew his conclusion. But Noah looked him squarely in the eye. "I do not speak of the Sun, but of the God of gods, who holds all things, including the Golden Orb, in his hand! And I do not speak of blessings and curses in the same way you do. For Yahweh's thoughts are not our thoughts, and before he sees fit to bless, he often reduces us to a fragment of our strength. Before he sees fit to redeem this earth, there will be a diminishing of all races, a loss greater than we can comprehend!"

When the preacher made this assertion, the marketplace became a clatter of whispers and murmurs. But Noah was not content to leave the subject. "Furthermore," he added, his voice strangely sad, "my people, the Sons of Seth, diminish because of their traffic with evil. They are no longer distinct from the hoards of Cainites who have absorbed them. There are but few Sethites who keep the old traditions, and it is for these that Yahweh will prepare his salvation when the great calamity descends!"

As he spoke these words, it was only intuition which drew his eyes skyward. He had no clear picture in his mind regarding "the calamity." But his gesture caused the multitude to lift its gaze with him; and as they wondered at his peculiar warnings they murmured and whispered angrily among themselves.

THREE

Shubag had sat in his chamber throughout the morning, awaiting an account of Noah's sermon. He had sent servants to the square as soon as he knew that the voice ringing forth was that of Lamech's son. And they had just returned home ahead of the young Sethite, where they anxiously repeated his strange message for their master's ears.

Now, as Shubag sat alone, contemplating the report, his eyes closed and he leaned back into his chair in silent meditation.

It was upon this quiet scene that Noah came when he returned from the square, and sought out his old friend and advisor. The young preacher stood awkwardly in the doorway of the chamber for a long moment, and thinking that Shubag must have fallen asleep, turned to leave. But the old fellow sensed his presence and called, "Do not go just yet."

The son of Lamech was surprised by the elder's call. The old man, whose hearing was somewhat dimmed by age, could not have perceived his quiet shuffle at the door. But now Shubag was motioning to him, his eyes still closed and his head resting against the back of his chair.

Noah entered the dimly lit room reverently. There was a hush about this place which he had encountered when in the presence of only one other man. When he had been a lad and his grandfather, Ishna, had summoned him for quiet chats, there had been the same peacefulness in their meetings. The boy had been awed by it. As he had grown older, and even now, when he remembered those times, the sensation was still there. And he had known, because of this, that Ishna was a holy man.

Shubag's face was younger than that of Noah's grandfather. After all, Shubag was of Lamech's generation. But the preacher realized in this moment, as never before, the holiness of the one who would now speak of the day's calling.

"Your words were well given today," the elder began.

"You were there?" Noah asked in surprise.

"No—but I received your message."

Noah studied the old man carefully, and his eyes grew wide. Was Shubag saying that the words had somehow been transmitted spiritually? In this setting and before this man, such a thing did not seem beyond belief.

But Shubag now looked at his young friend and his lips drew up in a smile. "No, no—servants, my lad. I sent servants to the square."

Noah relaxed a bit, and Shubag chuckled. "I am no wizard, my son. You have never thought so in the past and you need not think so now. No. I am quite human, but—" Here he paused. "I do have something to say to you, which I think is of Yahweh's prompting."

"Speak, then, sir," Noah nodded. "The role of preacher is very new to me, and I want to do all I can to improve myself."

"Oh, lad." Shubag smiled, reaching out a veined hand. Noah noticed the filmy white of the skin which enclosed it, and for the first time he was concerned for the elder's failing health. "Lad, I do not refer to your oratorical skills. I am assured by my messengers that they are honed to a flint-edge. How you have come by this talent is a marvel to me, for I know you have had little practice in public speaking."

Noah lowered his head with a sudden wave of humility. "You honor me," he said. "And truly, if this be the case, it is a gift of Yahweh, and none of my own."

"Yes," Shubag agreed. "And—for the most part—your message is directly from Yahweh's heart."

The preacher lifted his chin and studied the critic carefully. " 'For the most part'?"

"You spoke of the same great calamity which our Father Adam and the prophets Enoch and Methuselah predicted, did you not?"

"Yes, sir. . . ."

"And you spoke of the corruption of this age?"

"Yes—you received a correct report."

"And is the calamity not against all unrighteousness?"

"Indeed—"

"And salvation for all who are of upright heart?"

"Sir, of course . . ."

Noah was troubled at the inquisition. Obviously, Shubag was well aware of the themes he had addressed.

"There is but one weakness in your argument, as I have understood it today," Shubag asserted, leaning forward. And as Noah fidgeted, unused to being reviewed, the elder bid him sit on the chamber floor.

This was a familiar position for the son of Lamech to take. How often he had been privileged to sit at the knee of his elders at home, the great men who had raised him in the truth! He fleetingly surveyed the intricate tapestry of the carpet upon which he now reclined, and then he looked eagerly, though somewhat fearfully, at the one who would critique his fledgling sermon.

The old man had not been present in the market to study Noah's gestures, or to remark upon his tonal quality or use of emphasis. There was no exegesis of scriptures to debate, for there were no scriptures in this oral tradition. No—Shubag was about to inflict the analytical scalpel upon the very bones and marrow of the oration—upon its doctrine!

"It is true," said Shubag, looking kindly on the youngster who had won his heart so many years ago, "it is true that when our human father brought forth his first two sons, the stage was set for conflict. Until that point, sin had ravaged man's relationship not only with God, but also with his mate, our Mother Eve. But there was no social consequence beyond this, for there was no society. To this point pride and selfishness were the destroyers, but when two sons were born to work the garden beside their parents, the soil was made fertile for the seed of jealousy."

Noah listened respectfully, but wondered what point there was to all this. "Yes, of course," he replied, asking no questions.

"Though Cain and Abel were born to fallen parents, there is no evidence of sin in their lives until the dispute arose regarding their offerings of sacrifice. In fact, it seems likely that they were raised in a most righteous and God-fearing home, for Adam and Eve, though expelled from Paradise, were in close communion with Yahweh all their days."

"Yes," Noah assented. He stifled a yawn and blinked his bleary eyes. A night in the street and a morning in the square had wearied him immensely, and he hoped he could maintain interest in Shubag's seemingly aimless discourse.

The old man, however, appeared bent on some great purpose, and went on, his eyes riveted on the listener as he spoke. "Now, Noah, you addressed the matter of the two races well today. For it is true that the Sons of Cain and the Sons of Seth (who was given to Adam in the place of Abel) have demonstrated very different spiritual propensities. However," and here the speaker's voice grew more emphatic, "I fear you have missed an important understanding in your study."

Noah sensed that Shubag drew near making a point, and his interest was rekindled. "I have, sir? Where?"

"Look at the story of the sacrifices. Why was Yahweh displeased with Cain's, but accepted Abel's?"

The younger man did not have to think long on this. "Why, because the one was of fruits and grains and the other of blood. There is no redemption without the shedding of blood. This was a symbol!" Noah grew irritable. This catechism was known to any traditional Sethite. It seemed Shubag wasted his time.

"But," Shubag pursued the lesson, "did Yahweh punish Cain for lack of knowledge, for bringing the wrong sacrifice out of ignorance?"

The listener thought a moment. "No—I do not suppose so. He was punished for murdering his brother."

"And what prompted the murder?"

Noah rubbed his hands against the carpet in an angry fidget. "You know these things, Master. Why do you inquire of me?" But Shubag only waited, and at last Noah heaved a sigh. "Jealousy. Jealousy prompted the murder!" he exclaimed. "Cain was jealous of Abel, for he had found favor in God's eyes."

"And what was the punishment?" Shubag pressed.

"Cain was sent forth from his family and from God's presence—to the East of Eden—to be a vagabond and a wanderer in the earth!" the preacher replied. And as he did so, a smirk marked his lips—for he felt the vengeance of Yahweh in the description.

Shubag studied him a moment, and Noah felt something of an uneasiness in the old man's eyes—or a sadness. But the hoary head bent forward, even closer, and another question was produced.

"But—was he removed from the love of Yahweh?" Shubag inquired.

Noah perceived the weight of the question, though he did not understand its import. And he was careful before replying. "I assume so, yes. Otherwise the punishment would have little sting."

Shubag shook his head and raised a feeble finger. "In

this you are mistaken, young man. You would do well to think on the nature of Cain's expulsion. What was God's promise to him?"

The son of Lamech traced a line on the tapestry with his index finger. "Well—he feared that he would be set upon and killed for his crime. But . . ." He paused and marveled at the leading of his teacher.

"Go on," Shubag urged.

"But . . . in fact, God set a mark upon him to protect him, lest any man should try to take his life. . . ."

The young man's voice became a whisper, and yet Shubag was not content.

"Go on. . . ."

"And . . . Yahweh promised to avenge him. . . ."

At those words Shubag sunk back into his chair with an approving nod.

Noah sat for a long while trying to see the whole truth. He had been brought this far—but could see no farther. "But, sir," he objected, scratching his head, "given that all this is true, am I to conclude that there is no real difference between the Sethites and the Cainites? Why—look around you!" he demanded, gesturing toward the window. "The evidence is very clear! There are the good and the evil!"

"The privileged and the underprivileged!" Shubag corrected. "We must not assume that Cain's being driven from the presence of the Lord meant he was abandoned. For Yahweh is everywhere and in all things—and if any man seek him he shall be found. But . . . ," the elder explained, "for some this comes more easily than for others. And it is largely due to their surroundings. If a man is privileged, as you have been, to sit at the feet of godly men from his birth, and to learn the oracles from childhood, his path to the Lord of heaven is made much smoother. If, however," and his old voice broke, ". . . if a man is cut off from the communion of knowledge and his way leads to the Land of Nod, he cannot be expected to see the fullness of truth without great struggle. Such was the case with Cain. Yahweh did not so much abandon him as release him to follow the consequences of his heart's attitude. And Cain chose to remove himself from the communion of believers."

Noah still did not see how this should affect his sermonizing. "I agree completely," he said nodding. "So in what way have I been in error? Was not Cain's end of his own making? Did he not deserve what he received from the hand of justice?"

Shubag drew close again. "Your sermon did not do an injustice to Cain, but to his descendants. Cain's way was of his own making, correct. But not so for his sons and daughters. They were born into surroundings already alienated from the comforts of truth. The struggle for them and for their children and their children's children was to be monumental. And all because of the sin of their father. You have answered rightly when you say Yahweh did not punish Cain for lack of knowledge; nor should you be harsh on the Cainites for lack of knowledge. You have seen that jealousy was the goad which led to Cain's crime, and yet you stir up jealousy in the Cainites when you compare them to the privileged Sons of Seth. Just as Cain was jealous of Abel's favored position, so you would have the Cainites be provoked by the Sethites' privileged state."

Noah was dumbfounded. He sat for a long while in silence, feeling the sting of Shubag's critique. It had not been delivered as a reprimand, and yet the young preacher felt shame at the evidence of his shortsightedness.

"Almost you cause me to pity Cain," he said at last, an edge of sarcasm marking his self-defense.

"And perhaps you *should* pity him," Shubag insisted, his eyes full of conviction. "For, you see, the effect of sin in the human family not only expelled our first parents from the Garden, but is now expelling Cain and his generations from easy access to truth."

The son of Lamech had been thoroughly corrected now. He chafed under the exposure, and once more surveyed the intricate weaving upon which he sat. "So complex this calling is," he replied, shaking his head sadly. "It is like this tapestry. I shall never be worthy of it, for I shall never understand it as I should."

Shubag leaned forth and placed a hand upon Noah's shoulder. "But you *were* called, my son. You have the gift for what you do. Now you must develop the heart for it."

"But my heart is not like Yahweh's. It has no love for the people to whom I speak. I can only feel anger at their wickedness and a desire to call down wrath upon them!"

Tears welled in his eyes at this admission, and he was shamed to the core as he saw his true nature.

The elder listened patiently and then offered, "But your heart has been stirred this way only temporarily. You have the capacity to serve and to love, if you will only focus on the redemption God holds out."

"Redemption?"

"The 'symbol,' remember? You said that the blood sacrifice was a symbol, and that is why Abel was accepted. It was not through any righteousness of his own that he was accepted, but by the death of an innocent creature."

Noah waited for more, but Shubag did not go on. And when the younger could not draw a conclusion from the words, he stammered, "Explain, Master."

"Until you know in your heart that we all have sinned, and that no covering will suffice without the shedding of blood, you will not feel love for your brothers. You will be angry like Cain and your countenance will fall. Sin will crouch at your door and you will not master your heart. A murderous heart will be yours, my son, and the blessing of Yahweh will be a curse. Speak of the symbol," Shubag directed. "It will save you and your hearers."

FOUR

Noah was bone weary as he stood on the small balcony which availed his quarters of the west wind. Shubag had insisted that he rest before coming to work today in the accounting room. "In fact, I prefer that you *not* serve me as bookkeeper this morning," the old merchant had suggested. "Get some sleep and join me at noon on the sea-drive. I want you to meet someone."

The young preacher wondered what Shubag had in mind, and who the "someone" might be. But for now, he grappled with a larger issue. The thought of the old man's critique on his sermon brought a burning blush to his face, for it not only assailed his first public address, but a sizeable portion of the philosophy which had governed his attitude toward fellow humans. If he could no longer distinguish people on the convenient principle of racial origin, a major part of his life view must become completely reoriented.

The Sethites were spiritually superior by inclination, he had always thought. Where they had fallen away, it was due to traffic with the Cainites and their kind. To see all people as one race, equally gifted and equally fallen, was to alter his whole perception of things, for it would affect his view of . . . himself.

Noah pressed his thighs to the balcony rail and scanned the horizon of the Adlandian Sea. The ships which usually managed to catch his mind away held no attraction for him today. The more he contemplated his prejudice, the more exposed he sensed himself to be.

"But," he argued, "is pride of family—pride of heritage—not a blessed thing?"

There was no fellow human present to answer his unvoiced thought, but his spirit was nudged within.

"Perhaps not . . . ," something seemed to say, and Noah's ears burned.

He wheeled about, as if expecting to find an eavesdropper behind him. But, upon seeing nothing but his vacant room, he shook his head and turned again to the rail.

"But, of course . . . I have been greatly blessed!" he insisted, speaking this time in a whisper.

"You did not ask about your blessings," the Presence returned. "You asked about your pride."

Noah's skin stood in prickles, and he feared to look behind himself again. Certainly, someone or something had spoken. He could not be imagining this. Slowly he called up courage to turn his head and then his entire body. But, once more, there was nothing to be seen but his bed—not yet slept in, and his chair, draped by the cloak he had carelessly thrown over it. No movement or shadow betrayed a visitor, and the preacher feared for his own mind.

"I am overwrought," he reasoned. "I have pushed myself, and have required too much of my faculties these past hours. Besides," he concluded, "why all this introspection? If Shubag is right, and I am to have no pride of lineage—no certainty of who is right and who is wrong—I must doubt my own calling!" Striking the rail, he laughed aloud. "Aha! A trick of Lucifer! Certainly. That is what this is. He would win a great victory if he could cause me to doubt myself!"

But as Noah reclined upon his bed and shut his eyes, summoning sleep to his defense, it was not an easy rest he found. And when he woke it would be to the same debate and that old internal struggle—waiting like a set trap in the corner of his mind.

Shubag's residence had direct access to the wharves of Cronos by means of a long driveway leading down to the sea. His home, therefore, served many purposes. It housed his living quarters and the accounting rooms. And further down, along the drive, were the warehouses and loading platforms which received the imports he marketed in town.

Noah would have slept through his noon appointment had Shubag not told the housekeeper to wake him at the appropriate time. The old woman's rasping voice had been a rude jolt, but even so, Noah felt only half awake as he made his way down the long winding road upon which he was to meet his host.

As he journeyed, the tall vegetation bordering the byway cut off his view of the sea and the city, and he felt curiously alone, closed in again with the same conflict he had experienced upon the balcony. If only he could speak once more with Shubag. Yes—that would help. Surely the wise fellow would understand his confusion. When he found him, he would shout his questions in his ear!

But Shubag had other plans. As Noah reached the flat at the end of the road, where it broadened onto the main thoroughfare of the wharves, he saw the old man seated on a piling, a wide smile lighting his eyes and lips.

"Just in time!" the merchant greeted. "The ship is just now anchoring at port. See!" he cried, grasping Noah by the arm and directing his gaze to a slender white vessel whose sails were being rolled down and whose navigator was settling it into a narrow slip. "She doesn't carry much—but what she carries! Oh, the craftsmanship is wondrous!"

The son of Lamech could not help but be favorably impressed, as his eyes took in the sleek beauty with an appreciative sweep. "From whence does she hail?" he asked, his gaze lingering on the vessel's shiny fittings.

"From the east—around the peninsula," Shubag replied, and as Noah marveled at the ship, the old man secretly studied him.

"Like her—eh?" he inquired.

"Oh, yes, sir . . . ," Noah said wistfully. "What is her cargo?"

"Metal works—of many kinds. This time mainly cutlery—even some fine swords and scabbards. The owner is the greatest smith in all Adlandia!"

"The greatest?" Noah asked doubtfully. "Shubag, the greatest, so I have heard, is—"

"A Son of Cain . . . ," the old man agreed.

". . . Tubal-Cain . . . ," Noah said, his voice full of awe. "The son of Lamech the Murderer."

"The same," Shubag nodded.

Noah quivered with the memory of the tale. He had always thought it ironic that his own father, who had tamed a "wild" nature, bore the same name as the famed bloodshedder of Nod, who had killed a man and a boy. The plea had been self-defense, and the trial, which had drawn on for weeks, had been the subject of news around the world, for the man's situation had been peculiar: "If Cain was avenged sevenfold," he had argued before the court, "I should be avenged seventy-seven fold. For these fellows came upon me to rob and kill, and I only protected myself and my home."

Ultimately the Cainite had been freed, without penalty, and the case had set a legal precedent unmatched in history. To this day, his guilt or innocence was often argued, and Noah, because he despised the race of Nod, had always condemned him.

"But . . . I. . . ."

"You thought I did business only with Sethites?" the elder asked, winking.

"Well, of course not."

"Of course not, indeed! I would have little trade if I limited it to our dwindling race."

Noah turned again to the ship, whose deck was now swarming with crewmen, each busy with some errand, porting the vessel and preparing to unload her. "But—why would you have me meet this man?" he asked.

The old merchant watched the plank being lowered from the boat's side and began to make his way down the pier where his guests would soon be setting foot.

"Because—," he called over his shoulder, "it is important!"

Noah's prejudice against the Cainites was not based on much personal contact with the race. In fact, save for his occasional trips to Cronos where he had visited with Obad and the family of Shubag, his life had been spent in the highlands of a Sethite village.

He was, therefore, unprepared for the gentility and graciousness of the passengers who disembarked from the glistening eastern ship.

Tubal-Cain was, as could be expected, an awesome figure. He carried the name of his ancient ancestor very well, his fine chiseled nose and uplifted chin a credit to the line. No one could have mistaken him for anybody but the owner of this vessel. His dark head was adorned with a scarlet turban, fitted with a great jeweled clasp at the front, and his robes of multi-colored silk reflected the noon sun as he walked. He flashed a great, toothy smile at the sight of Shubag, and flung his arms wide.

"Friend!" he called, approaching the old merchant down the gangplank and embracing him with zeal. The Cainite was head and shoulders taller than the Sethite, but Shubag returned the gesture with equal enthusiasm.

"Welcome to Cronos!" the elder greeted. "I was so pleased to hear that you would accompany your shipment. My home is yours for as long as you are here!"

As the host led his friend to the wharf, he directed his

attention to the young preacher who stood a cautious distance away. "I have been wanting you two to meet," he explained, guiding Tubal-Cain toward Noah.

The newcomer's flashing dark eyes surveyed the son of Lamech quizzically, and Noah felt the awkwardness of his own rude appearance. Though he had spent several years in this town, he had never become accustomed to city attire and manners, and never had he felt less sophisticated than he did at this moment. For though Tubal-Cain was the son of the infamous Lamech, he was also one of the most renowned craftsmen of the day, truly the father of metallurgy, and the creator of its finest examples. His foundry, located south of Nod in the region east of the peninsula which separated the coast cities from the interior, was considered a Mecca for artisans of all sorts. For from its beginnings as a center for metal work it had developed into a haven for sculptors, painters, and inventors of all sorts. In Nod-Persia, as it was called, science and art blended into one. And, of course, it had become a sort of capital for thinking people, whatever their skills, for its atmosphere spawned the kind of climate which drew and produced philosophers.

Tubal-Cain, therefore, had risen above great odds, against the obstacle of his father's stigma to become not just a craftsman, not just a wealthy man, but an institution. And Noah was quiet before him.

As the three men made their way to the thoroughfare and Shubag's waiting carriage, Noah tried to reason what the host's purpose might be. Truly, it was an honor to be personally introduced to such a celebrity as Tubal-Cain. But, if the old merchant expected that fame and glory would impress the son of Lamech, he was mistaken. In fact, it surprised Noah that Shubag could be influenced by such superficial things. If these traits were supposed to prove some spiritual greatness in the Cainite line, they were not doing their job.

Noah held his tongue, however, and gave Shubag the

benefit of the doubt. He had known the old man too long to believe him capable of such shallow reasoning, and decided to withhold judgment for the moment.

Suddenly, however, his contemplation was broken. Tubal-Cain had stopped short in the path and turned about. "What can I be thinking?" he cried. "I was so taken with the sight of you, Shubag, I forgot my own kin. See—she looks for me now," he said, directing their attention toward the deck.

At the top of the gangplank, looking quite bewildered by their sudden desertion, stood a young woman, dark like Tubal-Cain, and just as handsomely dressed.

Noah could not repress the rush of response which welled within him at the sight of her. Never had he experienced such a sensation, so sudden, so unreasoned. His pulse, which throbbed strangely in his ears, nearly drowned the Cainite's words.

"My sister, Naamah," he pronounced, beckoning her. "She will be staying with us, if she may."

Shubag nodded graciously, and answered something affirmative. But Noah did not catch a syllable of his reply.

FIVE

Since Noah had been staying at Shubag's home, the courtyard had never been so lively as it was this evening. In fact, until now the residence had been a quiet retreat from the noisy city, and a place for business activity only.

Tonight, it had taken on a festive air, the halls and galleries and porches filled with light, sound, and laughter. Noah stood in an archway leading to the central patio, watching the preparation of the dining tables, and glancing now and then into the great parlor under the mezzanine. Tubal-Cain had brought with him more than his sister. His entire crew, it seemed, had been welcomed into Shubag's home and would be staying in the numerous quarters which stood vacant most other times.

The mountain man had never felt more out of his element, and did not know which way to turn. He supposed he ought to join the conversation in Shubag's big hall, but he almost felt he would be more comfortable assisting the servants who bustled about the court. In fact, it occurred to him, not for the first time, that his position in Shubag's world was frequently awkward. He was the old merchant's employee, and yet was more often treated like a guest or even a family member. And tonight, especially, this posed a predicament. The other bookkeepers would have retired to their own quarters by now, or would have gone to separate residences in town to join their families. Were Obad here, Noah would not hesitate to go with him into the sanctum of Shubag's most honored visitors. But as things stood, he did not know where he fit, and so lingered uneasily between the world of the hired help and the guests.

"Nonsense!" Matrina objected when she came upon him in the doorway. "You're a troublemaker for sure—but the master would not have you stand here like an oaf. Be as brazen as you were in the marketplace. Go in boldly to his side and make yourself known!"

And with a flick of the hand she dismissed him and scurried off to see to her workers.

The woman is right! Noah thought to himself. *Since when would I not be welcome in the parlor of my father's best friend, and my best friend's father?*

Lifting his chin he turned toward the spacious den in which two dozen male voices discussed the world of ships and cargoes, wealth and how it is attained, life and what makes it worth living. He caught Shubag's eye as he entered and the old man winked his approval.

"We have been looking for you!" the merchant called. "Do not wander off. We want to hear from you."

Hear from me! Noah thought. *What could Shubag mean by that?* The merchant was with the great metalworker—one of the most famous Cainites on earth, standing in the midst of Cainites. The son of Lamech shrugged his shoulders and bowed. Surely Shubag was extending a kindness, and he would acknowledge it, but not take it too seriously.

The doors to the veranda were open wide, admitting the evening breeze off the wide sea to penetrate the stuffy quarters. Noah peered out stealthily and slipped unnoticed onto the open porch. He would join the others in time, he reasoned. But he could not imagine what a mountain Sethite would have to discuss with the Sons of Cain.

He would not be alone upon the balcony, however. It was a feminine voice which interrupted his solitude. "I

146

hope you do not mind, sir," came the gentle sound.

Noah, whose gaze was to the sea, wheeled about—surprised, first at the greeting, and then at the wondrous creature who faced him. It was the woman from Nod-Persia, the Cainite's sister.

"Mind?" he stammered, taking in her beauty with a sharp breath.

"Yes—," she replied, smiling warmly. "I know it is not customary for a woman to invade male quarters, but the veranda was vacant, and I could not view the sea from my room below. I came up by the outside stairs when I saw no one was here," she explained, pointing to the steps which ascended from the women's chambers below. "I hope you are not angry."

The mountain man could feel no anger. He could feel nothing at the moment but clumsiness and speechlessness before the lady's soft black eyes and winsome tilt of the head.

"I . . . I am not the master of the house," he managed. "But I know you would be welcome wherever you wish to go."

The woman turned to the railing and asked no more questions. But for Noah the silence was not comfortable. He should think of some topic on which to converse; but his throat was tight, and he could only seem to stand back and allow his eyes to survey her graceful form as she watched the ships along the horizon.

"I am Naamah," she offered, still keeping her face to the wind.

All the earth spoke one language, and Noah knew her name meant "sweet and pleasant." *Fitting*, he thought. *Indeed, she is!*

"Noah . . . ," he returned. "My name is Noah."

"Ah." She smiled, wheeling excitedly toward him. "I heard Shubag speak of you today. You are the preacher!"

The mountain man felt even more awkward now. What could Shubag be thinking to spread this information among his visitors? He laughed uneasily and shrugged his shoulders. "Only today have I been called such. If I am a 'preacher,' I am a very new one."

"But you spoke in the square today," she objected.

"I did," Noah replied. "It was my *first* sermon."

The Cainite woman studied him closely, her eyes traveling down his homespun sleeve until they reached the hand which held the railing in a nervous grip.

"Well—first sermon, or hundredth—it does not seem to matter," she insisted. "You are apparently quite a gifted speaker." And with this she raised her gaze to his, punctuating her words with an earnest nod.

Noah was entranced. Her praise was sincere, he could tell. In fact, she seemed incapable of false flattery, and he almost forgot, for an instant, that she was not a Sethite.

He pivoted to the balustrade again and cleared his throat. The fingers of his free hand fidgeted uneasily with his cloak. He wished now that he had thought to dress more appropriately.

But . . . he must keep his thinking straight. This was a heathen woman. It would be best not to involve himself further, he knew. He could not seem to do the wise thing, however, and excuse himself from her presence. Somehow, he was compelled to fill the silence with conversation.

"I hear you have roofless houses in your country," he fumbled. And the minute he spoke the words, he wondered why he had not broached a more sophisticated subject. But the woman was not offended, and indeed responded as though this were an important observation.

"Yes," she replied. "Many Nod-Persians are so devoted to the Sun that they consider it sacrilege to roof a house. When the Golden Orb beats down into their chambers, they receive it as a blessing and do not shield themselves against the heat."

Noah listened respectfully, but could not discern whether she endorsed such an attitude or not. "And your family," he asked, "do they dwell in a roofless house?"

"Oh, no," Naamah smiled. "Indeed not. We are not Sun worshipers!"

Noah hardly knew how to respond to this revelation. He had thought that all Nod-Persians followed the Sun, and he wondered what strange cult Tubal-Cain and his people had adopted. But before he could pursue the matter, the woman was speaking again.

"I think you would enjoy my country," she asserted. "Thinking people feel at home there. And from what I hear, you are a thinking man."

Noah was honored by her comment, but wished he could tell her forthrightly that he would have nothing in common with the philosophers of her land. He studied the soft ringlet of black hair which hung free along her neck. The rest of her coiffure was an intricate bundle of curves and waves, wrapped turban-like about her head, and caught here and there with jeweled clasps. The entire look of her was disarming. But one ringlet—the way it moved with each sigh and each tilt of her chin—drew his glance over and over.

He barely followed her discourse as she explained that Nod-Persia was not the wilderness—that the wilderness of Nod was in the north portion of the Eastern Plain, and that the Persian region had been settled generations after Cain had entered the region.

"Nod-Persia is a reaction to the wilderness," she was saying. "My people knew they had been deprived, and fought valiantly to regain their lost dignity. Today Nod-Persia is a center of the arts and human searching."

Noah could detect no defensiveness in Naamah's critique. She seemed merely to be certain of her racial identity, and presented herself with definitive confidence.

He found himself losing against the urge to stay longer. Truly, he wished to hear more, and wondered if his spirit was weak, to allow him to linger so long at her side.

But before he could decide on the matter, a peculiar chattering ascended from the outside stairs. He could not imagine the source of the strange yelping, as of a very small. . . .

"Dog?" he marveled, as Naamah turned to greet the bounding, wriggling creature who had escaped its quarters below.

"Yes!" She laughed, bending over and lifting the furry white moppet in her arms. "This is Topay, my little companion. Tubal-Cain bought her for me when he began taking me on his voyages. I had no female friends to fill my hours, and Topay has served her purpose well."

"Dog?" Noah repeated, still incredulous. "What have you done to her?"

Naamah could not miss the disapproval in his tone.

"I have done nothing to her. What do you mean?" She bristled.

"Why," Noah smirked, "she bears as little resemblance to a dog as . . . as a mouse bears to a kangaroo!"

Naamah drew back and fought to control her tongue. "She was born this way—to a long line of ancestors—bred down to this size!"

Noah did care for the lady's feelings, but had never been tolerant of what he considered to be tampering with species.

"She has been manipulated!" he insisted.

But Naamah was no ignorant woman. "I think you are confusing breeding with the invasion of life-matter. There was nothing unnatural done to create this little dog. The parent line was simply chosen through several generations for size, color, and shape—until—this is the product!" she argued, cuddling the white fluff beneath her chin.

"Perhaps," Noah muttered. "But I see little difference in the techniques. The outcome is the same—the stripping of the original dignity God intended."

Naamah surveyed Noah with wide, round eyes. She could have taken great offense, but instead grew silent. "Why—you *are* a preacher . . . ," she whispered at last. And Noah was struck by her reverential tone.

He felt the blood rushing to his face once more, and found himself again painfully aware of his rude dress and unkempt beard.

"Well," he grunted, turning to the rail, "such things are not a matter on which we could agree."

"You are very sure of that?" Naamah queried.

"Of course," he asserted.

"Why?"

"Ha!" the preacher laughed, shrugging his shoulders. "Why, your frame of reference and mine are aliens."

"You speak of our beliefs?" she mused.

Noah studied her skeptically. "You know I do," he said. "What can a Cainite and a Sethite have in common?"

"Our God!" Naamah offered without hesitation.

Again Noah laughed and shook his head. "Dear lady," he condescended, "perhaps you have not understood. When I spoke in the square today, it was not on behalf of some pagan deity. I reject all gods but Yahweh!"

Naamah smiled brightly, her dark eyes gleaming. "Perhaps you are the one who has not understood," she laughed. "My brother and I worship the God of our father Lamech. We revere Yahweh, the only Deity."

SIX

Noah would find rest hard to come by when he returned to his chamber. Several troublesome thoughts would keep him awake. First, he wondered if Shubag would be unhappy with him for not rejoining the men in the parlor. After dinner, he had found himself speaking again with Naamah, and not until several hours had passed, and most of the guests had retired, had the two called it a night.

This was the second thing that troubled him: Never before had he found a woman so intriguing. And he did not know whether to revel in the new acquaintance or run from it. Surely his father would not understand his attraction to a Cainite female. Surely Lamech would not approve.

And this was the third thing that plagued his mind. He missed his father and his village. He wondered, as he sat alone in his room, why he was here—what purpose Yahweh really had for him, and if his sense of "call" was a deception. He had had little opportunity to put the experience in the town square into perspective. From the moment he had returned to Shubag's house, his mind had been bombarded with strange new ideas, questions on his view of life, his beliefs, his attitude toward his fellow humans. And then, to cap the day, he had been unexpectedly confronted with his manly needs and feelings, as a foreign woman, a Cainite, had turned his head.

All this, coupled with his experience of fear and revulsion in the Cronos street only last night, gave him vertigo, and he sat tentatively on the edge of his bed, his head reeling.

Just now, he wished he were home. He wished he could walk out his father's back door into the forest which hemmed the family estate. There was a little path he was fond of pursuing which led up the steep slope behind, and since childhood he had followed it countless times, over the rise to a small, round glen on the other side. Little-boy hurts, emotional upsets, or the simple need for solitude could always be appeased along that trail. He recalled now how often his cares had seemed to melt away when he had taken that short journey, and he lay back upon the bed, resting his spinning head and projecting his imagination to that private place.

At some point, imagination lapsed into unconsciousness, and as his soul slipped into slumber, the breeze off the Adlandian Sea ruffled the curtain at Noah's window.

Noah did not know what time it was when he was rudely shaken from sleep. It must have been well after midnight, for the darkness was at its blackest. All he knew was that some sort of rumbling had moved his bed so violently he was nearly thrown upon the floor.

In semiconsciousness he relived the earthquake of Baalbek, fighting the memory by burying his head in his pillow as he had buried it against the side of the mountain that long-ago night. But as he became fully awake, realizing the tremor was no dream, he staggered from the bed and threw open the door to his balcony.

The sea was calm enough. No one seemed to be stirring in the house below or in the nearby chambers. He turned and surveyed his room and found that everything but the bed was in perfect order. It alone was disheveled and had been wrenched from its place along the wall at an awkward angle.

He shook his head to be certain he was fully aware,

and wondered at his surroundings. Somehow he knew he had not imagined this, and yet how could such a violent shaking have moved nothing but the couch upon which he slept?

He looked seaward again, and as he pondered the phenomenon, he blinked his eyes firmly. What was this he saw? It appeared the night sky, the canopy which during the day was white, was breaking up. He shook his head again and the vision ceased. The sky returned to normal, and Noah shuddered.

He turned to take his place upon the bed once more, but as he did so a violent wind lashed up from the beach, and as he reached back to close the balcony door, the spectacle which greeted him froze his movement.

The sky had vanished in a torrent, falling in waves against the sea, and the sea was boiling, ingesting the canopy into its great maw.

"Lord God!" Noah cried, falling to his knees. "Spare us!"

But as he opened his eyes, once more the world was untouched, as though what he had just seen had been the product of a mad mind.

The son of Lamech gripped the doorpost and pulled himself upright. He stood for a long while on shaky legs, trying to regain himself.

The sea, again, was calm, the sky intact. No one in the house or in the street had responded to his cry, and apparently no one but Noah had been witness to the cataclysm.

He stumbled to his crooked couch, the only evidence of his experience, and sat rigid for hours, looking fearfully past the balcony. But there would be no more visions tonight. The rising sun, each morning's phenomenon, would be the only miracle to interrupt the remaining dark.

SEVEN

It was a holiday in Cronos, and in all the cities of the Sun along the Adlandian coast. It was the "Day of Blessing" in their calendar, and was an especially meaningful one for the inhabitants of marine towns. For this was the celebration of thanksgiving for the goodness of Lucifer and Poseidon, the solar deity and the god of the sea.

Great festivity marked the hours from sunup to sunset. By law, only foods of the ocean could be eaten on this day, and so the market was a paradise for fishmongers and seafood peddlers.

Noah rose from his crooked bed and pushed it back against the wall. His head was a blur, and had he been given to strong drink, he would have believed he was the victim of its morning aftereffects. But as he rubbed his eyes and insisted on equilibrium, he knew he was feeling the aftermath of his nightmare.

Tentatively he walked to the balcony, almost afraid to survey the world below. But, upon finding it to be stable and unchanged, he breathed a sigh of relief. Better to be a madman, he reasoned, than that the sky should really fall.

He remembered, as he saw the colorful streamers and banners of the festival along the wharf, that this was a holiday. Though it was a pagan celebration, he was glad that it would relieve him from a day in the accounting room. He was not certain he could function well, feeling as he did.

Since the household of Shubag would not be participating in the festivities, however, Noah would have to seek solitude away from home as well as town.

He knew that the nearby shore would be no place for privacy. The crowds would be immense in that district where so many of the traditional activities would take place—the games, the feasts, the parties. And by early evening the entire town would have congregated along the beach for the regatta, the boat races, and the Hour of Poseidon.

For this was the once-a-year day on which the great god of waters would sail up the coast from Sun City, to be hailed by his worshipers in the towns along the shore. They would see his stunning, fast-moving vessel as it sped from port to port, and they would actually have opportunity to observe the deity himself, as he hailed them from the deck.

It was believed that special blessing was imparted to anyone privileged to see him on this day, for the timing of his passage would coincide with the setting of the sun, the hour when the Golden Orb was closest to the earth. Believers contended that great energy was released to the sea on this day, as the rays of Lucifer blended with the waters of Poseidon along the sunset horizon, and anyone present at the sea god's passage would receive of its power.

So, for many reasons the nearby beach would be no place for solitude. Nor would any spot between Sun City and Cronos, the beginning and ending points of Poseidon's voyage. For folk from the interior, from far away villages north and south, would be lining the sandy shore, and indeed would have traveled great distances to do so.

If Noah wished to be alone, he would have to travel upland from Cronos. With this in mind, he recalled the day he had seen the dolphin, and wondered if he could again find the rock upon which he had rested.

Quickly he formed his cloak into a makeshift satchel and raced to the kitchen. It was still early enough that no servants were about. He foraged through the pantry for a bit of food and stuffed a few rolls, some cheese and butter into his crude bag. Then, running for the stable, he found his horse and prepared him for a little journey.

The other creatures in the stalls wondered at Noah's strange haste, but his own horse greeted him eagerly.

"I have neglected you of late," Noah smiled. "We shall have some time alone today. Remember the dolphin?"

With no more clarification than that the steed shook its head, and when the master had mounted, sped joyfully up the beach.

The horizon across from Cronos had been crowded with many ships which had come in from sea, anchoring themselves close enough to shore to catch sight of the festivities. Further north, at the rock of the dolphin, the sea was quite clear of vessels today.

For hours Noah sat perched atop the rounded rock, letting his mind stretch and roam freely. He could not, however, help pondering the peculiar and frightening events of the night before. Repeatedly he petitioned Yahweh for an explanation. If he were mad, let him know now and he would flee to some mountain cave, never to inflict himself upon society again. But if what he had experienced was a vision from God, let him have the interpretation.

He remembered how, when he had concluded his speech in the square, giving his warning of cataclysm, his eyes had been drawn skyward with some sense of urgency. Had that impulse been an omen reflected again in the vision of a falling canopy and a devouring sea?

As day wore on, Noah sat upon his rock, unmoving, except for his eyes, which worked their way first across the heavens, as though he might again see the vision, and then scanned the sea, in hopes that his dolphin friend might make its appearance once more.

His horse, tethered to a weathered root which protruded

from the sand, occasionally grew impatient with its master. And twice during their stay here, Noah had come down to him, unleashing and leading him to a patch of wiry grass growing against the bank which fronted the distant and vacant highway.

No travelers saw the lonesome pair as they passed the afternoon in solitude. Everyone was in the cities. And as Noah waited for his horse to finish grazing, he eyed the road with gratitude. Were anyone to pass by, he might be questioned, for it was so against tradition to neglect the holidays, one would be suspect for avoiding the throngs.

Besides, Noah thought, were people to know the content of his mind, to discover that he waited for the canopy of heaven to break or for a dolphin to speak, their suspicions might be well founded.

The sun would be setting within the hour. Noah could sense this as he sat on the rock, though he had brought no timepiece with him. There was that typical hushing of the always-gentle wind which blew in from the Adlandian waters this time of day, as if the earth prepared for the descent of dark with a kind of reverence.

Noah knew he must be returning to Shubag's soon. He did not want to be caught again in the fog which would be coming inland with dusk. But as he turned for the final time to leave his perch, his eyes were caught by the dark, box-like shape of an immense, many-tiered barge, wending up from Cronos along the line between sea and sky.

"Gigantic" was the only term for the vessel. Noah had seen such mammoth floats only a few times in his life, the products of the giant Nephilim, who used them to transport the machinery of war, or other colossal wares typical only of their class. The mountain man could not imagine what such a vessel would be doing on the sea at this time of day, or what errand could be taking it north on a holiday. Furthermore, as it drew straight ahead of him, he was baffled by its silence. The barges of the Nephilim were motorized. Their shape and weight would not allow them to catch the wind or to plow the waters by means of the currents. Oh, they could be moved by such methods, but so slowly that they were not economical transports without power.

As Noah gazed at the strange vessel, wondering how it was operated and what its purpose might be, he suddenly felt a warm wave of air rush up from behind the rock. Turning, he sought the source of the peculiar phenomenon, but found nothing. With the sensation, however, had come an even more unsettling impression of being watched—as though someone had stepped up behind to observe him.

And when he glanced seaward again, he knew he was not alone.

"Noah," the Voice came.

It was very soft, like a whisper, and it rode up to him on the soft warm swell which rose at his back.

This time Noah did not turn around. His skin tingled and he felt compelled to fix his eyes upon the floating vessel. "Yes . . . Lord," he whispered.

He knew it was Yahweh who had called his name, and he knew he would not see him, should he turn to look, for no man had ever seen God.

"Noah, son of Lamech," the hushed Voice called, "see and understand. The end of all flesh has come before me, for the earth is filled with violence. . . ."

The tone of the judgment was heavy, as if the very heart of Yahweh broke with its load. Noah shuddered, fearful to breathe lest God's anger single him out. But, as flashes of Baalbek and the assault of the rapists in the Cronos street flooded over the listener, tears rose to his eyes. And he assented with a quiver, "Yes, my Lord. . . ."

The soft wind became more insistent now and took on an eerie moan. "All flesh have corrupted their way upon the earth," the Almighty declared, and Noah trembled, wondering at the Voice which he had craved to hear all his life.

"Yes," he replied, thinking on the immoralities he had witnessed in his five years of wandering the byways of the city, and upon the pathetic creatures of man's manipulation and contrivance. "All flesh is corrupted." He nodded, his throat tight.

Now there was a lull in the breeze, as if Yahweh were appeased for a moment. But then the Voice came again. "Look and understand," Yahweh directed, the very breath of his nostrils filling the air around the preacher.

Noah drew his cloak in a bundle at his chest, gripping it with taut fingers. Suddenly, as he viewed the peculiar barge which rested upon the sea like a beckoning fortress, he seemed to be caught away—transported to the uppermost deck of the ship.

"Walk up and down in her, son of Lamech," Yahweh instructed. "Memorize her well—for it shall be your task to duplicate her."

Whether he was in the body or not in the body, Noah did not know—but he found himself walking from corner to corner of the vessel, and entering compartment after compartment.

It was evident that the ship was empty, and when he was returned to his rock, he shook his head as from a daze. "There is no one on board," he whispered, "and no cargo, my Lord." And then, daring to ask the interpretation, he inquired, "What is the purpose of this craft?"

For a long while there was no reply, and Noah might have thought he had imagined the whole thing—that indeed he was a madman. But he waited patiently for the words of his Lord.

When they came they were robed in majesty and holiness. "She is an Ark of Safety," Yahweh proclaimed. "She will be a symbol of my love—a resting place for those who trust in me. And she will preserve life as I have created it."

As Noah took in the message, pondering it and wondering at its full meaning, the sun began to melt into the sea, spreading its dusky paints over the water. He knew that along the shores of Cronos and Sun City folk would be marveling this moment at the ship of Poseidon, and hoping for the touch of Lucifer. But this one Sethite, solitary in his calling, kept his gaze upon the ark, thankful for the touch of hope he had received from the Lord's hand.

Though he was blind to the full import of what he witnessed, though he could not presently see the end from the beginning, he took courage from the promise which the great barge represented. And as he studied its silhouette in the red sun, his eyes were caught by the flutter of a small white bird which had appeared upon its top deck. It seemed not to be a gull, but a dove, and he wondered what such a creature would find of interest on the sea.

The dove did not stay long on board, but craned its neck in Noah's direction and then took flight, circling the ark and ascending—high above the waters, rising above the earth, until it vanished in the canopy of heaven.

When Noah's gaze returned to the sea, he found that the ark too had vanished, and with it the light of day.

EIGHT

Noah did not stop at Cronos when he returned from the rock. He sped past Shubag's town and went straight for the port of Poseidon, the City of the Sun.

It was the middle of the night by the time he reached the limits of the metropolis. He had traveled the coast highway, which was far enough from the waters to avoid the dense fog along the beach. But when he reached his destination, he found it necessary to wait until morning before proceeding into the city. He did not know his way about this place and, wishing to find the very temple of the god once again, he had to wait for the mists of the Adlandian Sea to dissipate.

It was very early morning when he made his way to the temple porch. This expanse of marble and granite stretched several city blocks along the shore, giving Poseidon's fortress a magnificent view of the blue-white waters. Ordinarily, if a man had a public issue to take up with the citizens, he would bring it to the marketplace, to be heard of the commoners. But Noah was not a citizen of this town. The issue he wished to address involved the coastal lands as a whole, and was therefore a subject on which the governor of the territory should be informed. It was a matter deserving to be discussed in the porch of Poseidon, Noah reasoned.

And this would be only a beginning, the Sethite assured himself. For he knew the issue merited even broader attention than the coastal territory could give it. It was of concern to all Adlandia, all earth. And since the porch of Poseidon was a thoroughfare for councilors from around the world, he knew his message would be heralded far and wide, through the interior of the continent, within days.

The porch was still decorated with banners and streamers from yesterday's festivities, and it was beneath the leftover trappings of a pagan celebration that Noah would take his stand for Yahweh and the vision which he was compelled to follow.

He did not know what words he would speak. As he opened his mouth he uttered only what came to mind, with no preparation. And what came forth surprised him, for it built upon the sermon he had given in the Cronos square:

"God has seen our wickedness!" he declared, his voice filling the temple court and reverberating off the mammoth rock walls of the heathen sanctuary. To his back, dividing the temple proper from the great porch, stood only the huge columns of red-gold orichalchum, the metal of the gods, erected by Poseidon. And before him spread only an empty stage, with no audience. But he cried again, "Every imagination of the thoughts of man's heart is only evil continually!"

The metal cylinders captured the vibrations of his cry as it rang through the porch, and they hummed an ominous chord. But soon enough, just as it had happened in Cronos, it began to happen here. People of the temple began to assemble along the colonnades and the edges of the wide veranda.

These folk were of a different sort than had congregated at Cronos. They were not commoners, except for the servants who crept out to listen. This audience, for the most part, was more sophisticated, highly educated, and of the ruling class. And as the Sethite continued to speak they were joined by some who had graced the court of Poseidon the day Noah and Obad had been inquisitioned.

"It has repented the Lord that he has made man on the earth, and it grieves him at his heart!" he shouted, the roofless veranda echoing. "The sky shall fall and the sea shall swallow it! The waters of the deep shall break forth to destroy the land!" he cried.

As he said this the court began to hum, not with sympathetic vibrations, as did the pillars, but with the murmuring of human voices. For a mighty throng was collecting, and their mood was not pleasant.

Since many of these people had heard Noah before, the day he was brought forth from prison, he was not a popular figure. And word spread quickly to those who had not been present the day of the hearing, that this was the notorious mountain man whom Poseidon had ejected five years before, and who had recently stirred up the town of Cronos.

Were Noah to have dwelled just now on the reaction of his audience, he might have reconsidered his position. But, closing his eyes, he threw open his arms and asserted, "Thus says the Lord, 'I will destroy man whom I have created, from the face of the earth! Both man and beast, and creeping things, and the fowl of the air. For it repents me that I have made them!' Yea," he cried, "the end of all flesh is come before me, and none shall be spared but the righteous!"

Now the patience of many present was short when it came to hearing what Noah had to say, for they had had opportunity to evaluate him before. But had the preacher been able to select a challenger from among them all, he would never have chosen the one who came forward. It was the old sorcerer whose familiar, the black raven, had tracked him to Baalbek—it was this one who would confront him. And when the wizened fellow stepped up to the stage, stroking his long white beard and peering at him gimlet-eyed, the Sethite trembled.

"Only 'the righteous' you say?" the wizard queried. "And who, pray tell, are 'the righteous'?"

Noah took a deep breath and looked, unflinching, into the piercing gaze of his opponent.

"The righteous are those who follow the ways of the Lord," he asserted.

At this a chuckle rattled up from the wizard's throat. "The 'Lord'?" he laughed. "We have heard you speak of your 'Lord' before. He is a very obscure one, if you ask me. 'Yahweh,' didn't you say? Very obscure indeed. At most, one of the least of the mountain pantheon. Certainly not akin to Poseidon or any of the heavenly gods."

"Yahweh is God of gods and Lord of lords!" Noah pronounced. "There is no god besides Yahweh!"

The throng howled at this, and the wizard took his staff, the heavy wand upon which the raven always sat, and shook it in the Sethite's face. The raven was not here today, and Noah wondered if he lurked somewhere in the rafters. He would have no chance just now to survey the site. "Aha, strange fellow," the sorcerer was challenging. "We can play your game! Let us say, for the sake of argument, that your God *is* the only god. . . ."

At this the crowd laughed and murmured yet more, but the wizard quieted them with a stern expression. And then, leaning his bent frame against his staff, he demanded, "See behind you—the stately pillars of the godly laws. The ordinances of our deities are etched upon them for all to behold and our system of justice depends upon this code. Now . . . if Yahweh were the only god, he would do well to inform us of his wishes. How can we follow him if we not only have never heard of him, but have no record of his laws?"

Though the congregation was pleased with the sorcerer's sagacity, Noah held steadfast. "The logic of your inquiry is sound, Wise One," the Sethite conceded. "But you are ill informed if you think the laws of Yahweh are unknowable. They are not written upon pillars of stone or bronze, it is true. But they are written upon our hearts. They are not changeable or subject to loss, for they are pressed into our minds and printed on our souls at birth."

The old magician was not prepared for such a statement, and while he faltered to respond, Noah drove home his point more firmly. "You, sir, are the master of elements. You cloak your manipulations with mystery, while you yourself know the truth behind them. But Yahweh is not so surreptitious. He is not cloaked, nor does he trick the eyes with illusion. His ways are knowable to any seeking heart, and his will is just beneath the veneer of our sin-hardened consciousness."

The crowd was troubled by the preacher's words, shuffling uneasily and whispering nervously with one another.

But Noah was not finished. "You refer, wizard, to the pillars of Poseidon, as though they were a sacred thing. And I know that to you they are. But I pronounce them a mockery and a sham against the truth, ministers for the Angels of Light!"

The throng was stirred to wrath by this, and the sorcerer peered at his cohorts with bared teeth. Then, growling up at the Sethite, he cried, "You inflame the souls of all who love the gods! Are the laws of Poseidon not good and just? What fault can you find in them?"

Noah was quick to reply. "Within most of the laws themselves I find little fault. For the purposes of justice and equity they serve well, and they have kept reasonable order upon this planet. Yes, Wise One, they are humane laws. But I contend that they veil the truth, for they would lead us to believe that Lucifer, the Prince of This World, is a just and equitable god. And yet, Lucifer has only *used* justice and equity, which derive from God Almighty, to cloak his identity and to deceive the masses. He has taken the very statutes of Yahweh and turned them to his own ends!"

Suddenly, from out of the corner of his eye, Noah saw something whirring toward him. Whether it was a brick, a rock, or a stick, he could not tell, and it came so quickly he could not duck it. It struck him on the temple, throwing him face forward against the pavement, and knocking him nearly senseless.

He staggered to his feet, but not before more of the ammunition was hurled.

"Lord God!" he cried, as the pain in his head mixed with the deafening roar of the jeering crowd.

He did not see the sorcerer as his dazed eyes scanned his enemies. The old fellow had disappeared into the masses. But as Noah spied a way of escape and headed for the outside stairs, his frantic gaze was caught by a majestic figure on the veranda balcony.

Poseidon himself had been summoned and stood now, staring iron-faced at the preacher. Noah remembered his glory, but never had he seemed so awesome as he did today. In gilded tunic, the god was flanked by a dozen Nephilim, all arrayed in battle gear.

The Sethite's heart was charged with fear, and with all the strength he could muster he darted for the street, away from the pursuing throng.

It was not until he had reached the shore of Sun City that he realized the crowd had been satisfied to evict him from the temple, and had ceased the chase once the prey was a comfortable distance from Poseidon's palace.

They could have caught him, Noah knew. Why were they content to let him go? And why had Poseidon been obliged to arm himself with militia against one lone mountain man?

The preacher could not determine the answers now. As he fled along the beach, he only thanked Yahweh that he was alive.

The pain in his forehead throbbed persistently, and he reined his horse to a stop long enough to rest upon an abandoned boat slip some way north of the metropolis.

The sun was just beginning to form its full circle above the horizon when he thought he was reliving his earlier vision. As the outline of a ship resting in the waters ahead took on clarity, however, he could see it was not the Ark of Yahweh, but the ship of Poseidon. It too stood strangely empty, and seemingly without purpose on the sea. It too revealed a bird upon its mast, as the ark had revealed the dove upon its upper deck. But when this creature craned its neck in Noah's direction and took flight, it did not soar toward heaven, but dipped toward the palace of the sea god. And its plumage was not white, but black—the plumage of the sorcerer's familiar.

NINE

The small ridge of hills which rose from the northeast of Cronos, gradually ascending into the highlands which Noah called home, provided a natural retreat for the fear-wracked Sethite. He was bruised in body and soul, his head throbbing, his heart aching as he tethered his horse and sought a niche on the wilderness heights in which to settle down and contemplate his condition.

There had been many times throughout his life when he had wished Yahweh were more tangible, that he would make himself known more clearly to those who believed in him. This was one of those times, the most lonely of them all.

Noah crept along a tangled hillside, miles from the nearest road, until all sign of human life was far behind him. These little mountains were heavy with vegetation. It would not be easy to find a cave here, but the earth was thick with leafy grottoes, bowers of vines and branches, in which he could find rest.

Selecting a likable spot, he sat down within its green shadows, and allowed the fragrance of the soil to console him.

But even as he lay his head against a mossy pillow, questions raged in his mind. He remembered what Obad had said that long-ago night in Poseidon's prison: "I feel you are a prophet. *The* prophet, chosen for these days."

It was some comfort to recall those words, especially

since Noah was prone just now to doubt his calling, to wonder if he had brought all this upon himself needlessly.

No, he reasoned. The call was real. And the persecution, rather than being a sign that he was out of God's will, was probably the surest evidence that he was perfectly on track.

But questions flooded him, nonetheless. Why, he wondered, had *he* been selected to carry out this mission? Surely there were others in the world who were more qualified. Not only had he presumed in the past few days to be a preacher, with no credentials or experience, but now he was being asked to take on a monumental task, for some purpose of which he was not even fully aware.

He contemplated the great floating barge in his vision and the words of Yahweh, "Memorize her well, for it shall be your task to duplicate her."

Noah pressed his aching head into the mossy cushion. His mind swam with the immensity of the order. "Memorize her? I barely had time to look at her," he whispered. And then, rising up suddenly, he shook himself and laughed.

"If Yahweh wants a boat built, he can build it himself!" he thought aloud. "This is madness!"

He felt as one who fought with a dream, half-waking. He could no longer distinguish what was reality. The whole notion of the boat project, especially with no real understanding of its purpose, was ludicrous.

Noah paced the jungle bower for a long moment, pounding his fists against his thighs in an attempt to bring himself back into the present. And then, as though a light had shone in his head, he fumbled with the pouch which hung from his sash, and drawing out a rumpled booklet of paper, smiled broadly.

He would record the events of the past few days in the little journal which had occupied his evenings at Shubag's house. Perhaps this would help clarify for him what was real.

Eagerly he sorted through the other contents of the purse until he found a stub of a writing pen, and he sat down to commit his recent days to black and white.

He began by making a simple list from the events of the past week.

"The night in Cronos . . . ," he wrote. ". . . the assault in the dark. . . ."

His fingers trembled as he validated the reality of that witness by spelling it out.

"The sermon. . . ."

"Shubag's critique. . . ."

"The vision of falling waters. . . ."

Here he paused, his fist clenching. But then, with a deep breath, he continued.

"Tubal-Cain. . . ."

". . . Naamah. . . ."

His face flushed at the thought of her, and he wondered what she would think of his experiences.

But then, as he was about to write "vision of the ark," he could not.

"I have not imagined all this!" he asserted.

He remembered having heard once that when a man begins to go mad, he does not hallucinate about things which have no relevance for him. Somewhere within each vision there is a link with the man's past or his personal experience. But, within the visions of falling water and of the great barge, or within the words which Yahweh had spoken to him, where was the link?

"No!" he declared again. "This did not arise from my own mind. It derives from . . . beyond myself. . . ."

Suddenly, as he drew this conclusion, a snapping noise was heard in the bushes just outside the bower. Noah gripped the little journal to his chest and stilled his breathing, strained his eyes in the direction of the sound, and waited. Fears of wild beasts, or . . . worse yet . . . of his pursuers, darted at him, and he sank as far into the green shadows as possible.

Again the snapping noise threatened, but this time the source revealed itself. A figure, at first a single silhouette, filled the opening to Noah's retreat. Discerning that it was a human being and not an animal, Noah stammered, "Who goes there—and what do you want?"

The figure made no response, but only entered the bower, and, as if perfectly at home, knelt down upon the leafy floor.

As Noah watched this behavior with speechless bewilderment, he could gradually, in the dim light, make out the even, gentle features of the face before him. It was a man's face, to be sure, but of such guileless character, the effect of it was startling. Above a neatly trimmed beard and slender nose were calm gray eyes and a smooth forehead. The cheeks, framed by a fall of dark, shoulder-length hair, were ruddy, as if the Stranger spent his days in the out-of-doors, and the man's hands were rugged but soothing. Noah knew they were soothing, because they touched him now. Yes—the Stranger, with no apology, had reached forth a hand to survey the wound on the Sethite's head. Had it not been for the gesture's matter-of-factness, Noah would have been offended at the intimacy. As it was, though, the familiarity did not frighten or alienate him, as he sat in breathless wonder before the newcomer.

"Uh—sir," Noah faltered, "who are you, and what do you want with me?"

The Stranger did not reply immediately. Instead, he foraged on the ground with his fingers and drew up a handful of pointed leaves. Stripping off the brittle tips, he crumbled the remainder in his palm and then ground a bit of it to a powder between his thumb and forefinger.

"See here," he replied at last, holding the residue in a firm pinch, "this will help the wound to heal quickly."

If Noah had been startled by his face, he was even more moved by the Stranger's voice. Full and manly, it was nonetheless very soft, like his touch, and compassionate, as though he empathized with the Sethite's pain and bewilderment. And now, his behavior became even more peculiar, as he took the pulverized substance and held it to his own lips, adding to it a small amount of spittle and then mixing the compound in the palm of his other hand.

When he had thus manufactured a little puddle of paste, he dipped his forefinger into the medicine and applied it directly to Noah's wound. Within a mere moment, the pain subsided, as though it had been drawn into the ointment itself. And as the patient marveled at the miracle, the Stranger smiled quietly. "There is much you do not know," he replied. "I taught the sons of Adam many things, and they have done great exploits, but they have lost much simple wisdom."

The Sethite was speechless as the Stranger sat down beside him and drew up his knees, resting his chin upon them. The gray eyes scanned the hillside below the bower, and Noah could see that his peculiar friend was deep in thought. When the newcomer at last spoke again, the implication of his question shook the preacher's soul.

"Do you recall my words to you when I showed you the Ark of Safety?" the Stranger inquired.

For a long, uneasy moment, silence hung between them. Noah's heart was lodged firmly in his throat, so that he could not reply. But as the Man turned to him, requiring a response, the Sethite managed, "Yes—my Lord. . . ."

"And did you memorize her, as I instructed?"

Noah swallowed hard, and blinked his awe-filled eyes. "Sir—the time was so short . . . I . . . I could not manage to memorize her. . . ."

The son of Lamech had not yet come to grips with his visitor's identity, and already the Magnificent One was demanding rational conversation. Noah trembled as he confessed his inadequacy to perform the Lord's wishes, and wondered now what punishment would be his for the failure.

But the Stranger seemed not to be angry. He only reached forth a confident hand and took hold of the journal to which Noah had clung tightly ever since hearing the snapping sound in the bushes.

"You have often written of me in this little book, haven't you, my friend?" the Lord asked, taking it from him.

"Yes . . . ," Noah stammered. "I have done so many times . . . though I have never seen you. . . ."

The Lord studied the leather binding on the worn volume and caressed it fondly. "Your spirit has known me since childhood, Noah. And of late you have heard my voice. Now you see me with your eyes, and you have felt my touch. Is it not enough?"

Tears rose and spilled over Noah's cheeks. He could not find a way to answer, but the Lord was satisfied with his silence.

"Did you wonder," he went on, "why the Daemon did not pursue you from Sun City?"

Noah trembled. "Sir—it was a miracle," he whispered.

"Were your eyes not blind you would have seen my servants all about you, greater far and stronger than all the hosts of Lucifer," the Lord explained.

"You mean. . . ."

"Yes—they were there. But you are called to walk not as the world walks—by faith and not by sight," the Lord went on. "The world's gods parade before them in shining raiment and in power. But the heart which seeks for me shall know me in the quiet of lonely days and in the hope of promises yet to be fulfilled."

Noah did not know where to begin with his own questions. He wanted to ask about the visions of the falling sky and the great barge, about the nature of man and the world system. About very great things and very particular things. But as he sat in the presence of this warm and kind companion, and as he realized that this—this was his God . . . he could only inquire, "Why, my Lord, have you chosen me? It is a fearsome and an unhappy mission to which I am called. How am I to master it? And who will hear me?"

"It *is* a fearsome thing to warn the world of judgment. It is an unhappy thing, indeed," the Lord agreed. The Master's shoulders stooped slightly as he acknowledged this, and Noah could read in his posture the gravity of his feelings for humanity. The Lord did not long dwell on this, however, before he spoke again, now with the fire of exhortation in his eyes. "But, friend, your mission is not only to preach judgment," he declared. "You are called to preach salvation to the great congregation! You are called to preach the righteousness which will spare any man from Yahweh's wrath!"

Noah contemplated the Lord's words with wide eyes, almost embarrassed to ask for an explanation. But the Master understood, and placing a firm hand upon his shoulder insisted, "Have you sought the truth so long, and yet it still eludes you? Do you not yet grasp the fact that righteousness comes only by faith? This is what you are to teach. Teach men to follow me by faith, for in this are they made complete."

Noah recalled Shubag's exhortation to the same effect. Of course—how could he have forgotten so easily?

"Oh, Master—it is a hard thing to hold onto. I have been taught such things from my youth up. But they seem to slip away so easily."

The Lord smiled at him knowingly. "This is because it is against man's nature to die to himself, to trust the unseen. But such is the road which leads to life, and few there be that find it."

The Sethite trembled. "Master—am I one who is counted righteous?"

The Lord knew the import of the question, and did not respond lightly. Focusing clearly on his chosen man, he replied, "You have found grace in my eyes, Noah. There are few men on earth who have such a seeking and an upright heart. You have walked with me, when you did not even know it, and your heart is blameless, for you have the righteousness which comes by faith alone."

TEN

It would be the cool of evening when the Master departed. All that day he would spend with his friend. The words which the Lord would speak would be retained in Noah's memory to be called up throughout the days and years which lay ahead. He would not be able to recount them all immediately, for there would be too much given to him this day. But certain aspects of the discussion would be especially meaningful to him just now.

They left the bower at noontime and walked through the forest together until they reached the ridge of the hill, and from their seat beneath a pine they watched the sea glisten far out from the coast.

Noah would never forget how the subject of the cataclysm was approached. His own inquiring mind led directly to it, though it was a question of theology and not geology which plagued him.

"Master," he asked, as they came to rest from the long climb, "those who have not sought you—who do not know the righteousness you offer—do you intend to destroy them?"

Noah was respectfully cautious as he broached the topic, but the Lord seemed to sense his underlying courage and answered with equal honor. "Every man knows the essential truths from birth—so that there is no excuse," he began. "Those who do not believe are condemned of themselves, for apart from faith there is no righteousness. Do you see? Though I speak of my judgment, it is man himself who brings his *own* destruction. And though I speak of my anger, all creation groans under the abuses of sin, and waits for my redemption."

Noah was convicted by the Lord's logic, and pondered the last words carefully. "All creation, Lord?"

"Indeed," the Master said with a nod, surveying the sky and sea. "The earth itself is gathering force to rebel against man's oppression."

Immediately Noah drew the corollary between what the Master addressed and the cataclysmic visions he had received. "The sky shall fall and the sea shall swallow it up . . . ," he whispered, remembering his own words to the people of Poseidon.

The Lord studied him compassionately. "It is I who have told you so," he asserted.

Noah bowed his head and closed his eyes. On his own he had consoled himself that the visions were not the product of a mad mind—but that the Lord should thus confirm this brought great relief.

Relief and sorrow. For, indeed, the visions were prophetic of disaster, and as Noah raised his gaze to the sunlight, tears shimmered along his lashes.

"The earth of late has trembled," the Lord continued. "You have felt her rumblings?"

Noah nodded, recalling the quake at Baalbek, and the Master explained, "Though the judgment shall be by my hand, all elements conspire to fulfill my commands. The planet prepares to serve my bidding. For I am about to destroy the wicked by means of my own handiwork. I will destroy them *with* the earth."

The way the Lord phrased this last pronouncement connoted a partnership: Yahweh and the planet. He would bring judgment not only by means *of* the earth, but in league *with* the earth.

Noah suddenly felt the immensity of it all, and was acutely aware of his own frailty. What, he wondered, did the Lord have in mind for him? How could someone so insignificant as he be used in such a universal drama?

He hardly needed to voice the question. The Lord drew out of his sleeve the little journal which he had carried from the bower and handed it to the son of Lamech.

"Write," he said. "What I am about to tell you must be written down."

Noah took the volume and, with trembling fingers, pulled out the small writing instrument nestled in the back cover.

"Remember the great seacraft which you watched from the rock of the dolphin?" the Lord asked. "What I am about to tell you applies to her. Since you could not memorize her, let me set the matter out for you."

Then, closing his eyes and leaning back, he began:

"You are to make for yourself an ark of gopher wood. You shall make the ark with rooms," he instructed, "and shall cover it inside and out with pitch."

Noah listened wonderingly, and when the Lord looked up, glancing at the little book, he quickly jotted down the words.

"And this is how you shall make it," the Master continued, giving the specifications slowly and deliberately, as would a customer to a contractor. "The length of the ark three hundred cubits, its breadth fifty cubits, and its height thirty cubits."

Noah wrote down each order, remembering the many times he had read over such statements in his father's account books.

"You shall make a window for the ark," he went on, "and finish it to a cubit from the top and set the door of the ark in the side of it."

The Master paused, to be sure Noah had caught all this, and when the contractor nodded, he continued.

"You shall make it with lower, second, and third decks."

Noah's eyes grew large as he marveled at the dimensions and the volume of the vessel. Quickly he began to calculate in his mind the time and expense it would take to build such a craft; and then, remembering his brief walk through the barge at the dolphin rock, he shook his head at the enormity of the project. He remembered that the Lord had explained the purpose of the vessel at that time, but he still did not have a complete grasp on it.

He need not ponder this long, however, as the Master declared his intentions once again. "And behold, I, even I am bringing a flood of water upon the earth," he affirmed, "to destroy all flesh in which is the breath of life, from under heaven! Everything that is on the earth shall perish."

Noah shuddered and, contemplating the magnitude of such destruction, he feared to look at Yahweh. Hadn't he been told that it would be his mission to preach of the Ark of Safety? Was there *no one* who would believe?

The Lord would not answer that question just now, but did hold out his purpose for the man of God. "But I will establish my covenant with you, Noah, and you shall enter the ark—you and your sons and your wife, and your sons' wives with you."

Now the Sethite was even more baffled. *Wife!* he thought. *Sons! Does the Lord really know me! Surely he must be aware that I have no family!* But he dared not interject his questions, for the Master's demeanor was profoundly serious.

"And of every living thing of all flesh," the Lord continued, "you shall bring two of every kind into the ark, to keep them alive with you. They shall be male and female. Of birds after their kind, and of the animals after their kind, of every creeping thing of the ground after its kind—two of every kind shall come to you for you to keep them alive."

Noah was still recording all this in his little journal. Word for word he captured it. But its meaning went past his head. He could not begin to dwell upon it, for it was full of mystery. So he kept his eyes to the paper and was not even tempted to make rebuttal, for his soul was numb with awe.

"And as for you," the Master went on, "take for yourself some of all food which is edible, and gather it to yourself. And it shall supply you and the animals."

Something in this last command struck Noah strangely. How very practical! If all species of animal life were to be cared for, all forms of diet would be required. His face broke into a broad grin and he began to laugh. His shoulders shook with hilarity as he was overwhelmed now not with mystery, but with the incredible earthiness of all this.

Of course such logistics were only reasonable! This was not just a spiritual drama being planned out, a way to save the righteous when the wicked were destroyed. If the dry land were to be deluged, provision must be made for created life! And in making that provision a craft must be built, the chambers designed, the order of entrance and the log of daily matters scheduled and inventoried. Who would stay with whom, who would eat what, how much space must the elephant have, where would the kangaroo get her exercise, would the cat be content to leave the mouse alone?

Yes—he was laughing! The tension of prophetic bewilderment gave way to the simpler considerations of gopher wood and water, feed and stock, smell and survival and compatibility.

Something in such fundamentals relieved him. It would be his mainstay of serenity for years to come—when the pain of the prophecy settled in, when the burden of sorrow became too great, when his heart broke with human rejection or was devoured with fear for his own mind— such things as the dimensions of a waste tank or the placement of a pigeon's roost would ground him in sanity and rivet his heart to the present.

But now he heard his own laughter, and it frightened him. Had he offended God?

Stifling himself, he brought his hilarity into submission and choked back his smile. He cocked one eye, glancing fearfully at the Master. But what met him was more awesome than rebuke. It was approval, for the Lord himself was smiling.

Yahweh stood up from the pine-needle cushion where they sat, and held out his hand. Noah reached forth tentatively and the Master lifted him to his feet with a playful jerk.

Soon they were laughing together, and as they descended the green hill the Lord placed his arm around Noah's shoulders.

P A R T I I I
THE ARK OF SAFETY

The end of all flesh has come before me; . . . and,
behold, I will destroy them with the earth.

But with thee will I establish my covenant; and
thou shalt come into the ark, thou, and thy
sons, and thy wife, and thy sons' wives with thee.

Genesis 6:13, 18

ONE

It was sunset when Noah returned to Cronos from the eastern highlands. The evening tide had washed its coral sheen across the sand, and the shadows of pebbles and shells reached out long and thin toward the rider who passed them.

The Sethite, who had crawled off into the hills, was no longer weary. His spirit had been renewed, his calling confirmed. What he longed for now was someone with whom to share his story. To keep such an incredible message to himself was unthinkable.

It seemed logical that Shubag should be the first to hear it. Intending to go directly to him, Noah spurred his horse toward the white walls of the city.

But had there been a ready and trusted ear available anywhere between the hills and Cronos, Noah would have related his story sooner. It must have been more than chance, therefore, that a female was the first to receive Noah's tale. Under any other circumstances, such an intimacy would have been out of character for the son of Lamech.

But when he saw her strolling in the twilight along the shore, he could not pass by without a word.

"Naamah?" he called. "Is that you?"

The figure was framed by the departing sun in dark silhouette. But the Sethite felt he would recognize that gracefulness anywhere.

"Noah?" she replied, turning about at the sound of his voice and raising her hand against the red sunlight which bounced off his harnesswork. The shawl which draped her head against the evening breeze slipped from her black tresses as she did this, and her hair, which had always before been gathered high and intricate, was unfettered tonight. In fact, in the twilight, it was not easily discernible where her long hair left off and her flowing gown began, for the picture of her against the ruddy sky was a harmony of line and wind.

The Sethite dismounted and led his horse across the strip of sand which separated them. A peculiar caution, almost a reverence, marked Noah's gait as he approached the woman, as though he feared too firm a step would destroy the moment.

When he drew near enough that he could clearly see her features, touched now by the descending glow of evening, the tightness he had known only in her presence rose once more to constrict his breath. What power she had to perform this wickedness, he did not understand.

It *was* wickedness, was it not, this ability to rivet his soul? Or was it what old men spoke of in their parlors with other old men—the magic of youth which they had long since ceased to experience?

The Sethite could not unravel the mystery. He knew only that he longed to share with this foreign woman— this Cainite—what had charged his heart and given him purpose. He longed to tell her, above anyone else, what Yahweh had done for him.

"Walk with me," was all he said. And as if it were only natural, he took her slender hand in his, and, leading his horse with the other, continued down the beach. The woman was silent, allowing her fingers to meld with his as though they had been made to do so.

"Where is your dog this evening?" Noah asked, awkwardly introducing the subject which had sparked their last conversation.

Naamah smiled and turned laughing eyes to the ground. "Topay is in my quarters. She does not enjoy the night breezes."

The preacher relaxed with his levity and felt free to be a little vulnerable. "I wish to apologize for my critical attitude when we last spoke. Your pet is a fine animal. Not a wolf, mind you—but fine for her purposes."

The woman warmed to this show of masculine humility.

"Thank you," she returned. "But I have thought much on your exhortation, and do now see your side of things. Topay is not what Yahweh intended."

Noah nodded respectfully. "Nonetheless," he added, "it is difficult to know just how much is allowed. I was wrong to pass judgment."

With this, Naamah drew closer and, sighing, acknowledged, "Many things are not as they should be. It would be wonderful to see the world as it originally was." The mountain man paused and studied her intent expression. For the moment he wished to set aside these matters, to speak of what was growing in his heart. But then, thinking better of it, he continued the stroll.

"I have my own ideas," he said, perhaps a bit too determinedly, "regarding what the world was like. For instance what would you say if I told you animals were able to speak?"

Naamah was captivated by the little boy behind Noah's serious nature. She knew he struggled against a man's impulses, and these weighty topics were his shield. But she stifled what would have been a much-too-broad smile and nodded appreciatively. "I would say it is a marvelous thought. There are many legends about such things."

Suddenly Noah dropped his horse's reins and grasped the woman's hands in both of his own. Then, gesturing wildly up the coast, he exclaimed, "Oh, lady—I must tell you! I heard a talking dolphin. Yes—I did! It was years ago—but I know it was no dream!"

The woman studied his enthusiasm. Part of her wished to laugh—but her soul was at the preacher's mercy, and she longed to please him. Knowing that her response could determine her place in his life for years to come, she summoned all her will and nodded agreement.

"You believe me? You do not think me mad?" he cried.

Naamah was lost in the depths of his flashing eyes. "No—my lord," she whispered, a smile touching her lips. "I could never think anything of you but the highest thoughts. If you say a dolphin talked . . . a dolphin talked!"

The Sethite, who had momentarily doused his tension, succumbed to the woman's praise. His palms were sweaty now, and the constriction returned to his throat. He ran his hands over his cloak, trying at the same time to ease the bands about his heart. But the moment he allowed his eyes to find hers again, he could not restrain himself.

Reaching forth, he drew her into his bosom, enfolding her anxiously in his arms.

"I feel," he stammered, "I feel you would believe anything I told you."

"Tell me anything you wish," the woman replied, pressing the beat of her heart against his own. "I could not doubt, should you tell me the sky would fall and the sea would swallow it up."

Now it was Noah who wished to laugh. Raising her face to his, he smiled broadly down at her. "Oh, lady, prepare yourself, for the tale I have to tell surpasses even that!"

And with these words he bent over her, caressing her lips with his own, again and then again.

TWO

Naamah never returned to Nod-Persia. She married the son of Lamech after a full year's courtship in the city of Shubag, and all with the blessings of her brother, Tubal-Cain.

It had been nearly a decade, now, since they wed, and Noah had never regretted his choice of a woman. His only hardship in wedding Naamah had been in his father's rejection. He had known the old Sethite would never consent to his marrying a Cainite, the daughter of a murderer, but he had nonetheless sought approval, as a dutiful son. When it was not forthcoming, he had gone against his father's wishes, being an emancipated and self-governing entity. And it would be a long time before the mountain patriarch softened.

However, a small fissure in the old man's shell widened to a crack when Naamah bore her first son, Shem. The couple would have remained with Shubag, but at last Lamech could resist no longer, and one day sent word that he longed to see the child.

So it was that Noah and his little family came to dwell at Lamechtown. For when the grandfather sent this invitation, Noah left nothing behind. He not only loaded Naamah and the toddler in the family wagon, but all their worldly goods in three others, knowing full well that the old man's heart would receive them openly once it was touched by Shem's dimpled smile.

Since before their marriage, Noah and his wife had

wished to live in the north country. It had been Naamah's idea, really. "The ark should be built in the mountains," she insisted, "away from the cities, away from your enemies. The lumber mill is there, and workers aplenty."

At first Noah had laughed. "The mountains! A boat in the mountains? How would we get it to sea?"

Naamah had only grinned slyly, waiting for the light to dawn in her husband's mind. "Ah, yes," he had conceded, a blush coloring his cheeks, "the sea will come to us. . . ."

"And the sky . . . ," Naamah had added, delighted at his slip of mind.

It was such moments which made the thought of the coming cataclysm endurable. And it was hope.

For the ark represented hope. The hope that some would be saved, and that all who were willing to believe would have sanctuary.

"Besides," Naamah had reasoned, "if the ark is in the mountains, it will be more accessible to those who flee the cities when the deluge descends. The high country will be the last to be flooded, and its location there should allow more to reach safety in time."

Noah had agreed, and neither of them had spoken of the fact that only they and their family would be spared, as Yahweh had said. Neither wished to voice that part of the prophecy—perhaps because they hoped for another interpretation—perhaps because they hoped that Yahweh might . . . change his mind.

This had been Noah's dream over the past year since they had come to Lamechtown. He had often tried to skirt Yahweh's words. And he had cleverly conjured up a number of possibilities which could allow for a large number of survivors.

What, for instance, if "Noah" might be interpreted as all those who follow Noah's preaching? Or what if his "sons" might be interpreted as all their children and their servants and their servants' children?

There were a dozen ways to stretch the meaning. Though the prophecy seemed to groan under the redefining, the practice gave intellectual ballast to Noah's dreams. And Yahweh did not seem bent on squelching such hope.

So it was that today, as Noah sat atop a rib of the ark's wooden skeleton, he had the heart to continue with the work.

It was amazing how much humidity could be felt at the higher elevations, the mountains where the land was closest to the vaporous canopy of earth. And the thirty cubits which the ark rose above Lamechtown gave a man even more reason to wipe his brow. As Noah sat on the highest point of the vessel's squat gable, the handle of his wood-plane slipped now and then against the sweat of his callused palm.

Working just below him on the third deck was Jaseth, his younger brother. As the preacher worked at the whittling of a great beam, attempting to bring it into a smooth, square angle around a stubborn core of knot, the younger man peered above.

"Careful!" he called, smiling with a gleam of perfect teeth. "The way you're going, you're bound to drop that tool directly on my head!"

Noah glanced down at the lad and chuckled. How Jaseth reminded him of his mother. No one else in the family had inherited her fine shock of red hair, or her fair complexion. "Don't worry," the elder replied. "It wouldn't hurt any more than the sunburn you've sported for weeks. Poor Paleskin! One would think you never spent a day outdoors!"

At this Jaseth reached into a nearby bucket of cold drinking water and threw a handful on his accuser. "You know better!" he cried. "Just because my skin doesn't look like a tanned hide does not mean I work less than you—Leatherface!"

Noah laid aside his plane and bounded down from the

beam, grasping his brother by the waist and throwing him to the floor of the deck.

Over and over the two tumbled, laughing and cursing one another, until they rolled indecorously into the ramport. Noah had Jaseth in a threatening lock, his right arm twisted behind him and his head forced up against the preacher's chest.

"Enough, Powderface?" Noah bellowed.

"Enough!" Jaseth agreed, crying and laughing at once.

The elder released him and Jaseth shook his head, working his jaw with one hand to see that it was intact. And then, eying his brother sideways, he suddenly threw an elbow to Noah's stomach and set upon him with a vengeance.

Again they tumbled until neither had the strength for a challenge, exhausted as much by hilarity as by exertion. And they crawled over to the water bucket, dowsing one another with great handfuls.

"I know," the elder said at last, "that you have worked as hard as anyone here." He wrapped his sturdy arm around Jaseth's slender shoulders and drew him close. "And I remember how Mother used to suffer with the heat. Her skin would redden just like yours, and sometimes it would blister if she stayed out too long. The sun does not affect most of us that way. I guess we can be grateful for the sky-canopy, or your skin would be even more tender."

"It is not so bad," Jaseth conceded. "I must be out for many days before I feel it. Besides—there is much for me to do."

"Indeed," Noah replied, surveying the work crews below. The men of Lamechtown's mill had been a real boon to the project. Due to a small miracle, they had been ordered to include Noah's ark in their work schedules. As the preacher observed their labors now it seemed only yesterday that he had approached his father with the strange story of Yahweh's contract, and of the great cataclysm which would necessitate its fulfillment.

The three years between Noah's sermons in the cities and his move to the mountains had been silent ones for the preacher. He had kept a low profile on the coast during his courtship year and the infancy of Shem. Word had trickled to Lamech about Noah's peculiar discourses at Cronos and Sun City, but the news had been diluted by the time it reached the old Sethite, and with the intervening quiet, he had not thought much further on it.

Therefore, the day Noah had come to him, soon after bringing his family to dwell on the estate, his presentation had been of great surprise to the patriarch.

"You are to build what?" the grandfather marveled.

"A ship," Noah repeated. "A great barge, for the preservation of life."

The concept of universal destruction was not new to Lamech. The Sethite tradition was full of references to such a time. But it took awhile for the old man to digest the full meaning of his son's vision. He had dwelt on it for several days before he called Noah to sit with him by the fire of his chamber.

"Did you share these dreams with Shubag?" the elder inquired.

"Often," Noah replied. "And with my wife's brother, Tubal-Cain."

Lamech winced. It had been hard for him to accept Naamah into the family, though he had eventually grown in to it. But any reminder of her notorious Cainite lineage still pained him.

"They are both . . . great men," Lamech admitted.

"Yes," Noah agreed, surprised at his father's magnanimity. "Both of them."

"And . . . they were persuaded of your vision?"

"Indeed," the son responded.

Lamech's gaze drifted between the flames of the fire-pit, and when he spoke it was in a whisper. "Perhaps this is the meaning . . . ," he said.

"The meaning?" Noah asked.

Lamech shook himself from his private reverie. "The meaning of your name. . . . I have wondered about it all your life."

Noah recalled the story of the peculiar naming and how all the local folk had pondered the interpretation of the word "rest."

"You have some new insight, Father?"

"Yes—it must be that in this calling lies the fulfillment of the prophecy which Yahweh bestowed when he gave your name. For if the ark is to be a place of safety, a refuge for the righteous, and you are to be its builder, then you will have gone the length of your journey. You, in fact, shall be for your people 'a rest' from the weariness of the sin-cursed world."

Noah surveyed his father's time-worn face where the fire emphasized its crevices, and his heart warmed with love. "Would such a thing make you happy?" he inquired.

Lamech turned glistening eyes to the young preacher who had once sat upon his knee. "It would bless me, my son."

The two were silent as they pondered the magnitude of the mission. And then, suddenly, Lamech was standing, pacing the floor and making gestures as if to calculate some formula.

Noah watched him without a word, until the old man at last asserted, "You know that a father usually reserves his blessing for his deathbed. But you have so pleased me tonight, I must give you some portion of your inheritance this day!"

The son was awestruck, not having expected any such thing. And when the father explained, he was even more surprised.

"Workers!" Lamech offered. "You shall have access to my workers whenever you need them, for as long as it takes. And materials. . . . They are yours for the taking!"

Such a gift surpassed anything Noah could have asked. It was true that he and Naamah had discussed the availability of such resources in Lamechtown, but never with thought that they could be had without dipping into Naamah's rich dowry.

As he marveled at the bestowal, seeking words to approximate his gratitude, his father spoke again. "I may not live to see the deluge," he was saying, "but I shall see the ship of Yahweh! I shall not die until I see her."

The preacher listened respectfully, but objected, "See her? You shall sail her with me!"

Lamech understood Noah's heart, but set him right. "Do not question Yahweh's words, my son. The ship is for you and yours; not for me. I shall not sail with you, for I shall be gone. And no one else will sail, but those whom Yahweh has prophesied."

Noah sat with Jaseth on the deck and grasped him a little too securely about the sunburned shoulders. The younger brother winced and drew back, but Noah asserted, "Imagine! Won't it be grand—to work this craft together? You and I, captains of the biggest life preserver ever to float!"

Jaseth gave an obligatory smile, but wondered why Noah must include him so determinedly. "Of course . . . ," he agreed. "We'll sail together."

Noah held onto the lad's promise like an anchor, and forced Lamech's words to accommodate it.

"If I am called, all mine are called. Right, Jaseth? And you are mine!"

The young man nodded, studying Noah's fevered eyes with apprehension.

But then, the preacher was distracted. Below walked Naamah, and his heart stirred with pride.

"Have you noticed, Jaseth?" He nudged his brother. "Have you noticed how her belly swells? She will bear me another son before the year is out."

The lad turned his ruddy face in her direction and nodded. "Who could not have noticed? I am most happy for you. But. . . ."

"But what?" The Sethite smiled, tracing Naamah's steps with his gaze.

"But how do you know the child shall be a boy?"

Noah chafed. "Why, Jaseth! How often have I told you Yahweh's words to me? Did he not say that I and my *sons* would be saved, before I ever had Naamah *or* little Shem? We should never doubt the word of God."

The youngster was strangely quiet. The preacher caught this, but tried to ignore it. "I know you believe!" he insisted.

"Of course," Jaseth laughed. But his laugh was empty, as was his heart.

THREE

When Noah's second son was born, he was not fair of skin, as was Jaseth. Neither was his complexion olive-hued as the preacher's. He bore a closer likeness to Naamah's kin. He was a dark and handsome character, darker than Noah—resembling his other uncle, Tubal-Cain. And as he grew, his skin became even deeper in tone, until he and his brother Shem contrasted in the sun.

One would almost wonder, to look at him, how his flesh remained cool, as it absorbed the sun's rays more readily than Shem's. And therefore, though it was a misnomer, he came to be called Ham, meaning "hot."

As for Shem, he began to live up to his name, meaning "renown or fame," shortly after he began to toddle. It seemed Noah could go nowhere without the little one beside him, or following close after like a shadow. The child mimicked everything his father did, from the way he stood to the way he lifted a tool. Noah would never forget the day Shem attempted to drive his first nail with a hammer fully as long as his arm. Determined to lift the heavy instrument, if not swing it wildly, he succeeded in striking his own toe, and then in suppressing the tears which exerted themselves against his closed eyes.

"A sturdy one he is," Noah boasted. "He will do his father proud all his life."

As Ham grew, he came to admire his elder brother, Shem, as much as Shem admired Noah. And the second son desired to please the father as much as the firstborn. But his attempts to meet Noah's expectations were designed as much to put him on a par with Shem as to win him paternal approval. And perhaps this was where it began—the rivalry, the jealousy between brothers—even at such an early age.

Eventually, Ham's attitude contrasted with Shem's as much as his skin color.

Noah might have handled it all better. Naamah often wished the father could appreciate more deeply the struggle of her second child. She spoke with him about it, but the Sethite would only shrug. "Ham knows that I love him just as I love my firstborn," he would insist.

"Then pay him more mind, Noah," the woman would warn. "Do not dote so much on Shem. Remember that he had the advantage in keeping you to himself for nine years. Ham needs your attention now."

But it was difficult to deny time to Shem and give it to the younger. Shem knew best how to attract his father's eye and hold it—with little gestures and pleasing acts. As much as Ham might try to compete, there was little chance of his measuring up to Shem, who was always several steps ahead in development.

And then, about the time the father began to see the need—to realize Ham's discouragement and try to help him—there was yet another interference. For the third son of Yahweh's prophecy was born to Noah's wife.

This child was Jaseth's godson, his look-alike. And the moment he was born, Noah bestowed on him a name reminiscent of the uncle. "Japheth," he was called. "Just as Jaseth was 'God's appointment,' so Japheth shall carry on his beginnings. He shall be the 'widespreading one,' and his seed shall fill the earth." So much did Noah love his brother, that he chose to think of his third son as a type of the uncle. And it was not difficult to do so, for Japheth was as pale of skin as Jaseth, and both were reminders of Noah's mother.

The disparity in the naming of his sons did not seem to occur to Noah. Shem was promised great renown, and Japheth great prosperity. Ham, who was born between, had missed the privileged firstborn status, and by the time he had developed enough problems to be a thorn in Noah's side, Japheth came along to capture the father's frustrated heart and draw it once again away from Ham.

And so, Ham was left with a name that was virtually meaningless. "Hot" they called him—nothing more than a poor attempt to describe his experience in the flesh. But in the ironic way names have of fulfilling themselves, Ham grew into the appellation. He became hot of spirit, hot of temperament, angry and with a bitter sense of humor. It seemed all the world had conspired to thwart his future. And by the time he was a young man, he had set himself apart. Though he lived with Noah, though he dwelt with Shem and Japheth, he was a solitary fellow.

The Sun, which seared his dark complexion with glistening sweat, became his companion. He was a wilderness man, and lived on the fantasy of conquest. One day, he swore, he would prove his worth, though he must sell his soul to do it.

FOUR

All Lamechtown relied economically on the commerce generated by the lumber mill. Therefore, though Lamech had given Noah access to his workers for the building of the ark, the preacher made certain that the schedule on that project never interfered with the routine of the factory.

As a result, progress on the mammoth ship was very slow, and added to the time delay was the fact that Noah preferred to manufacture the vessel by hand, rather than by machine. Noah did not know what stressful conditions the ark might have to endure or how long after the deluge it might have to serve as shelter for all life on earth. So he wanted it built perfectly, with craftsmanship as fine as possible. Therefore, except for the cutting of the lumber into prefabricated lengths, all was done manually.

It was on Japheth's twentieth birthday that Ham voiced his discontent for the first time. And it was over thirty-five years into the building of the boat. There was a great party in Lamechtown to celebrate the anniversaries, and Ham chose not to participate.

Instead he left at early morn for the high country behind the village. There was a pad of granite high on the side of one hill which sat naked between the trees and yet was secluded from the valley's view. It was to find this seclusion that Ham wended his way through the forest. His aim was to sit in the exposure to the sun which the place afforded.

As he put distance between himself and the celebration below, the sound of music and dancing became fainter until he could hear it no more. The private retreat lay only a few feet ahead, and his heart raced as he watched the morning light play through tree shadows across the rock face. Soon he was positioned atop it, sitting with feet brought close to his body between spread knees, hands resting palms up upon his thighs, and eyes turned heavenward.

For long hours he sat thus, until the Golden Orb stood directly overhead in its noontime arc, and his brow was shiny with perspiration.

It was possible that someone might come upon him here, but highly unlikely. For years he had found uninterrupted privacy at this place. But even if the unlikely were to happen, he never expected it to be Naamah who would intrude.

She stood now on the boundary of the granite pad, just inside the trees, and studied her dark son as he glistened in the light. His torso was bare, and streamlets of sweat trickled down his back, catching the sun.

She had seen the men of her own country in such meditations, where they sat in the palm groves outside her hometown, doing obeisance to Lucifer. They had raised stone structures to house such worship, as well, in the form of granite pillars arranged in a circle. And it was said by those who understood such things that the pillars told the calendar and the time, by the lines of shadow which the sun cast from them.

Naamah had spoken to Ham about these matters, as he had grown up closer to her than to his father. She had always dealt with the issue in the negative, teaching Ham that such religion was pagan, and not of God.

Now she wished she had never spoken of such things at all.

When she could still her heart no longer, she crept forward and approached her son, who was oblivious to anything outside himself. It was not until she had placed a cool hand upon his wet shoulder that he lurched into consciousness.

"Mother!" he cried, when he had wheeled about. Naamah's sad eyes met his in a whisper of inquisition, and he turned his own to the ground.

"What are you doing?" was her simple question. "Tell me, please, that you are not given over."

Ham sighed and scanned the forestline absently. "I cannot answer that, Mother. I would like to think not. I do not believe in Sun-worship. . . ."

"Then what?" Naamah persisted, her voice breaking. "Are the traditions of Yahweh not enough for you?"

Ham looked at her with great round eyes, and his full lips parted with an expression she could not interpret. It seemed half of surprise and half a sneer.

"Mother," he stammered, "I believe in Yahweh, but I struggle."

The mother knelt down beside him and listened as carefully as she could, refraining the impulse to scold. "How, son? Tell me of the struggle."

Ham ran a nervous hand across his ebony face and sighed again. "Somehow," he began, "I do not feel the part of a Sethite. Though I am the son of a Sethite, I feel I belong . . . to Cain."

Naamah drew back and let the strange pronouncement sink into her heart. She did not wish to jump to conclusions, and so proceeded cautiously.

"What does this mean to you—this 'belonging' to Cain?" she queried.

Ham pondered this a moment and then reflected, "I have never felt close to Noah."

Naamah noted, not for the first time, his avoidance of the term "father" when referring to her husband, but she did not correct him as he continued, "And I look more like those of your country. Were my uncle, Tubal-Cain, to be here, I sense I would feel very close to him."

The mother shook her head. "Perhaps you would, because he would love you as a son. But no one in my family
has ever been . . . a Sun-worshiper. Tubal-Cain would
scorn the comparison!"

Ham sat slump-shouldered at this rebuke, and nodded.
"I know that, Mother. I scorn it as well. It is just that I
cannot identify with my elder brother's God."

The dark beauty scrutinized the lad with compassion.
"Why do you call Yahweh your *brother's* God?"

"Because," Ham said, punctuating his response with
a clenched fist, "that is how Noah refers to him . . . 'the
God of Lamech,' he says, and 'the God of Shem.' Never
the God of Ham or of Japheth. My younger brother does
not seem to mind, but I always have resented this!"

Naamah drew close. "This is tradition you balk at,
Ham, not your father's heart. It is tradition to refer to
one's God as the God of one's father and one's firstborn
son. It simply shows the handing down of faith from one
generation to the next, and to the next. It is not intended
to slight the other children of a family."

"Ha!" Ham cried. "Tradition be damned! It is tradition
which has stripped me of all opportunity. Not only was
I born the second son, and so by tradition am inferior,
but by tradition my name is my designation, and my
designation is meaningless. I am a meaningless man!"

"Child," the woman whispered, tears rising to her
lashes, "this is not true. You are neither inferior nor meaningless. A name does not make a statement regarding a
man's worth, so much as it describes him or states some
hope for his future. And a man can make his own name
glow with meaning. If you are 'hot,' be 'hot for Yahweh,'
'hot of spirit'!"

Now Ham laughed derisively. "No, Mother! You strain
the interpretation! If I am hot, it shall be after gain and
after glory! Thus shall I fulfill all hope concerning me!
And when my father is on his deathbed, I shall heat his

blessing to a white flame, or I shall melt his curse with my breath!"

The woman had always known that her son cut his teeth on discouragement, but only now did she realize that this discouragement had turned to hate.

"You speak of blessings and of curses? Be careful, my child," she pleaded, "lest your resentment mark you with Cain's *curse*. If you feel close to Cain, it is in the similarity of your feelings toward your brother. His resentment of Abel led the way to sin, and so shall yours if you do not curb it. Then your dream of conquest will end in slavery, and your hope of glory shall end in shame. So did it happen for my countrymen and their patriarch. And it was generations being undone."

FIVE

From the beginning of the boat project, Noah's work had not gone unnoticed by the world beyond Lamechtown. At first, as the ship's skeletal structure had taken form, travelers passing through the village or customers coming up from the cities assumed it to be a mammoth advertisement for the mill's products.

Even the workmen assigned to the project by Lamech were unaware of the barge's ultimate destiny. "Some eccentric whim of the old man," they would laugh among themselves, presuming that Lamech had gone a bit off center in his thinking. But all hours spent on the craft were overtime and, hence, well paid. For years the millworkers had labored on the project without question. And so the ribs and beams had been completed and then the great strips of gopher-wood siding had been applied. It was not until the interior work had begun that the men began to murmur.

"If this is nothing more than a display, why are we asked to supply such detail?" they wondered. "And what are these plans?" they marveled, perusing the maze-like blueprints of cellular rooms and stalls.

So it was that the curiosity began to grow first in Lamechtown, among the workers, and then spread down to the cities as travelers passed word of the strange project in the hills.

Within a few weeks the inquisitive began arriving, to

213

see if the rumor were true. Why was a boat being built in the mountains, where there were no rivers or lakes and the closest body of water was a turtle pond? And why was the boat so immense, so peculiar in its internal arrangement?

This month there had been more tourists visiting the site than ever before, and the workers were coming under great strain as they were bombarded daily with inquiring eyes and with questions for which they had no answers. What had been a virtual secret in the Adlandian wilderness, the property of one village, now demanded an explanation. It had been over thirty-eight years since Noah had preached a sermon, but today he must do so. After almost four decades of peace, he must bring himself to herald his cause once more before the public. For the quiet hamlet was quiet no longer.

The laborers had organized themselves this morning, determined to have their satisfaction. If Lamech would not speak with them, Noah must. And since the patriarch thought it best that his son do the explaining, he directed them his way.

The best place to speak to the millworkers, who numbered in the hundreds, was from the high, open doorway of the ark. When Noah had ascended the narrow ladder leading to this aperture, he had not expected the even larger crowd which had assembled. Foreigners passing through town, and the always-present tourists here to see the renowned ark, had joined the villagers to learn what the preacher would present.

In family hours by the evening fires, Shem, Ham, and Japheth had heard the story since childhood, of their father's call and his visit with Yahweh, of the devastation which was imminent, and of the purpose of the ark. The eldest and the youngest were clearly visible on the edge of the crowd, where they stood, confident in Noah's ability to handle the situation. But the Sethite's dark eyes scanned the throng, which even now grew in numbers as more onlookers joined its ranks. Ham's face would have been easily distinguishable, were he present. Even among Cainites, whose skin tended to a deeper pigmentation than Sethites', Ham would have stood out, for he drew his lineage from the purer race of Nod-Persia, and harked back to his mother's ancestors in appearance.

But Ham was not in the crowd, and Noah was disappointed. His job would have been easier had all three sons shown their support in this moment.

Just now Noah wished he had devoted more time to prayer since coming to Lamechtown. He longed to duck into the vessel, to hide himself and seek Yahweh's counsel as to what he should speak.

But he gripped himself and reasoned privately, "This is the Lord's project. He must give me the words to defend it."

He surveyed the audience, and tried to recapture the serenity of the time when the Lord had walked with him.

Summoning courage which came from that memory, he opened his mouth and gestured to the walls of the ship. "It is supposed that this vessel is meant to highlight my father's mill—to bring commerce to our village. This is not true. It is surmised that we are investigating some new model in ship-building. This also is untrue. The craft you see before you," he said calmly, "is not Lamech's design—neither was it his idea to produce it in this isolated spot. This ship is not the product of Lamechtown alone, nor of a mad mind. It is not, indeed, the concept of any *man*. It is a vessel contracted by our God!"

The Sethian villagers eyed one another in surprise. Some recalled the vague rumors regarding Noah's strange sermons in the coastal cities years before. But they had never connected those rumors with the project on which they had labored all this time.

As the murmuring grew, and the questions, Noah tried to regain their attention.

"You have heard of the great cataclysm prophesied by

our fathers Adam and Enoch, which would mark the end of this planet as we know it!" he cried.

Instantly all eyes were on him, as the fearsome subject with which they had been familiar since childhood was resurrected. The preacher met the opportunity with full force.

"Nowhere do these prophecies state that all *life* will be destroyed. This vessel," he hailed her, "shall be guardian of the species God has ordained, protecting them from the deluge and from the Destroyer's hand which shall press sore upon the earth!"

The foreigners and city dwellers who witnessed this speech grew restless now. This was not just a Sethian issue, they perceived. It was clear the implication involved *all* Adlandian life.

As the Sethites whispered among themselves, shaking their heads in laughing doubt or serious contemplation, the Cainites on the edge of the crowd grew angry. One of them, an aged merchant from Cronos, waved vigorously over the heads of his fellow listeners, and at last Noah called on him.

"Sir," the merchant inquired, "I heard you years ago, when you spoke in the marketplace of my city. I did not like what you said then, and I like it even less today."

Many present hooted agreement, but Noah let him continue.

"So you intend to house all species within this vessel? Have you made calculations? Granted, your ship is immense, but the zoo of Poseidon in Sun City is a mile square and contains a mere fraction of the animal types. How, pray tell, do you plan to accomplish such a feat?"

"Yahweh has asked only that I bring one pair of each unclean and seven pair of each clean animal type on board," Noah explained. "The various species are contained within the life-matter of the *kinds* or *families*, and it is estimated that there are at most 800 *kinds* on earth. I figure, given the diversity of clean and unclean, that I must accommodate less than 2,400 individual creatures in the ark, which has the capacity for more than forty times that number of the medium-sized." With this he took a deep breath and concluded, "As you can see, not only will there be ample space for each, but for many supplies and potential offspring. And if Yahweh sees fit to board more, there is more than enough room!"

The congregation stood amazed at Noah's calculations. It was apparent much foresight had gone into his plan for the interior.

"As to the exterior of the vessel," he continued, "this ship was not made for sailing, but for floating; its shape best suited for stability and endurance against the most threatening conditions. It is simply not capsizable—a storehouse for survival!"

Now the crowd was very still. Even the challenger shrank meekly into the throng.

But Noah was not satisfied to stop. Yahweh had given him courage for more than a technical explanation.

"The questions you have asked are wise ones," he commended his enemies, "but there is a matter more important than these. What you should be asking is *why* Yahweh sees fit to destroy the earth!"

His voice picked up conviction as he reminded the audience of humanity's sin, of the violence of the planet, the destruction of mankind's habitat, and the arts of manipulation. He spared nothing in singling out those responsible for the oppressions of greed and warfare, promiscuity and lust. The capacity of the human heart for evil had been enlarged, he proclaimed, by its trafficking with strange gods—with the minions of Lucifer and their halfbreed descendants.

Suddenly, though the crowd had listened well to this point, the atmosphere was seared with a sinister spirit. Faces here and there displayed it, and all present could feel it in the air. From somewhere deep in the throng came a rattling challenge.

"Who—then—shall be saved?" it inquired.

Noah sensed the origin of the confrontation, though no one else seemed to identify it, and his skin tingled. But, squaring his shoulders, he nodded agreeably toward the strange utterance. "I am glad you asked that question," he declared. "For Yahweh would not have anyone be ignorant of his salvation!"

Then, leveling his gaze at the congregation, he proclaimed, "The Lord says the just shall live by faith! There is none righteous! No—not one! All have sinned and fallen short of God's glory. But he has, in his grace, prepared an escape for those who confess their unworthiness and turn to him!"

The spirit of antagonism had not fully crested, when another voice interrupted Noah, drawing his attention to one of the project's most devoted workmen.

"Speak, Seltan," the preacher deferred. "You have been a good friend. What is your question?"

The Sethite was a little hesitant, but finally spoke forthrightly. "Noah—do you mean to say that this vessel is large enough to hold progenitors for all animal species, along with all *people* who wish to escape the flood? How can such a thing be?"

The son of Lamech was touched by his friend's naivete. "Seltan," he replied, "I recall our days together, growing up in these mountains. You were one of my closest companions, and have become a community leader. I respect your concern for humanity, but you have not heard me correctly."

Noah's boyhood comrade listened quietly as the preacher reiterated, "It is not all those who *wish* to be spared, who *will* be spared. Only those who admit their need of salvation and trust Yahweh's provision shall be saved." At this the preacher shuddered and looked skyward. "But the time will draw short for salvation. God's hand will not always stretch forth to save, nor will he always strive with mankind. There will come a time," he cried, "when the door to the ark will be shut, and no one shall enter in—despite many petitions and many tears!"

SIX

The cool of evening was ascending the sides of the great vessel, as Noah gathered up his tools. Once, when he was a child, he had made the mistake of leaving his father's hammer outside overnight. By morning, it had developed a fine coating of rust from the dense dew which settled upon the ground where it lay.

Ever since, he had made sure to leave nothing out which would be endangered by the nightly fog of Adlandia.

His childhood had been on his mind since Seltan had spoken up today. As Noah arranged his chisels in their leather sheath, he reminisced on those more carefree days, and he wondered if any of his old companions would live to see the world beyond the coming destruction.

A warm tear spilled down his cheek and splashed onto the back of one hand. He lifted his fingers from the sheath, which he had just bound with a cord, and he brushed away the salty trickle. It was good that he was alone just now, he thought. He would not want anyone to see him cry.

But at that instant, he heard footsteps below, and being on the roof of the ark, he crawled to the rampart and peered over. It was difficult to identify who stood silent in the fog beside the vessel. He waited a moment, and when the figure did not move, he called, "Who is it? Did you need something?"

"It is I, Seltan," came a husky reply. "I was hoping to speak with you, Noah."

The preacher quickly thrust his tools into the work-chest and shut the lid. He then scrambled down the long ladder which led to the ground and stood face to face with his old friend.

"I thought you went home hours ago," he greeted.

"I did," Seltan said. "But I could not rest."

"Come," Noah directed, bundling an extra cloak about his own shoulders. "It is much too damp out here. There is probably a fire still burning in the men's hall."

Seltan complied gratefully, and soon they had crossed the village to the small retreat frequented by the laborers of Lamechtown. Noah did not often resort to the place, but knew Seltan would feel most comfortable there. And so, when they entered, he called for a table nearest the still-glowing hearth.

Wine in Adlandia was a rare commodity. There were brewed drinks available, but naturally turned beverages were very expensive, for the canopy of heaven obstructed all but the most persistent aging elements of sun and air. Therefore, the fruit of the vine and its juices were extremely slow in fermenting. And if a man treated a friend to such a luxury, it was an expensive treat indeed.

Therefore, it was evidence of Noah's great affection for Seltan that he ordered for him one of the most costly nectars of the mountain vineyards.

The millworker's eyes misted at this show of generosity, but Noah's kindness seemed to make his task even more difficult. The preacher leaned forward and prodded him a little. "Now, friend, you said you wished to speak with me?"

The little tavern was very quiet. Only the shuffling of the servants in the kitchen broke the silence, for tomorrow was a workday and all the other customers had gone home with the dark.

"You handled the crowd well today," Seltan began, his voice betraying nervousness. "And you replied well to my question. But. . . ."

He hesitated and Noah spurred him, "Yes—go on. . . ."

"But . . . and you must understand that I am not mocking you, as some persist in doing. . . ."

"Of course." Noah smiled.

Seltan bowed his head, and Noah's heart ached for the heaviness he perceived on his weathered face. He recalled the lighthearted laugh which had always characterized this fellow, and he was sorry it seemed so buried.

"But," the craftsman went on, "I think you mislead the people."

Noah studied the accusation briefly, and rebutted, perhaps too quickly, "Seltan—if you speak again of the limited capacity of the ark—it is only because you have led a sheltered life in these hills. You have not seen the wickedness of the cities. Most of humanity will never turn to Yahweh!"

But Seltan was shaking his head. "I fear you have spent too *much* time in those places, Noah. You forget that there are still pockets of life where sanctified folk dwell. Why, your ark will not hold even half of Lamechtown, and our village is full of those who keep the ways of Seth!"

"Ah," Noah reflected, leaning back in the squat chair which cradled his tired body. He fingered his own wine glass and considered Seltan's viewpoint carefully. "I see what you are saying," he admitted. And then, proceeding gently, he explained, "I once felt as you do, my friend, about the holiness of our race. And it is true that we have been the most privileged men on earth. We have the oracles of Adam and the prophecies of Enoch. We have the traditions and the laws of righteousness."

"Yes—we do!" Seltan asserted. "And yet you say we shall not all be saved!"

Noah cleared his throat. "Not for those reasons, Seltan. Any more than a Cainite will be lost because he is a Cainite!"

Seltan's eyes flashed and he scanned the low rafters with a grunt. "I see that your wife not only turned your head years ago, but also your mind!" he muttered.

Noah bristled, but restrained his anger. "It is not my wife who has convinced me of such things, though she has a heart for Yahweh that would put many a Sethite to shame. No . . . ," he said emphatically, "it is not Naamah, but Yahweh who has taught me that not one work of right-eousness shall save a human soul! And," he declared, wondering at his own boldness, "my friend, if it is upon tradition or good works that you rely, I fear for *your* future, as I fear for those who have forgotten God in Cronos and Sun City and the Wilderness of Nod!"

The words hung bitingly in the air, and Seltan's face grew red with their impact. For a long while the two men confronted one another in silence, the declaration swing-ing like an invisible flag between them.

As Noah marveled at their newfound animosity, the millworker rose from the table. Without a word he pulled his cloak over his shoulders and picked up his wine glass. He tipped the container toward his mouth, emptying it with a gulp. Then, setting it down carefully, he glanced once more at the preacher.

Noah watched his exit numbly.

SEVEN

When the sons of Noah began to seek wives for themselves, Ham was the first to marry. And the day he announced his choice to the patriarch, Lamech, seeking his blessing, the final wedge was driven between himself and the grandfather, who had never been warm toward the lad.

From the time Ham had been born, and especially when his skin had begun to darken like Tubal-Cain's and his brethren of Nod, the old Sethite had found great difficulty in overlooking the reminder of Naamah's race. Intellectually the old man knew there was no difference between Shem, Japheth, and Ham. But it was an emotional blindness which caused his prejudice—not an intellectual one.

And Ham's choice of a woman was no inducement to change Lamech's thinking.

Carise had captured Ham's heart the moment he first saw her with a bedouin caravan outside the village. Her people were not city-dwellers, nor were they mountaineers. They were free wanderers, claiming no particular nation or origin. They lived off transient labor and wily connivery. They were an amiable, but fiercely loyal tribe, and abided by no law but their own. "Stranger beware" was their operating code, and they lived for song, dance, and nomadic freedom. Their racial distinction had become blurred by years of wandering. Not one of them knew whether his tribe should be considered Sethitic or Cainitic, and nothing was of less importance to them.

Ham had come upon the caravan one evening as he returned from a day in the hills. Most Sethites, as well as Cainites, had long since given up the strict vegetarianism of Eden, and during his years of solitude Ham had developed mastery of the hunt, being a fine archer. He rarely failed to bring a feast of game to Naamah, who enjoyed cooking whatever he presented and who had developed a fine collection of recipes for wild meat.

This evening, as Ham descended the last low hill bordering Lamechtown, with a small doe dressed out and slung over his broad shoulders, he was caught by the glint of warm light and the sound of music in a hollow just off the road.

Creeping to the edge of the vale, he hid within the fog-rimmed trees sheltering the little camp, and watched as a woman spun and swayed around the fire, her colorful garments flowing with her wild but graceful movements like a flashing aurora.

High in her right hand a tambourine shimmered, as the heel of her left palm struck it in cadence with the music's beat. Earrings, bangles, and chains added their own chorus as she spun, and a dozen bracelets danced on her arm in silver chime.

The eyes of the men tried to catch hers, but she played them for fools with her fickle glances.

When at last the music reached a crescendo and she turned herself to a pivoting step, tumbling from outstretched arm to outstretched arm, each admirer strained to hold her to himself. And when she rested, it was with a breathless laugh.

"No—let me be!" she cried. "I belong to none of you!"

With this, she gathered her skirts about her and sashayed to the edge of the camp, where they knew she wished to be alone.

"Carise!" they called, but she did not reply. And when she found a quiet retreat she sat within the shadows, waiting for the stilling of her heart.

She could not know that a stranger watched..She could not know that the grandson of this village's founder studied her a stone's throw away.

Where moonlight found her as it filtered through low branches, it showed an aquiline nose and high cheek-bones, set in a complexion made earth-dark by the sun. The woman could have been Ham's cousin, or Tubal-Cain's daughter. From a crowd of thousands she would have been picked as the twin of Naamah's second son.

Her obsidian eyes flashed like those of a startled fawn when she heard Ham move behind her.

"Do not be afraid, my lady," he whispered. "It is a friend—perhaps even a brother—who approaches."

"I have no brother but the wind," she replied. "And I belong to no man!"

"So I heard you tell the others," he said, a smile in his voice as he stepped closer.

"Friend or foe, come no nearer!" she warned, drawing a slender blade from a strap upon her thigh.

Ham caught sight of the glistening skin beneath her skirt, and he stood still, as much in admiration as in fear. "I mean no harm," he repeated. "See, I am unarmed." He stepped out from the shadows, his hands extended. "I am a hunter, only now come down from the hills. When I heard your music, I stopped to listen. . . ."

"And to watch," she presumed, tossing her head coyly.

". . . Yes—to watch," he granted. "My bow and quiver are in the wood, with my game."

At this the woman was silent, glancing enviously in the direction of his gesture.

"Game?" she whispered.

Ham studied her furtive expression, and, now that he had drawn closer, could make out the sunken hollows beneath her cheeks and the hunger behind her carefree ambiance.

"When did you last eat?" he inquired.

The woman lifted her chin scornfully. "Eat? Do you

question our fortunes? My people are well fed!"

"Then," he said gently, placing a hand on her smooth arm, "they will not mind if you join me for supper. Unless, of course, you have already taken your evening meal." Carise turned a nervous glance to the caravan, and Ham prodded her again, "Or perhaps you have some jealous lover who would constrain you?"

"Hmmph!" she sighed. "I told you I belong to no man!"

"Very well, then," he laughed. "Come!"

Taking her by the hand, he led her up the foggy hill to his cache of venison. Finding a nearby cave, they built a fire, and within a short while the scent of meat, laden with herbs collected from the underbrush, wooed her.

When she had well eaten, he knew she was his for the taking. Drawing her close, he breathed upon her neck and she melted into the warmth of his embrace.

"A shame to the line of Seth!" Lamech was raving, as Naamah flew from the patriarch's chamber. She sped down the long hall of the estate and out onto the veranda, running squarely into her husband.

"Noah!" she cried, throwing herself into his arms and then pulling back angrily. "Where are you when I need you?" She glared at the rough calluses on his open palms and declared, "The boat project! Always the project! It has taken your heart all these years—and your sons grew up without you!"

The Sethite muttered his exasperation. "What troubles you, woman?"

"Did you not see the damsel in the garden as you passed? The bedouin?"

"I did not." Noah shrugged. "What damsel?"

"She shall soon be your daughter-in-law, if Ham has his way. And if she is a poor choice, you must live with the fact that you never instructed him in matters of taste, or in matters of life!"

Then, pushing past him, Naamah rushed toward the
wing of the estate which had been their home since they
came to Lamechtown years before. The preacher watched
her exit and noted her swift glance into the border garden.
Her angry shake of the head spoke volumes. He would
have peeked into the bower himself, had he not heard the
voices of his father and Ham spilling from the house in
heated disagreement.

"Perhaps, indeed, you have never been one of us!"
Lamech was shouting. "You are of the line of Cain—of
the family of the other Lamech!"

At this Noah rushed to the chamber, in time to see
Ham turn in a fury for the door. "Stop, son!" he cried.
"What is this about?"

The handsome ebony face met his in a cloud of resentment. "It is about tradition, Noah!"

"Call me, 'father,'" the preacher insisted, grasping him
by the arm.

" 'Father' . . . ," Ham spit viciously. "It is about tradition! Do we not all honor tradition in this family? By
tradition I approached our patriarch for his blessing on
my forthcoming marriage. And he refused it. So I shall
do as you did, when you took a wife! I shall defy my
elders!"

Noah was stunned by his rebuking tone. "Why . . . ,"
he stammered, "did you not come directly to me about
this? Why did you go to Lamech?"

"Ha!" the son roared, his head thrown back and the
veins in his sleek black neck thick with urgency. "When
could I ever talk with you?"

At this, Ham's tormented eyes moved toward the door
and he rushed for the garden, to the one who had spurred
his rebellious soul.

Ham would not find Carise in the little bower. Skittish
as a wild doe, she had retreated up the mountain at the

sounds of turmoil in Lamech's house. It would, in fact, be Noah who unexpectedly came upon her along the trail to his favorite glen of solitude.

In his brooding mood, shoulders stooped and fists clenched, the preacher kept his eyes to the ground, as he hiked into the outback, speaking to himself in characteristic manner, hoping to collect his wits and analyze the domestic furor. He would not have noticed Carise lingering beside the trail, had she not spoken directly to him.

"Do you sense it? " she called.

Noah stopped abruptly and found the mysterious girl staring at him full-faced.

"What?" he asked.

"You must be the preacher. Ham has spoken of you these past days." She smiled. "I am Carise."

The Sethite was awed by her natural glamour and cleared his throat with new understanding. "So . . . ," he concluded, "you are the lady who has turned my son's heart."

"Oh," she laughed dryly, "I would guess his heart was turned years ago. All I have done is catch in its shadow."

Noah studied her and clicked his tongue. "You underestimate your powers," he observed. "Now—what did you ask as I came upon you?"

" 'Do you sense it?' I said. The stillness in the air? You speak of my powers, but I have only a few. I know you have many more, for your son insists you are a prophet, that you have seen the future in your mind."

Noah was surprised at Ham's endorsement, but did not grasp at it. "I do not consider myself gifted," he hedged.

"Well—that depends on your point of view." Carise nodded, her eyes twinkling with interest. "Now—as for this strange stillness in the air—have you noticed it?"

"I cannot say that I have—until just now."

"At dawn, as Ham and I came down from the hills, I saw the deer and the birds take flight into the high country. I perceived their fear—not fear of our approach—but of something greater."

Noah surveyed the jungle growth and a shudder crossed his shoulders.

"You feel it. The nearing of the end," she whispered, leaning toward him.

Noah did not like to admit, especially to a stranger, that he had of late experienced a kind of urgency, as if the visions neared fulfillment. Again, he shrugged and was silent.

"Did you know that animals sense the movement of the earth?" she inquired, her voice heavy with conviction. "Just as you discern things which other men do not, so they perceive the changing of the times. I have observed that they have a second sense," she asserted, raising a finger to his face. "I have an affinity for wild things."

Noah swallowed hard. "I can believe that you do." He smiled.

"Then believe this," she said soberly, "that of late the beasts are wary."

Carise turned from him now, vanishing into the depths of the wood, and as he watched her go he pondered the truth she spoke and wondered how Ham had found such a creature.

EIGHT

For nearly a century Noah, the son of Lamech, Noah the preacher of righteousness, Noah, who would be among only ten generations recorded from the time of Adam to the deluge—for nearly one hundred years he had proclaimed judgment and salvation to the Adlandian world. By now the story of the peculiar north country wildman and of his strange ship had quite literally reached the entire continent. It was safe to say that there was not a soul on the planet, human or superhuman, who had not heard the message.

And though this fact verged on the miraculous, for there were millions of folk spread across earth's single land mass, it was even more astounding that it had happened without Noah setting foot outside his mountain village since the ark was begun.

The preacher found wonder in this knowledge, but also sadness. For though he had longed to tell the world, he also sensed that once each soul had the message, the end would not long be held back.

During these years of exhortation, however, the hope that many would believe and be saved had kept Noah's zeal at a high pitch. When any other man would have long since given up, he still carried on with evangelistic fervor.

But the way had not been easy. Obad had predicted that the prophet's path would be extremely hard. And the words had proven true time and again.

Noah rarely lifted a hammer or drove a nail these days. For many months his waking hours had been consumed with preaching. The throngs who daily filled the little valley necessitated this. For the great landlocked vessel of Lamechtown was now simply known, worldwide, as "Noah's Ark," and tourists from every nation made their way daily up the mountain highway to view it, and to listen to the peculiar teachings regarding it.

The preacher's safety and health had more than once been subject to danger during these months, as his words provoked anger in most listeners. After the first few times he had been pummeled by stones or sticks, he had constructed a scaffold far up the side of the vessel from which to preach.

This had not done away with the threats to himself and his family, but it had made it possible for him to address the hoards who perpetually came before him.

The boat project which, after over nine decades, had been nearly completed, now suffered major slowdowns. Progress had never been speedy, but now, due to continual social pressure, many of the Sethites who had been committed to the extra earnings if not the philosophy behind the ark, were dropping out of the force. And if they were not persuaded to quit by social assault, Seltan and his kind had infiltrated their thinking, persuading them that Noah's doctrine was contrary to tradition.

"He does not teach the laws of righteousness by which we have always distinguished ourselves," Seltan argued. "He teaches some insipid form of salvation by 'faith alone'!" His comrades laughed at the thought, nudging one another with pious scorn.

Often now, except for the work of Shem and Japheth, and an occasional lift from Ham, labor on the vessel was at a virtual standstill. When others cooperated it was for monetary gain only, and Noah wondered where the Lord was.

All these years he had sensed God's presence in the

work of his own hands, and in the slow but steady materialization of his dreams. But sometimes now, when he realized how few on earth believed in his vision, he despaired.

Save for the faith of his eldest and youngest, and the lip service of Ham, Noah could count none of the younger generation who trusted in the word he taught. And among his peers there were even fewer, if any, whom he could call believers. Not only was Seltan a stumbling block, but Jaseth, his own brother, was cool toward the project.

Just a month ago news had reached Lamechtown of the death of old Shubag. And Noah marveled at his father's diminished generation. Moricahn was still a devoted kinsman, but tended, on his rare visits, to sympathize with Jaseth, who increasingly questioned the validity of Noah's calling. While Moricahn had rebelled against Sethitic tradition quietly, retreating into the wilderness for peace, Jaseth turned his eyes toward the pleasures of the coastlands, and spoke of travel a bit too often.

Somewhere there was Tubal-Cain, who apart from his sister Naamah, was likely the only Cainite on earth to express faith in Yahweh.

Noah sighed, thinking on his wife and her patience. Had it not been for her persistent support, he should have given up many times. And now, even she was put out with him.

The Sethite sat in the cool of evening on the veranda of Lamech's estate. The crowds had dispersed for the day, many returning to homes far away, and others quartered in the tourists' camp which had sprung up and remained in semipermanence within the Valley of Turtles.

On his lap he held the little journal in which he had entered his memoirs faithfully over the years. The leaves had been replaced countless times as the leatherbound volume had been filled again and again, and the numerous booklets had been stored in a cedar chest.

He thought just now on the sweet face and pleasant

ways of his wife, considering the numberless times she had brought him cool drinks on hot days and joined him with a basket of lunch at the work site. He wondered if he had, indeed, slighted his family through the years. Could he have managed his time better, to be more attentive to their needs?

As he pondered this, he did not hear Naamah's footstep behind him, but when she placed a warm hand on his shoulder, he turned happily to greet her.

"I was just thinking of you." He smiled. "Sit with me."

The woman was quiet this evening, her face marked with sadness. She nestled beside him, sitting at his feet and resting her head upon his knee. With one finger she stroked the top of his sandaled foot where the dust of the day's labors had settled.

"Husband," she whispered, turning soft eyes toward him, "forgive my harshness this morning."

Noah caressed her dark head and shook his own. "No— it is I who must ask forgiveness. You are right. I have not been all I should have been to you or the boys." His voice broke and he looked far off to the hills where Ham so often retreated. "If only there were some way to go back," he sighed.

Naamah did not refute his self-castigation. But she wished to speak of matters even weightier. "You have been a good man," she insisted. "Your calling has been heavy on your shoulders. What more could you have done?" And turning her gaze to the journal, which she had always honored as Noah's private property, she asked, "Has Yahweh spoken to you of late? Do you think we have much time?"

Noah could feel her tremble at the question, and wondered if she really wished to hear the answer.

"There are rumblings," was all he would say. "Rumblings in the earth."

Naamah sat erect and drew her knees to her chin. A

tear glimmered at the corner of one eye, and Noah leaned forward quickly. "Oh, wife, what is it? Do you fear?"

"I fear, husband," she replied, her voice a quiver. "I fear for our . . . for Ham."

The preacher slipped from his chair and knelt beside her on the pavement, taking her hands in his. "As to Ham," he began, "I have met this lady of his. Naamah, she is an intriguing creature."

The woman drew back and studied him narrowly. "Intriguing? Is that the word men use for such females?"

Noah's eyes grew wide and he laughed heartily. "No, no! I do not mean that. I mean—I have spoken with her, and. . . ."

"Spoken with her?" Naamah bristled.

"Yes—indeed," he said, trying to soothe her. "Do not take it this way. Now listen—I have met her and I sense she is a girl of some depth. She is unusual. . . ."

"Ha!" Naamah retorted.

". . . unusual . . . ," he repeated, "in her perceptions."

The Cainitess rebuffed him squarely. "It sounds as though you have come to know her very well in so short a time!"

Noah laughed again, and drew her rigid body close. "You will see," he insisted. "She will be of value to us in time."

The woman tried to absorb this assurance and yet still shook her head. "But, what of Ham? His heart is so rebellious! Is Yahweh offended?"

Noah could read beyond her words to the true fear of her mind. "Do you worry that Ham will be left behind—that he will . . . perish?"

The mother turned her face away and did not answer. But Noah reached for the little journal which he had left on the chair.

"Here," he directed, turning to his favorite passage. "Listen to the promise of our God." And then he read,

"But I will establish my covenant with you, and you shall enter the ark—you and your sons and your wife, and your sons' wives with you."

Naamah longed to see the words for herself, and when he obliged, handing her the open volume, she scanned the writing urgently. Yes—it did read thus!

She closed her eyes and sighed deeply, serenity easing the tension in her face.

"You see—," Noah went on—"this is the grace of Yahweh. For my sake, he has made this covenant. My sons are not perfect—they may even be unbelieving. But for my sake he has made this exception."

The woman listened carefully and pondered the meaning a long time.

"Then," she marveled, "the new world will not be perfect. It is destined for strife from its beginning, for the deluge will not wipe out selfishness or pride."

Noah wondered at his wife's conclusion. "No—," the man agreed. "For that to happen—there would not be one soul left alive."

P A R T   I V
RAIN AND THE BOW

All the fountains of the great deep [were] broken up, and the windows of heaven were opened.

And the waters prevailed upon the earth. . . .

And God said . . . I do set my bow in the cloud, and it shall be for a token of a covenant between me and the earth.

Genesis 7:11, 24; 9:12, 13

ONE

Though Noah was now 595 years old, the lines upon his face were not from age. For his generation, six centuries did not represent an extraordinary life span, nor did it qualify him to be an elder. It was not unusual for a man to have his first child after he had passed 500 years, as Noah had done; nor was it peculiar to marry after having lived nearly five centuries.

The Sethite was not an old man. But his face was marked with strain. The toll which life had exacted on him had become increasingly evident, as day by day for over ten decades, his burden had grown heavier and his rejection by the world had intensified.

Today, however, the marks of stress were joined by lines of deep sorrow. He stood beside the great white cave of his ancestors, the sepulcher where Enoch, Methuselah, and Ishna were buried, and he watched as Shem, Ham, and Japheth rolled the mammoth stone across its maw, sealing the repose of his father, Lamech.

The venerable patriarch, after 777 years of faithfulness, had passed away three days before, marking not only the end of an exemplary life, but the close of a generation. Though, as he had prophesied, he had lived to see the ship of Yahweh, he would never sail in her.

Noah, supported on each side by his eldest and youngest sons, and followed close behind by Ham, descended the mountain of sepulchers and reentered the village whose

243

very name spoke of his father. All too quickly, it seemed, the mourning which had marked the community with the old man's passing had been replaced by business-as-usual. And rising above the sounds of daily routine were the perpetual revelings of the tourist camp in the valley below.

Shem noticed Noah's scornful glimpse toward the enormous tent compound which filled the plain. He pressed his arm gently and nudged him toward home. But the preacher resisted, gazing through his grief on the raucous camp.

"A valley of flesh-pots!" he muttered. "Our peaceful plain—a valley of sinners!"

The sons looked quietly at one another, stung by his pain. But at last, with a snort, Ham protested, "Come—let's be going."

As they neared the village, they were obliged to pass by the great gopher-wood ark which loomed like a gigantic phantom through the rising fog. For nearly a century the ship had stood as a dreadful ensign over the town which had produced it. And it was even more dreadful these days, as the sermons of Noah carried more bite than ever before.

The preacher had not changed his message, but the world had changed, becoming ever more vile with passing time, and ever more sensitive to the prophetic declarations of doom. For though hearts were hardened, many people experienced, with the hardening, an intuition—a knowledge of certain judgment which could not be denied, placated, or drugged away.

The ship stood as a ghostly reminder of doom, empty and still. The work on her was slow, the sounds of industry muted. And in the evening, when strangers came upon her as she quietly waited, they were awed by her brooding spirit.

For *wait* she did. Anyone could feel it. And she did bear a spirit—an aura of foreboding aloofness. She waited through years of war which sprang up and died down across the continent—and through rumors of further wars which sapped the souls of the fearful, and charged even the staunchest hearts with dread. She waited through the comings and the goings of daily life, while men and women died and gave birth, married and gave in marriage, ate and drank and ran to and fro upon the face of the earth. She waited for one generation to pass away and another to replace it, and still she contained herself.

But while men came and went and the world about them declined, there were other Beings who watched the signs of the times with awareness equal to Noah's. While the specter of the ark haunted the souls of humanity, the gods of earth served to speed the planet on its destructive course.

Tormented Beings they were—for while they were consumed with their own successes, they knew each victory moved them toward their inevitable overthrow. Yet, perverse as they were, they seemed compelled to race to their own demise, like the sands of an hourglass which chase themselves more quickly as the draining nears its end.

The pantheon of legendary figures born to the gods and mortal women were usually male—"mighty men of old, men of renown." But there were a few Nephilim born female. And one of the greatest was Artemis Beyond the North.

This magnificent creature, long of leg and skilled with weaponry, had enjoyed frequent liaisons with Poseidon, but had of late crossed him sorely in commerce and her city's technological advances. Her land to the north of Nod had been favored by alliances with both the coast and the Persians, and she had connived to bring great advantage to her followers.

Now she was at war with the cities of the sea, a confrontation which endangered the entire planet.

One could not set foot outside one's door without hearing of it. The streets and taverns, shops and marketplaces in every earthly city buzzed with news regarding the most recent battles and strategies of the opposing forces. All nations had taken sides, allying with either the "Huntress" or the "Sea God."

And the camp at the Valley of Turtles had become a place to trade news from north, south, east, and west, as folk of all nationalities convened to seek Noah's predictions and opinions on the subject.

Strange, he often thought, that he should be considered a prophet of such temporal things. He had never presumed to speak out on Adlandian politics. Always he replied with reference to the end of all things—to the message of Yahweh and the certain annihilation which would come upon the planet.

But his shortsighted audience seemed incapable of applying his words to anything beyond worldly conflict. And, try as he might to lift their eyes to greater dangers, they were satisfied to receive his eccentric message in a narrower context. Thus he became, in a peculiar twist of public opinion, a popular oddity—an object of curiosity, when not in actual danger of the scorning masses.

As he passed, this evening, beneath the eerie shadow of the ark, his sons urging him home, he recalled the day he and Obad had come to the foot of the humming pyramid in Poseidon's hall.

"The ark does not hum," he noted. "The things of Yahweh need not announce themselves with vibrations and thunderings."

Shem followed his father's gaze to the top of the empty ship, and as he did so he moved closer to Noah's side.

"Do you see how quiet she is?" the father repeated. "She is patient, while the world winds down."

Shem trembled a little and stood riveted to his father's arm. "You speak of the vessel as if it were a living thing," he whispered.

"In a way, she does live," Noah replied. "She is the

Word of God in material form. His Provision for the souls of men."

The young man glanced at his brothers and the preacher detected his apprehensiveness. "Oh, son, I know you do not believe as I do. . . ."

"I believe!" Shem objected, shaking his head firmly.

"Well, yes—of course—," Noah conceded. "I do not mean to say that you doubt. I only mean that your belief is based on my word only. And you cannot be expected to see things with the same conviction I possess. But," he affirmed, "one day your faith will be invincible— founded on experience."

The oldest son did not question this. He knew his father referred to the coming deluge, and that he would, indeed, experience God's hand directly.

"No, the ship is a quiet thing," the preacher continued. "But there are rumblings in the planet. The wars of Poseidon and his kind and the cry of humanity are only part of the throes of sin. The greater part is the rebellious earth itself. Have you not felt it?"

He turned to his sons, and Japheth, feeling obliged to fill the silence, interjected, "Yes, sir. Only yesterday, as I was in the hills, I heard a distant thunder, as of the ground swelling. And shortly after, a rumbling at my feet. My very body quaked with it!"

Noah smiled and placed a soothing hand on Japheth's slender shoulder. He studied the fair skin and blue eyes of his smallest son. "You are beginning then, already, to feel the touch of God," he acknowledged. "The earth is his handiwork, and responds to his broken heart."

Casting one last glance toward the valley, the Sethite shook himself and began the final steps toward home. But suddenly, the air was split by the droning of engines and the flash of silvery lights. A rush of wind from the heavens swept over the four Sethites, and Ham, his arm shielding his eyes, cried out, "It is the sky Daemons!"

Noah and his sons were pressed to the ground by the force of the machines' whirlwind, but just as they flew past, the preacher was able to catch a clear glimpse of them through the swirling fog. They matched those he had seen years before, darting and diving over the plain at Baalbek. Sky-machines were nothing rare in Adlandia, but these were military vehicles, not seen except in wartime. A wheel within a wheel, each had a metallic rim which revolved about a stationary plate, and within the rims were rows of eye-like, circular windows, lit brilliantly by interior lumination.

When they vanished in the mountain vapors, Noah knew they would return. And so they did, in a startling dash and sudden halt, buzzing and flashing above the four men's heads. Then, slowly, they descended, their pulsing vibration filling the hamlet and bringing a flood of onlookers out from the houses.

"We are being attacked!" Japheth shouted above the roar.

"No!" the preacher declared. "Poseidon only wants to shake us with a show of power!"

"Poseidon?" Ham asked, watching the crafts as they settled to a drone. "Why do you imagine it is he?"

Noah bid him follow, confidently brushed the swirling dust from his own garment, and went forth to greet the visitors.

By now campers from the plain and villagers alike had joined along the ridge where the great machines, half a dozen in all, hovered just inches above the ground. Within moments the gangplank of one was lowered and the scarlet-robed sea god appeared on its platform. His brooding eyes scanned the congregation until he spied the object of his journey.

"Noah, son of Lamech," he called, hailing the preacher with a stern demeanor. "Come forth!"

The Sethite, chin lifted, did as he was bid, but not from fear. And as he stood before the machine, the Overlord descended the plank, confronting him face to face.

"I would speak with you," the god demanded.

"Speak," Noah offered.

Haughty as the day the preacher had last seen him, standing on the temple balcony, Poseidon glowered down at the man whose height came only to his sternum. "I have heard your message often enough," he began.

"Yes." The prophet nodded.

"There are tremors in the earth."

"Yes."

"Can you account for this?"

Noah weighed his words carefully, but risked danger as he suggested, "Do you not credit yourself with them, great Daemon? Your warfare and its thunderings have split mountains in the past. Could it not be that the earth shudders under *your* power?"

The god could have been flattered. It was true that his weaponry was so advanced, it threatened the very core of the continent. But he read more than flattery in Noah's suggestion.

"You mock me!" he roared, and his underlings stepped forward like guard dogs. "The tremors of which I speak register on our instruments from far below the planet's surface. These cannot be the effects of war!"

Noah squared his shoulders. "You come against me with soldiers and machines, as if I were a threat to you," he observed. "What do you wish to hear me say?"

The governor fidgeted with the heavy neck chain which bore his insignia, a crimson dolphin. "It seems," he laughed, "that all men come to you for answers. You must, by now, be in the habit of giving them. Tell me, O prophet," he snarled, "what is the omen in these rumblings? Do they portend the disasters of which you spoke in my court?"

Noah studied the glittering, gem-studded dolphin on Poseidon's breast, and sensed the desperation in his bearing. He remembered the suffering of his sister Adala at the hands of this tyrant, and the death of his friend, Obad. A tear shone along his lashes and he said, "Once a dolphin spoke to me. Do you believe this, Poseidon?"

The god's eyes widened, and he cleared his throat. "Such things have been known to happen," he assented.

"Then I will return the favor this day, as I speak to the god of the sea. Indeed," he declared, "you know the answer to your own question. You know the end draws near, for this world and your dominion. You know the quakes beneath the ocean portend your demise—the destruction of all Beings such as yourself who wrest creation from Yahweh's will!" And then, turning toward the ark, he cried through the descending dark of night, "You come to me, Mighty One, in the safety of steel and the shine of combat, but I will trust in the ship of my God! One day I will rise upon waves of wrath while you sink beneath the sea, and the waters of your own domain shall be your grave!"

TWO

It had not escaped Poseidon, on his visit to Lamechtown, that Noah had very few, even among his townsmen, who championed his cause. Perhaps the god took consolation in this fact, for though the prophet's words troubled him, it was with his ever-haughty demeanor that he returned to his ship and flew back to the coast.

The villagers and campers, while awed by Noah's confident manner, had still received his message skeptically, and had seen little more than an intriguing show in the whole affair. Their star-worship was directed at the Overlord, whom many had secretly wished to see and never dreamed he might come to them.

Noah sadly watched the congregation depart, until his sons, frustrated in their attempts to take him home, left their father alone on the mountain trail. "I will come shortly," he promised, and when they had gone he sat down beside the ark, leaning against her with a sigh.

He thought on Lamech and a hot tear nudged at one eye, but he suppressed it. Then he thought on his calling and his heart was wrung with heaviness as he tried to remember Obad's prediction: "Your message may be only a glimmer now. But the day will come when the door is thrown open wide. And then all men will see the brilliance of your words."

Often over the years that assertion had consoled him. Perhaps, he reasoned, when the door was flung wide, many would enter in.

Tonight as he dwelled on this hope, renewing his courage, he did not expect a kinsman to threaten his confidence. It was Jaseth who came to find him after the densest fog of evening had settled across the hills.

"Brother!" he called as he stumbled upon the preacher, "we have been worried. The mourners have all gone home and the house is quiet. Won't you come and eat?"

Noah was surprised at this show of concern. He knew his younger brother loved him, but for months their relationship had been marked more by silence than affection.

"Sit with me," Noah offered, patting the ground at his side.

Jaseth cast a wary glance at the enormous hull of the vessel, as if he did not trust it. "Must we sit here?" he asked.

"Come!" Noah laughed. "You have spent years with the ship. Are you afraid?"

Jaseth hunched his shoulders and drew his cloak over his head. He bent his knees and squatted nervously beside the preacher, peering at the ramparts high above.

"So strange it is. Eerie in the fog," Jaseth whispered. "Sometimes, as I have passed her of an evening, I felt I could almost hear her breathe."

Noah surveyed him sideways and chuckled, "Oh, Jaseth. Your imagination runs with you!"

"Perhaps so, brother. But she is a peculiar craft, don't you think?"

"How so?" Noah inquired.

"Why—just see! She towers like a fortress. Only one door . . . and the only window set in the roof and shuttered!"

"Those were the specifications," he asserted.

"Hmph!" Jaseth snorted. "Do you really still believe Yahweh designed her or is that just a story to keep the masses happy?"

"Indeed, I believe!" the Sethite declared. "And you do not?"

Never before had the issue of Jaseth's waning faith been directly confronted. Both men had known of the matter, but neither had wished to speak of it.

Jaseth fidgeted anxiously. "I began to doubt long ago," he admitted, flicking the dew-laden dust from his sandal tops. "If your message is true, this ark symbolizes countless tragedies."

Noah nodded his head sadly. "We were taught to accept God's word. What else can I preach?"

"I should expect nothing else of you," the younger sneered. "But it seems you teach that not only will scoundrels and dreadful sinners be destroyed, but some very fine people will also lose their lives. Uncle Moricahn, Seltan—anyone who does not believe as you do!"

"I have never named those who would be saved and those who would not," Noah objected. "I have only declared Yahweh's righteousness. My hearers can do with it as they please."

Jaseth turned burning eyes to his brother and lashed out a stinging challenge. "And you, Noah—will you be able to shut the door to the ark when the damned cry out for salvation?"

The preacher shuddered. The thought of having to do this had never crossed his mind. It had been enough for him to seek ways to stretch Yahweh's words so as to include a ship full of humans. The idea that he might be responsible for shutting out souls was anathema to him.

"How can you suggest such a thing?" he cried. "I am here to call the world to repentance—not to condemn it!"

"Ha!" Jaseth snarled, throwing his head back defiantly. "How you exalt yourself! You thought you were called to save Adala, and you only stirred up the crisis of her death!"

There. It had been said. All the pent-up antagonism, phrased in an instant.

Noah's face went white, but Jaseth was not finished. "Besides, brother, if you are such a literalist, you had better reconsider. According to my calculation if your prophecies are true, there will be only eight souls saved off the face of the earth!"

Noah's heart pounded like a hammer. He could barely think of a response before Jaseth was on his feet heading for home, calling over his shoulder, "Ah-ha! That would be why there are no open windows! To spare you the sight of the wicked clinging to the sides of the ark! Clinging while the waters pull them, one by one, to their demise!"

His laugh was hollow, rising on the fog with sinister wings, and settling over Lamechtown with a shudder.

THREE

Very little remained to be done before the ark would be completed. But these days Noah found it extremely painful to pursue the tasks involved. For each nail driven, each plank set in place, brought him closer to the appointed hour—the hour when life as he knew it would cease to be and the souls of humanity would hear the message of salvation for the last time.

Day after day, however, he roused himself and went to the ship. Day after day he performed the necessary duties, Shem and Japheth following his instructions, and Ham lingering a little closer, recently, to the job site.

Noah had sensed a mellowing in Ham's heart. Perhaps it was Carise, the fiery bedouin, who had, ironically, brought about this transformation. For she was showing herself, more and more, to be in tune with the spirit of the family calling. Maybe it was her sensitivity to nature and to the vibrations of the earth which impelled her cooperation. Whatever it was, she was proving an asset to the project at every turn.

Sensitivity to nature was manifest in a different way by Shem and Japheth, who of late had followed their masculine need for companionship and had begun to seek wives from among the Lamechtown villagers.

Shem was the first to fulfill the calling of husband. A quiet and delicate woman named Sindra had captured his heart, and they had been wed only a few months after

Lamech's burial. With this event, Noah had seen ever more clearly the closure of time. It remained only for Japheth to follow suit, and the last requirement for entering the ark would be in place.

In fact, if the words of Yahweh were literal, there could be no grandchild born before the flood. And therefore, since Ham and Carise might any day announce a coming family, Noah knew the hour grew short.

As the ark neared completion, and the work began to consist of finer details—the arranging of the family's compartments, the building of beds and stationary furniture—Naamah's involvement became more crucial. It was at this point that she took it upon herself to include Carise in the preparations. Her initial objections to the gypsy woman melted away as she did so, and she found that what had begun as a sacrifice of kindness reaped rich rewards.

Soon Sindra, Carise, and Naamah were spending hours together, designing the interior of the cabin, selecting fabrics, sewing bolsters, deciding which household goods they would take aboard and which to leave behind. Though a sense of urgency sped their labors—for they too felt the shortness of time—their tasks were happy ones and they developed an amiable fellowship.

Carise, especially, sparked their days with lively conversation. Tales of her childhood and her times with the caravan, of the many places she had been and strange sights she had seen, entranced the other women. Particularly her experience with the wilderness intrigued them.

This afternoon Naamah and her companions sat beside the fire in the private quarter of Lamech's house. His large chamber, now vacant, had been established as their headquarters, as they gathered in supplies and laid up special treasures for the coming days. This seemed no dishonor to his memory. In fact, they believed the old patriarch would have been pleased to know they fulfilled Yahweh's plans in his own room.

Naamah worked a large loom, weaving a rug for the cabin floor, and as the shuttle sped up and down, the daughters-in-law watched its hypnotic movements. The matron eyed her two young ladies covertly and proudly. Sindra leaned more toward the Sethite line in appearance, and the women contrasted like nuggets of gold and iron, their natures fine and coarse as their opposite backgrounds.

"I have led a very sheltered life," the mother-in-law confessed. "Except for a few sea journeys with my brother, I have seen little of the world. But you, Carise—you have seen a great deal." The bedouin girl nodded her head and the woman asked, "What, of all you have seen, was the most wonderful?"

Carise studied the loom quietly. "The animals," she replied.

"Animals?" Sindra repeated.

"Yes—they are the closest to the Creator. They have never lost their innocence. Even the most vicious beast is purely a survivor."

Naamah scrutinized this dark jewel whom Ham had wrested from the hills. Carise was qualified to speak of survival, she was certain. Though the girl had never shared the more sordid elements of her past, Naamah knew she had overcome much.

"I once was quite attached to an animal," the mother-in-law commented. "A little white dog. It did not survive our move to the mountains."

"How could it?" Carise asserted, in a brave burst of conviction. "A dog should not be small and delicate. It was made for hardier things."

Naamah smiled and gave the shuttle a quicker push. "How you sound like Noah!" she laughed.

"He would say this?" Carise marveled.

"Indeed, he *did*."

The two had never felt closer than in that instant, and Naamah confided, "Perhaps you can tell me. How can this prophecy of my husband's be fulfilled? How shall all the animals come to be on board our ark? It is a mystery I cannot fathom."

Carise gazed out the west window, where the gloaming was just about to settle. "A mystery is only in the mind of man," she whispered. "With nature there are no mysteries. When the animals sense the closing hour, they will move."

As Naamah contemplated this, Sindra was caught by her faraway look.

"Perhaps, Mother, you have been sheltered," she agreed, "but I have never been beyond this village. From your sea travels, what do you recall best?"

The wife of Noah stopped the rhythmic loom and studied the red yarn wound upon the spindle.

"I recall most of all my brother," she said wistfully, "one of the greatest men who ever graced the East."

The inquisitive girl sat amazed at the answer, and at its phrasing. "Why do you speak of Tubal-Cain as if he were no longer living?"

Naamah stood and walked toward the chamber window. The sun had dipped past the Lamechtown hills.

"I have an instinct for it," she said matter-of-factly. But her posture belied her courageous tone. "Noah always dreamed that my brother would join us on the ark. But just as wilderness creatures perceive the end of things, I know this. Tubal-Cain is gone, and with him our last hope for earth."

FOUR

Naamah's premonition was confirmed only days later, when a messenger from Nod-Persia, lean and dark, his skin glistening with sweat, ran into Lamechtown. Tubal-Cain had chosen to send word of his illness and imminent death by this personal means because he wished to honor his brother-in-law's simple dignity.

Finding Naamah and her husband, the runner brought forth a small scroll, written in Tubal-Cain's own hand. "By the time you receive this, I shall have gone on before you," it read. "Meet me on the other side."

The sister, tears glimmering on her cheeks, fingered the little parcel fondly and handed it to Noah. "Keep it with your journal," she smiled. "It is the only entry necessary for this matter."

And as they sent the messenger away, they knew a shadow had descended, not on their past alone, but on the waning time.

The day of Japheth's wedding was one of signs and omens. As the fair-skinned son of Noah walked toward the marriage canopy flanked by his two brothers, and as his bride, Elsbeth, a buxom lass with shining brass hair, awaited his promises, the earth shook.

Everyone in the wedding party, and all the village guests felt it.

The day had been a strained one. Noah knew that,

except for the godfather, Jaseth, who had an emotional investment in the event, those attending did so out of obligation, or out of a hankering for good food and music. Especially since the death of Lamech, devotion to the mill's founding family had fallen off. For years previous, dissension over the boat project had stretched familiar ties to the limit, and only loyalty to the town's patriarch had kept matters stable. Today, smiles on once friendly faces were drawn like rigid lines and eyes were vacant.

But when the earth shook, these facts paled to insignificance. The preacher's mind was instantly pulled to the ship, and its readiness. He had to force himself to concentrate on the two who stood beneath the wreathed and flowered canopy awaiting his blessing and his patriarchal injunction.

As he placed his callused, labor-hardened hands upon their heads, speaking fatherly words and commending them to Yahweh's care, a flutter of wings drew their attention upward.

A white dove had descended upon the trelliswork like a benediction, and she sat there preening herself and chortling on the canopy's rounded crest, as though satisfied with some completed task.

Noah took this as a sign from the Lord, a pronouncement of approval and consummation, and his heart surged. But just as quickly, his eyes were caught to the ark which sat against the distant hills, and to the sky overstretching it. A black dot, soaring and dipping, circled the air above the ship.

No one else noticed the raven's shadowy flight. Only the dove craned her gaze toward the creature, and as she did so, the plumage of her neck ruffled, poised like an eagle's pinions.

FIVE

The dove and the raven were only the beginning signs which the sky would bring forth. Over the days following the latest rumblings of the earth, when the valley was swollen again with tourists, the white heavens were invaded repeatedly by Poseidon's spying vessels.

Indeed, Noah considered, the Overlord knew the hour was at hand.

"They frighten us," Naamah confided one day to her husband. "The women and I see them many times when we cart supplies to the ship, when we gather wood for the cabin stove, when we bring your lunches to you."

"They will not harm you," he assured her. "Their mission is only to report what they see. The Daemon must fear the shortening time far more than we fear him!"

Though all these things—his sons' marriages, deaths of great and good men, tremors in the ground, and the response of the wicked—spoke of the nearing end, there was yet one thing remaining before the cataclysm would descend.

The first evidence of its fulfillment appeared after the last peg was driven into the last stall of the ark and the final bolt fastened to the last gate of the cages.

The completion of the project, nearly a hundred years in the making, brought an intense moment of mixed emotions for Noah. Shem would never forget the unreadable look on his father's face that day. As the firstborn

261

knelt on the floor of the second deck, squaring and steadying the stall door against its jamb, and as Ham drove the bolt through the hinge while Japheth swept up wood chips from the cage's interior, Noah cleared his throat several times.

"Is there something wrong, Father?" Shem asked, expecting some correction on their work.

"No," he replied. "I only. . . . Nothing, son." And then, turning a furtive glance up and down the stables, as if seeking one more uncompleted task, the preacher walked slowly away. As he exited down the corridor, his hands gently caressed the woodwork. And in his bearing was a strange sadness.

"We are done!" Japheth announced proudly, as he swept away the remaining chips.

"Shhh," the firstborn gestured, pointing to the departing figure.

"Oh," Japheth sighed. "He is not pleased?"

Shem and Ham looked at one another knowingly, the second son's dark face marked with rare compassion.

"He needs time alone," he remarked. "Perhaps we will not see him for a while."

Ham was correct. Noah disappeared into the hills that day. The job was done. The years of labor completed had left him suddenly empty. And a pallor of depression began to fill the void.

As he neared the crest of the village's last ridge, he remembered when the Lord had come to him in the highlands east of Sun City. How he longed to feel his touch again!

For some reason, as he looked back on the ark, where it nestled in the distant valley, a desperate fear swept through him. What if it were all a lie? What if he had spent a lifetime fulfilling a madman's dreams?

He had experienced such doubts often, before the Lord had touched him. It was evidence of great weariness today that after more than ten decades he would again entertain such a notion.

He crawled into a small, mossy ravine and covered himself with the giant leaves of a low-spreading palm. He would let the forgetfulness of slumber work its healing.

But all night he was troubled by dreams of an endless quest, of the seeking, rounding up, and corraling of countless animals; of long journeys through unknown territories, of fearful battles with vicious beasts.

He woke in the darkest part of night, just before dawn, with beads of sweat upon his brow. How could he be expected to locate, much less bring across innumerable miles the representatives of all animal species on earth? He had never had a problem believing the ark could contain them, once they were found. But he had not allowed himself to ponder the logistics of collecting.

Now he was confronted with the matter—the final requirement of Yahweh's plan.

He knew that the Valley of Turtles contained a magnificent cross section of animal types. This would be helpful, and he could see Yahweh's foresight in so providing. But there were many other varieties, especially in the Wilderness of Nod, the Region Beyond the North, and the upper reaches of the Olympian heights, which he had never seen, perhaps had never even heard of. Even if he were to manage, over many months and with much personal risk, to gather two of each kind from the valley, he would be at a loss to begin elsewhere.

"The time grows short, Lord," he whispered, peering through the dark forest with narrow eyes. "I know the hour is at hand. How am I to accomplish your will?"

This time, when he heard a snapping noise outside the green cover, his heart leaped with expectation. "Yahweh?" he whispered.

But as he pulled back the leaves, he was greeted with

a blast from the shining nostrils of some creature, and he drew away, terrified.

The sun was just ascending, and as his eyes adjusted to the faint glow of morning, he made out the buff coats of two deer, a male and a female, grazing just beyond his cover.

Such a sight was common in these hills. But, surely they knew he was here. Why did they not raise their tails and run for the depths of the wood? Instead, they seemed to wait for him, watching the greenery where he had moved.

Noah clicked his tongue several times, but they remained unfrightened, and as he revealed himself outside the bower, they stood still.

"Hello, fine folk," he greeted, holding out a hand. "What is your pleasure?"

He recalled that within a little pouch upon his belt there was an apple, left over from yesterday's lunch. Drawing it forth, he cut into it with his knife and held the two pieces before him, one in each hand.

Without a quiver, the deer came forward, nuzzling the fruit and gingerly lifting it with their teeth.

As he headed home, they followed close, and along the trail they were joined by a she-bear and her male cub, a wild boar and his sow.

By the time Noah had reached the village, a herd of creatures had fallen in behind him. And as he led them, tapping the trail rhythmically with his staff, his shoulders thrown back and head held high, a hearty laugh rose from his throat, and a smile, like that of a child, stretched across his face.

"They shall be male and female," he chanted the Lord's words. "Of birds after their kind, and of the animals after their kind . . . two of every kind *shall come to you* to keep them alive!"

SIX

The vale which gradually ascended from the pond of giant turtles below Lamechtown had been populated by tourists for years. As men had intruded into that wilderness, the animals, generally benign in their behavior, had been pushed back, until they dwelt mainly on the far side of the plain, toward the heights where Baalbek loomed, flat and ominous.

No conflict had ever erupted between the displaced creatures and the humans who had invaded their domain. But, as the valley was now being entered daily by little streams of animals from distant parts of Adlandia, the people who had established temporary quarters in the place grew uneasy.

The creatures were well behaved—even the most innately vicious of them. But their mere presence—lingering, haunting around the edges of the valley—was a fearsome thing.

Strange it was to waken to the sounds of a tiger's roar or to the vibration of shifting ground beneath the feet of lumbering elephants.

One by one the tents began to disappear, the tarpaulins to be folded up and packed away, and no residents came to replace them.

"I would think that the creatures' arrival would only convince your listeners of the truth," Naamah marveled one day. "Instead, it drives them away!"

She sat beside her husband on the top deck of the ark this afternoon, as they watched the scrambling activity in the plain below. Just last evening seven enormous white wolves had descended from somewhere high in the Olympian mountains, and their howling, which had lasted well past moonrise, seemed to portend the coming disaster. It had stirred the same premonitions in all the other beasts, until the vale had become a din of growling, roaring, trumpeting, and screeching. Now most of the human occupants were anxiously preparing to leave—determined not to spend another such clamorous night.

"They operate from hardened hearts," the preacher explained. "Still, I pray for their salvation."

Naamah glanced across the pond to a small rise where the huge wolves sat erect, ears pricked, surveying the scurrying humans below. "Magnificent," she whispered. "I see why you scorned my little Topay, who was like them in color only."

Noah drew her close, and studied the mighty canines. "Their bodies contain the life of all dogs to come," he stated.

"Does that mean all dogs will be enormous?" she asked.

"I am certain the variety will be endless," he explained. "The potential is within them as it was within their ancestors who dwelt in Eden."

The beasts seemed to be aware of the attention they attracted and looked toward the ship where the man and woman sat. The sun reflected off their coats in a white fire, and Noah shook his head. "I have heard that in the highest points of earth, the canopy sometimes condenses and leaves a layer of frozen dew, very deep, along the mountaintops. The wolves must have come from there."

"Why do you assume so?" Naamah asked.

"Before the first sin, there was no need for camouflage," he explained. "But in the world which followed, Yahweh made all things practical. The wolves' white coats are more than just beautiful. They are meant to protect them from their enemies, as well as from the cold."

Naamah shuddered and sat closer to her husband. "I would not like to dwell in a cold world, where the dew remained past morning," she said.

The preacher smiled and caressed her head where she leaned it on his shoulder. He wondered what the deluge would change, and how altered the planet would be. But he did not voice his speculations to his wife.

SEVEN

The howling of the wolves continued night after night at a more frantic level until the valley was completely empty of human inhabitants. The cries were spurred by a peculiar waxing of the moon, which appeared to be coming closer to earth each evening. And then Moricahn arrived from the retreat of his hilly farm.

Jaseth was delighted. Moricahn only made such visits when he had something to discuss, and the younger son of Lamech hoped he had thoughts on the signs which stirred the wolves, and the heavens.

"Night before last," Moricahn began, as he settled before the fire in the family estate, "the moon seemed unusually large. Did you notice this, Noah?"

The preacher, who prayed his uncle's arrival meant he was reconsidering the prophecies, nodded his head. "Yes," he asserted. "The entire creation groans and travails. The sky readies itself."

"Brother," Jaseth laughed, "must everything be related to your fantastic dreams? Perhaps Moricahn is more studied in such matters."

"Very well," Noah agreed. "You have read the stars for years, Moricahn. If you have a different theory, tell us. Why does the earth tremble and why do the heavenly bodies alter?"

The farmer hunched his shoulders and suggested, "I am not surprised that you see, in all this, the hand of

Yahweh. I, for one, perceive the signs to be omens bearing on the war."

"Between Poseidon and the Huntress?" Jaseth marveled.

"Indeed," their uncle went on. "The moon is the lady's symbol, and I predict this portends her growing strength. The skies are telling us she shall defeat the sea god and extend her domain to the shores of Adlandia!"

Noah leaned back and slapped his knees, releasing a hearty laugh. "Your reasoning is peculiar," he objected. "Why, we all know that when the moon waxes, the sea boils and has its strongest hour. How could such a sign hail the demise of Poseidon?"

Moricahn was stunned by Noah's logic, and Jaseth waited for his reply, but he had none.

"Of course," Noah continued, "those of you who attach the earthly Daemons to celestial bodies must read things this way. But, I assure you, there is no such interpretation warranted. The moon, as well as the sun and earth, are in Yahweh's hands. Poseidon does not rule the sea, nor does Lucifer rule the Golden Orb. In these beliefs, uncle, you have always spat upon Sethite tradition!"

Jaseth was astounded at his brother's gall. "How dare you speak to our kinsman this way?" he cried.

"The time has come," Noah asserted, "for men to reckon kinship and brotherhood by different ties." He studied his uncle's wounded expression and steeled himself. "Though I had hoped otherwise, I see now that Moricahn is still no more kindred to Lamech than any servant of Satan!"

The room was very quiet. Only crackling firelogs interrupted the silence. Moricahn cleared his throat and steadied himself, maintaining the gentle demeanor which had always been his hallmark. "Very well, then, nephew," he offered, "how do you interpret the signs in the heavens?"

Noah stretched his legs and rose to pace the room,

while Jaseth's face reddened. "The moon will participate in the cataclysm. I believe it is breaking this planet's orbit, and when it does, it will usher in the final throes."

The uncle turned a furtive face to the door where Noah's sons had congregated, listening in on the discussion. "Lads," he called, "what do you think of all this? Are the Daemons not in charge of earth and does the Sun not guide them?"

Shem entered the room and placed a gentle hand on the man's shoulder. His eyes were like Noah's—like Lamech's—dark and penetrating, but full of urgent love, a quality which Noah could, in moments of evangelistic fervor, neglect. "You are a fine man, uncle," he said, beseeching him. "But your folly is great. Turn from the rebellion which you cloak with intellect. The hour draws short."

EIGHT

There were very few listeners the morning of Noah's last sermon. The famed orator who had stood fearless before crowds of commoners, and before gods and demigods of earth, spoke from the vessel's little platform this day with only a few Lamechtown villagers attending.

His heart was not really in the delivery anyway. He would have made a poor showing before a larger crowd. His heart was not in it because it had broken the night before, when Moricahn and Jaseth had spurned his warnings once again, and walked arm in arm from Lamech's chamber, shaking their heads and murmuring between themselves.

His speech today was short, and redundant. It said nothing new, and fell on deaf ears, though the listeners received it by choice.

As the audience dispersed to their work at the mill, Noah descended the ladder with bent head and sorry eyes. When he reached the entry of the ark, he pushed open the heavy door for the thousandth time and peered absently into the ship's dark interior. The familiar odor of waterproof resin, pitched along the walls, greeted him, and he fondled the lantern which hung beside the jamb. In moments a soft, swinging light spilled from the lamp and Noah scanned the hall to the stairway of the family quarters.

All along the sides and halfway up the walls of this

corridor were sacks of grain and dried fruits. Behind these, and leading down the halls fronting the gates and cages of future residents, were bales of hay, bags of oats, heavy cisterns of water; and on the lower deck, which would be cradled in the cold sea, were caches of preserved meats for the carnivores of the crowd.

The meat had been the last provision gathered in. Ham had been the greatest help in that department, lending his wilderness skills to the capture of deer, wild turkey, rabbit, and fish.

All these preparations had demanded precise calculations, and Noah's accountant training was invaluable. Though the animals would estivate, he must be prepared to feed them in their more wakeful moments, and he must determine the proportions for each kind of food. But when the hallways and storage areas were filled to capacity, he knew the gathering of provender, one of Yahweh's commands, had been accomplished. If God had designed this vessel, he had also known how much room would be left for supplies once the cages and perches were completed. Noah could trust his judgment.

Waste would be contained in the lower deck, far apart from the meat-storage area, beneath the cages, which were equipped with floor grids. And the central area of the third deck would house the family. Noah thought on Naamah's fear of the cold, and he was glad that—on the heaving sea, in the freezing gales of the tempest—the human passengers would receive the warmth which rose from the creatures beneath and surrounding their own chambers.

He let it sweep over him now—the reality that they had stored up only enough food to last eight passengers for the same length of time for which the animals were provided. He knew that even with estivation, the fodder on board would stretch a year at most. And, by his calculations, there had been room to bring only enough to last his family that same amount of time.

It was clear that Yahweh's words had been literal. Only Noah, his wife, their sons, and their wives would be spared.

His throat grew tight and tears threatened. He snuffed out the lamp and turned for the ladder again. As he began his descent, however, the sun caressed his back with unusually warm fingers, and it seemed the atmosphere close to the ark hummed with tension. It was then that he heard the voice of Yahweh for the first time since their encounter in the eastern hills—since the day God had set forth plans for the ark.

This time, as at the dolphin rock, the Lord was invisible. Only the impression of his presence preceded his words.

"Enter the ark," his instructions began, "you and all your household; for you alone I have seen to be righteous before me in this time."

The Sethite trembled and scanned the ground below, seeing no one. And then his eyes surveyed the valley, where the representative creatures of all Adlandia had congregated. They stood, the horde of them, watching and waiting, their bodies great and small, furry, fleecy, scaly and feathered, poised for instruction.

"You shall take with you of every clean animal by sevens," the Lord repeated, "a male and a female; and of the animals that are not clean, two, a male and his female. Also of the birds of the sky, by sevens, male and female, to keep offspring alive on the face of the earth."

The air was filled with even stronger tension now, and it seemed Noah could sense the Lord's broken heart, a pain which he himself had endured the likeness of only last evening. "For after seven days," the Voice declared, "I will send rain on the earth forty days and forty nights. And I will blot out from the face of the land every living thing that I have made."

NINE

Seven days? The chance for men's salvation would close in seven days!

Noah stood alongside the door to the vessel that night, watching as Japheth, Naamah, Carise, Sindra, and Elsbeth herded the stream of sevens and twos, the river of hoofed, pawed, and taloned creatures into the mighty ark. For each beast he had a word as it passed him, a pat or a caress. His heart sounded with the thunder of their tread up the spacious foot-thick plank which, despite its strength, bent beneath the weight of the greater ones.

From inside the vessel could be heard the shouts of Ham and Shem as they ushered, prodded, and cursed the more stubborn beasts into their appointed dens. But apart from an occasional blast of objection or cry of complaint, the creatures were miraculously cooperative.

Of course, Noah mused, everything about this adventure was a miracle. Who would believe the tale a thousand or ten thousand years from now? Who would believe that the entire planet could be devastated by water, or that the wild beings of God's creation could be subject to one little man and a few goading staffs?

Noah believed, not only because he witnessed it, but because he had communed with nature in his time. He knew the earth sympathized with good, and that animals could think. He knew the creations of Yahweh's fingers, celestial, terrestrial, or bestial were not automatons, but operated from a syncrony of soul, a spirit of innocence in harmony with divine will. Only mankind and the Fallen Ones had been perverted, and where the rest of creation appeared to fall short of perfection, it was only in response to this perversion.

Above him, on one of the ramparts of the third deck, the gentle white dove who had overseen the wedding of his third son, cooed a little anxiously. "What is it?" Noah inquired, studying her uplifted beak. Her small, round eyes were directed toward the sky-canopy, through which the moon shone in swirls of evening fog.

"Yes, I see," he agreed. "Bigger than ever, it is. And I suspect it shall come closer yet before the seven days are past." He watched the silvery orb with a tremble of fear, but then turned again to the beasts who passed before him.

A pair of lizards, very small and green, scurried up the plank, and then two dragonflies, whose eggs would not survive the flood, droned their dog-sized bodies above them. He could not know that one day such insects would be smaller than lizards, and would provide a portion of their diet. For now, he was concerned only for the safety of both kinds, and hurried the green slips ahead of two web-footed geese, while helping one of the shining blue dragons to fit beneath the lintel.

Next, lumbering up the gangway were a pair of large simians, followed by two other pair, of different variety. Conspicuously absent were any individuals who looked like the great hairy giant he and Lamech had seen in the hunting hills when he was a boy. "Perhaps it was a Nephil," he speculated, "or one of the Overlords' mistakes."

It seemed the canopy was altered tonight, its vapors condensing where the moon caught them. Noah blinked his eyes, but knew the truth of what he saw. He had no name for it—what would one day be called "cumulus"—what would one day be called "clouds."

It took a full five days for the animals to be herded and settled. The sixth day, Japheth stood with his father on the ramparts of the top deck and studied the pale gigantic satellite which loomed ever closer to earth. From the cabin beneath the squat gable, where the rest of the family was quartered, could be discerned the sounds of dinner preparations, but the two men were absorbed in analysis of the sky.

"I wish we had Uncle Moricahn's telescope," Japheth admitted. "I would like to get a closer look at those strange lights about the moon."

"I think they are only trails of dust, broken off from its surface," Noah guessed. "I believe the pull of this planet is taking its toll on the moon's face."

"Will it break up completely?" he asked.

"The moon was established when the sun was made," Noah assured him. "As long as Yahweh ordains night and day, it will remain to rule the darkness."

"But what is it doing now?" his son whispered, his voice full of awe.

"Its dissolving surface will seed the canopy," the Sethite suggested. "See how the vapors accumulate where the moon dust rains?"

Japheth thought he could, indeed, see a denser cover where silvery shafts of light filtered through the tent of heaven, and alongside, areas where the shield seemed to be thinner.

"I am afraid, Father. Why do the others—those in the cities, and even in our village, refuse to believe?"

But before Noah could respond, their conversation was interrupted by a cry from below. Peering over the side of the vessel, they could see lantern light, and within it the form of Seltan, who had come looking for them.

"When will you give up this madness? Will you spend the rest of your life in that tomb?" he shouted, gesturing toward the ark.

"You only come seeking me, Seltan, because you sense

the end is near," the preacher replied. "You have seen the evidence, but you have less sense than the brute beasts who have come for shelter."

"You are insane!" Seltan shouted. "Even your uncle and brother say so. If you have any power over the animals it is because you share a kindred mentality!"

Japheth tensed angrily and bent over the rampart, thrusting a fist through the air. "Come up *here* and say that!" he challenged.

But Noah drew him back with a firm hand. "He speaks from a tormented heart," he whispered. "Do not encourage him."

"But he has seen it all! All of them have seen it! The coming of the animals, the heaving of the earth, the signs in the heavens! Are they *blind?*"

"Yes." The father nodded. "They are blind."

TEN

In the six hundredth year of Noah's life, and on the seventeenth day of the second month—seven days after God had told him to enter the ark—all the fountains of the great deep burst open, and the floodgates of the sky were rent asunder.

It was difficult to tell which came first, the splitting and falling of the canopy or the wrenching of ocean depths and erupting of the continent's crust. Altogether the beginning seemed instantaneous. Noah and his family would remember only the clamor and cry of the villagers who, when the rain began to descend—the first rain ever to fall on earth—came running for the safety of the ark.

Noah had been standing at the doorway, waiting, listening to the ominous calm which preceded the storm, and watching the eerie gathering of the canopy into dark billows and folds so that searing seams of sunlight penetrated in vivid ribbons across the landscape. "It must be now," he realized. "The end will be within this day, and, I fear, within minutes."

A gale had sprung up from the valley, where the heat of the greenhouse floor rose to meet descending blasts of cold from beyond the torn curtain. It lashed at Noah's garments and at his beard, and he had the voice of God as he cried, "Repent! The end is upon us! Repent and be saved!"

The people of Lamechtown emerged from the mill and

from their homes at the sound of his cry and at the peculiar moan of the wind. Never had they seen or heard such a wind. Never had the sky been black and gold—only white. Amazingly, they still laughed, still shook their heads and pointed at him together.

Until the rain began.

When the rain came, they were terrified. They had reasoned away all other evidence. For nearly sixty-five years they had resisted Noah's prophecy, taking comfort in their traditions, as city-folk took comfort in another brand of folly.

When the rain began, they huddled outside the village, along the trail which led to the ark, and the men murmured among themselves while the women and children cried.

Suddenly, as their garments were drenched, and as they heard the distant rumble of some terrible avalanche, they began to shout and scream, and as a body, ran for the ark. Among them were Seltan and Jaseth, and being vigorous and strong, they were the first to reach the plank which led to the ship's door.

Noah had ceased to warn the people, to plead for repentance, when he had seen their first reaction and their mocking, pointed fingers. By the time they fled toward him, he had ceased to call them forth.

But when he saw Seltan's determination and heard Jaseth's cries, when he realized that even Moricahn followed close behind them, intent on entering in, his heart leaped. "They shall be saved!" he told himself. And he reached down from the doorway, ready to raise them to safety—along with all others—men, women, little ones, the elderly, any who would come.

The plank was full, Seltan nearest the top, and his pursuers scrambling over one another. Lightning rent the heavens. Thunder pealed. Noah shivered violently and reached forth, clinging to the doorpost as the wind tore at his fingers.

But, suddenly, the plank gave way. The sturdy gopher-wood ramp which had borne the weight of elephants, broke into slivers and shattered to the ground, taking with it all who climbed upon it.

"My God!" Noah pleaded.

And yet they would not give up. They sought footholds on the ark's siding, and Jaseth, stepping upon the backs of his companions, nearly reached the door once again.

Noah, straining to help him, could feel the nearing warmth of his brother's crabbed hand, before the tempest pushed him back—back into the ship's interior.

Sprawled upon the floor, the preacher sat up stunned, hearing the cries of his fellow villagers.

And then the door was shut. By the hand of God it was slammed and locked!

He leaped up and threw himself against it, but it would not move. He beat upon it with his fist, and kicked against the bolting bar. But the door would not open.

Outside, the storm was rising, mixing its lament with the terror of Noah's people.

"God!" he shrieked, digging his nails into his scalp and weeping.

His sons had seen it all. They had come upon him just as the door was closed, and they drew around him in a circle. Shem reached out and touched his shoulder, but he wrenched away with an angry cry.

"Come, Father!" Ham demanded, bending down and lifting Noah's rebellious, knotted body to its feet.

The three men led him to the cabin, where the eight passengers of Yahweh, the only remnant of Adlandia, would wait out the holocaust of God's tears.

ELEVEN

For months Poseidon had watched the changes in sea and sky. His sophisticated instruments and the word of his wise men had kept him keenly aware of the alterations.

It could not be said that he or any of his fellow Daemons had ever been *deceived* by Lucifer. They had willingly followed his rebellion against Yahweh in the mists of history, before the earth had been populated. They had simply believed that Lucifer *could* be raised to the throne of heaven, and that such a thing would benefit them in their prideful longing for power. And so they had supported him. Even after they had been evicted from the heavenly realms with their mentor, they had for eons operated from this premise, their rebellion continuing in an insane assumption that they would ultimately prevail.

Humankind had been the unwitting victims of this madness. Unwitting but not ultimately innocent. They had been caught up in its wake, without a full understanding of its origins or extent. As humanity went about its daily experience, it realized only vaguely the part it played in the universal drama, as pawns of the mercenary Overlords and objects of Yahweh's unflagging love.

As to the question of *why* Yahweh had allowed such victimization, the Edenic tale held the key. It seemed that, of all the planets in the universe, earth was the only one on which such a drama of temptation, fall, and redemption would be played out—for it was the only one

285

whose Prince had rebelled against the Lord, and whose original parents would be forced to make a choice by faith alone.

Poseidon and his kind had the full story. But in their pride they continued to follow their leader, Satan. And only now was the imminence of their demise drawing upon them.

The sea god stood within the expansive porch of his temple, where years before the simple mountain man had stirred his wrath with insane predictions. He knew now that the prophecies were true. The pillars which rose to the unroofed sky trembled. Inside, his minions had taken refuge in the underground caverns of his aquarium. But, as he watched the deepening gloom of the canopy, as his eyes were seared by sunlight piercing through the veil to the shining sea, he knew there was no safety.

He looked to the shore, where the beach was disintegrating. Tall plumes of steam rose from the magma beneath as cold waves spilled over it. When the torrent began, crashing unhampered through his roofless home, he started to quiver. And it seemed he could hear the cry of the dead as they called to him from the eternal pit, the everlasting fire "prepared for the devil and his angels."

"You who have kept not your first estate, who have done the great abomination, shall be judged!" they shouted. "Reserved in everlasting chains of darkness! Hell from beneath is moved for you to meet you at your coming!" they railed. "We await, Poseidon. We stir up the dead for you, even all leaders of earth, and all kings of past nations!"

The Daemon fell back, wiping the rain from his mighty brow and lifting his face to the sky. "Lucifer!" he cried. "Save me!"

But the chants and the taunts of his spirit-comrades filled his ears. "Your glory is brought down to the grave!" they cried. "How art thou fallen, O Lucifer, Son of Morning! And how art your minions destroyed. How art thou cut down to the ground, who did weaken the nations! You and all those who made the earth to tremble and did shake kingdoms with your rule!"

The sea was boiling, lifting hot fingers toward the temple's marble steps.

The voices from the pit mixed in an eerie chorus with the warring elements. "Tartarus!" they called. "Tartarus is prepared! Hades, home of the tormented. Tartarus, domain of the doomed!"

And as the steps broke up, as the mighty Daemon lost his footing, his magnificent body drawn irresistibly toward the sulfuric stench of the underworld, no one mourned him. The red shimmer of his tunic melded with the licking flames, and his helpless cries with the song of the damned.

TWELVE

The pull of the moon against the earth and the pull of
the earth against the moon had set in motion a chain of
geologic, subterranean, volcanic, and tectonic events
which would not cease until the planet was torn asunder.
The waters of the great deep, all the oceanic currents and
boiling fountains beneath earth's crust broke forth as the
canopy dissolved. The deluge which would envelop all
land and all mountains not only descended from the skies,
but rose from the depths of the sea and from the cavernous
reservoirs and hot cisterns of the convulsing magma.

Sea beds rose and fell; granite pinnacles toppled to valley floors; shale plates were heaved atop shifting strata
of sandstone; streams of molten lava, running like rivers,
sought the lowest levels in which to cool—in brine, in
marbly sheets of hail—and it sent up shoots of steam,
hundreds of feet high, where it touched the rising flood.

Gigantic tidal waves swept over the lip of the continent,
which had cracked along its natural faults. And great
clumps of terrain broke from the mainland and drowned
beneath the heaving sea.

Life clung to whatever would support it, insects riveted
themselves to passing reeds, birds to limbs of uprooted
trees. Four-legged creatures hid in caves and scrambled
for higher ground, ever higher ground.

Human beings in towns distant from the ocean sought
refuge atop tall buildings, and turned their eyes to the

highlands as they saw the waters encroach steadily from sea level.

But in all parts of the world, the deluge was imminent. Even at the highest elevations, the terrain slipped and washed away, eroded for the first time by unharnessed elements.

Within the ark, the passengers—people and animals— rode the billows in a craft which alternately lunged prow downward toward something bottomless, or shot straight up, a slick bullet of resin and wood. Or they were rocked back and forth, thrown against the walls, clinging to whatever was handy.

Because the ark was a floating barge, and not a sailing vessel, it was indestructible. The ship cooperated so well with the movements of the sea, molding herself like a leaf to the convulsing surface, that she was impervious to the giant waves, no matter how violently they sought to overthrow her.

The passengers suffered from the thrashing, but in the end, no one would be the worse for it. For the tossing they received was more a heaving and a lunging than a crashing and a battering.

The first six days of Yahweh's wrath were the most terrifying. It was impossible to discern, most of the time, what was the crying chorus of fear-filled creatures and what the howling of the elements. Noah longed to walk the halls of the ship, to peek into the cages and speak reassuringly to the beasts. But so erratic were the movements of the craft that no one could make such a journey. He only hoped that the creatures were lying low, keeping close to the floors of their compartments, as he and his family had learned to do. Fortunately, no cage was large enough to allow an animal to be thrown great distance. And the little apartments, lined with hay, were reasonably safe for the storm-tossed occupants.

After the sixth day, the waters seemed to level out. The torrent could still be heard on the cabin roof, and distant rumblings indicated that the planet was still in upheaval, but the ark's movement had calmed to only a perpetual rising, as the craft was borne higher and higher by the ascending flood.

As soon as the ship ceased its violent tossing, Noah made his way down the stairs from the family quarters. The soft yellow light of his hand-held lantern illumined the corridor lined by cages, berths, and perches. The animals were surprisingly quiet, he thought.

He gently thrust his lamp toward the first cage, and found a huddle of brown fur clinging to the lattice which ranged up one side. This was the koala den, and a soft whimpering could be heard where the animals hung together, not sure the worst was over.

"It is all right," Noah spoke soothingly. He unlatched the gate and reached in to rustle a pile of eucalyptus leaves upon which they would feast soon enough. Then he wandered further, hearing the bleating of sheep a few doors down. He remembered visiting village fairs, where the finest farm animals were displayed in competitions. They had had much less room than these fellows, and had managed well enough for days at a time. But the fear in the large round eyes of these wooly creatures was not due to confinement. Noah pushed the upper shutter aside and bent over the waist-high gate. The sheep fell back, skittish, the whites of their eyes flashing as they strained against one another.

"It is all right," he said again, holding his hand steady above their heads until they ceased to flinch.

And so he continued from cage to cage—from the tunnel holds of the burrowing creatures, to the sandpits of the scaly ones; from tall aviaries containing numerous feathered species to the even taller spaces of giraffes and ostriches. Every compartment had been outfitted, zoolike, to resemble as closely as possible the natural habitat of each type. Everything had been considered, from adorning vegetation which approximated home, to the gravelly ground or mossy rocks which would be more comforting to some. Such accoutrements were permanently affixed to walls and floors, and during the most violent moments of the catastrophe, had added no hazard.

After all, years had been afforded for thinking out the most minute details. And Noah had not known how long his cargo would be obliged to dwell in the craft. Therefore, he had spared no lengths in preparing for their needs.

Still, their natural fear of it all distressed him. This was his first contact with them since the door of the ark had shut. And their wide eyes, their occasional troubled cries raised his skin in gooseflesh. For they reminded him of the lost ones, the panicked beings, human and animal, who had drowned in a sea of terror.

As he made his way back through the hall, stumbling up the stairs, the thought of what might be floating outside nauseated him. He was glad the ark's only window was shuttered. He was grateful he could not see the destruction beyond, and that he had been unable to witness death's victories.

THIRTEEN

The rains continued forty days and forty nights. And when they subsided, the ark continued to rise on the ascending flood. Apparently the continent was sinking and the waters beneath the earth's crust were inundating the planet.

The passengers of the ark could not see that all the high mountains everywhere under heaven were being submerged. But the eight occupants knew that Yahweh's will would not be satisfied until this was the case. They were not able to watch the waters rise a full fifteen cubits above the loftiest peaks, but with their timing instruments, one advancement Noah had allowed himself, they were able to calculate that the flood prevailed one hundred and fifty days before abating.

The resined walls of the cabin, hardened to a shellac, reflected in their golden surface the stove light which the women kept burning day and night.

Day and night, Naamah thought silently, as she studied her husband's sleeping form. *I wonder if there is day outside, or night? I wonder if the sun has fallen with the sky, and if this fire is the only light we shall ever see again!*

At least there was no more storm. Rumblings of the collapsing earth could be heard now and then, and occasionally the waters heaved ominously. But life upon the ark had settled to a maddening calm for the past weeks.

The routine Noah had established was the only thing

which helped maintain sanity on board—that and the camaraderie which the family, as well as the animals, must abide by.

But even with the schedule of daily inspections up and down rows of cages, the lighting and extinguishing of many lanterns in the corridors to provide the creatures a semblance of night and day, and the ongoing cleanings and feedings, there was an oppressiveness which sometimes threatened mania.

Naamah's husband rested peacefully on one of the upholstered divans which she and the three daughters-in-law had designed, and which the men had bolted to the cabin walls. She marveled at Noah's strength of purpose and the inner peace which he seemed to maintain so easily.

Her mind drifted from his composed face to thoughts of her children and their wives who slept in adjoining rooms. The sons had done well in choosing life partners. Carise, especially, had served the family commendably. She seemed to know, by instinct, when the various animals were in need of attention. And they followed her willingly from their cages for moments of exercise up and down the narrow halls. At the end of each deck was an open space, meant for such purposes, and even the largest beasts looked forward to their stints with the energetic nature lover.

When Naamah had married the Sethite a lifetime ago, she had known the years would bring experiences worth far more than all the normalcy she might sacrifice. She loved him with a zeal unquenched by trial and test. But of late, she felt her mind slipping. How long could they endure the prison of the ark?

Naamah had never roused her husband from sleep out of selfish need in all their married life. But today she reached out a hesitant finger and nudged him from slumber.

"I fear, my lord," she whispered as he opened his eyes.

"What is it?" he asked, starting anxiously.

"The walls are closing in on me." She trembled.

Noah drew her close. "God is with us," he offered, caressing her cold hands.

"How do you know?" she pleaded, shaking her head. "Perhaps he has forgotten us. Perhaps after all is said and done we have kept our part of the obligation, but he will forget his."

Noah smiled tenderly. "How can we doubt, when everything he said would happen has come to pass?"

Naamah was silent, choked by frustration. But suddenly, Noah sat up rigid and straight. "Listen," he said. "Do you hear it?"

The woman heard nothing, but did as he asked, cocking her head to one side.

"Listen!" he insisted.

And then she could discern it, the faint, distant sound of a mighty wind.

"The storm!" she cried, clutching him. "It is upon us again!"

"No—listen!" he commanded.

It rose steadily, coming nearer. And its droning seemed almost musical—a symphony of exultation, sweeping over the waters.

"He has not forgotten us!" Noah exclaimed. "This is the Voice of God!"

The wind continued five months. The fountains of the deep and the floodgates of the sky were closed. The rain ceased. During the cataclysm the ocean basins had dropped, and steadily the water receded into them.

And in the seventh month after the rains had begun, on the seventeenth day, the hull of the ark scraped solid ground and the great barge rested on the mountains of Ararat.

FOURTEEN

"Is it day outside, or night?" Japheth asked as the dishes were cleared from the table.

"I believe it is day," Noah replied, noting his son's wistful expression. "We will go out soon."

"Can we not just peek outside?" he begged. "Surely by now the mountaintops are visible."

"Yahweh has not told me it is time," the Sethite explained.

The prophet ached for his children. Shem, busily helping the womenfolk, hid a frustrated longing for action; and Ham, who had called Noah "Father" when the rains began, now sat in a corner of the hold, his ebony frame blending with the shadows, a mirror of his spirit.

The dark son watched his wife, Carise, bending over the low oven to feed the little fire. Whenever he looked on her it was with the same stirrings he had felt the day he first saw her at the bedouin camp. And, as they had lived in close quarters with his brothers, suppressed seeds of jealousy had sprouted. He grew suspicious of any lingering glance on the part of Shem or Japheth. He was possessive toward the wild beauty he had captured, and dreamed of the day they would have personal space once more.

He would build an empire! he told himself. Carise would bear him many sons, many daughters, and the world would be his to conquer. The fact that his progeny would have to procreate with Shemites and Japhethites troubled him only a little. The Hamitic strain would dominate, he reasoned. And they would rule the earth.

Noah scrutinized the lift of Ham's chin. He wondered what his son fantasized, and he feared to know.

But their thoughts were interrupted. "Have you noticed the roebucks' antlers?" Carise expounded, as she prodded the fire's smoldering embers. "They are in velvet. Soon the feuding for the does will begin. It is an instinct we cannot hold down."

She hoped Noah had a solution. But he could only say, "The Lord will tell us when to go outside. Then the bucks will stake out their territories and take their ladies where they will."

The dove and the raven were fighting again. It was happening too often, and the women feared the black scavenger would one day kill the gentler bird.

Naamah had strange feelings about the pair. There were six others of each kind, and none possessed such personalities as these displayed.

She had noticed it the day they entered the ark, when the raven pushed past the dove, choosing the highest perch for himself, battling all others for the dominant position.

"He seems to have a spirit," she had commented to Noah. "It unnerves me."

The preacher had said nothing, but kept the knowledge to himself—the understanding that the ark must bear the seeds of good and evil, as had Eden. And the knowledge that human choices would once again be required to lay the foundation of history.

FIFTEEN

The day came for the window to be opened.

The two feathered antagonists roused the ship that morning with their quarreling, and Noah strode to their cage, thrusting his hand into the din of squabbling, cawing creatures and grasping the raven by his bristled neck.

"Out with you!" he cried. "But you shall do a service before receiving freedom!"

He carried the struggling bird to the top deck, followed closely by Naamah and the family. Excitement marked their bearing as the long-confined humans trod the last steps to the bolted window—the only window on the ark.

Their enthusiasm passed to the caged creatures all about them, giving rise to cries, barks, howls, and chittering—until the whole ship was a cacophony of anticipation.

The Sethite, his brow furrowed, lifted the heavy bar which held the shutter fast, and with a mighty heave, he flung wide the aperture.

Blazing sunlight flooded the dank interior, and the passengers fell back with sighs of wonder. Noah shielded his eyes, unaccustomed to such glory, and flung the dark emissary through the opening. "Go to!" he cried. "Seek dry land, and if you must return, do not reenter the ark! Wait on the upper roost, until you can be gone for good!"

The raven, staring back at him hatefully, did as he was commanded, objecting with a wicked screech.

Then, trembling, Noah ascended the ladder until he could see the world beyond. A hush came over the family.

"What is it, Father?" Shem cried at last. "What does it look like?"

Noah had no word to describe the sky. "Son, do you recall the color of cornflowers? The hue of Japheth's eyes?"

"I do," he laughed.

"The sky—the sky is no longer white, but vivid as lapis lazuli."

The family murmured their amazement, and Naamah pushed forward. "And the sea, husband. What of the sea?"

"It is calm," he assured her. "But it is a mirror of the sky, a sheet of turquoise."

The passengers scrambled for the window, tugging at Noah's skirts. But he reached up and shut the window with a slam. "Another day," he commanded. "You will see it all another day."

The family shouted their objections, but Noah would hear none of it. And he kept the ugliness of the world a secret. Only he had seen the raven swoop for carrion—the flotsam of death which still lingered on the waters. He would show his people their new domain when the old was fully gone.

It was the dove who would find the first sign of new life. Twice, in secret, the prophet ascended the window ladder to see if the waters had abated. The first time the lovely white bird, whom he released for this mission, flew out and back, having found no resting place. With a disappointed flutter, she landed on Noah's outstretched arm. He cupped her to his bosom and returned her to the cage, but a week later sent her forth again.

This time she disappeared for the entire day, and he anxiously awaited her return, sending away his sons who came looking for him.

Toward evening he spied her flying back from some distant place, a shining object in her beak. His heart leaped as he recognized it, a fresh-plucked olive leaf—wet, but green and tender!

Grasping the dove to himself, he raised the leaf in thanksgiving and called for his family.

"See!" he cried. "Life has returned to the land, and so shall we!"

SIXTEEN

When the ground was dry, one year and ten days after the rains had begun, the eight passengers of the ark, the only human survivors of the Great Deluge, set foot on earth's surface.

They left the vessel as they had entered it, at the command of Yahweh. And it was to an alien and eerie world that they descended. They might as well have been transported to some distant planet, so foreign was this place.

First to strike the family, as it had Noah, was the blinding blue of the sky. And then the desolation of the landscape, sculpted as if by a madman's hand, with gorges and fissures and heaps of clay rubble. The ground had literally turned inside out, leaving mountains where valleys once had been, and replacing hills with plains. Terrifying streams coursed down the sides of the Ararat range upon which the ark had settled, and ran through a wilderness devoid of green.

Only the barest hint of new shoots, scattered about the ground as far as the eye could see, gave evidence of returning vegetation.

And across the planet's surface, from which clouds of steam still rose to the naked sky, whistled a dry, relentless wind.

The animals, released from their cages, followed the family down a new ramp, one which Noah and his sons had created from a few pieces of dismantled siding. At first eager to be free, most of the creatures paused before exiting the ship's door, as if stunned by the strange environment. Some of them, actually preferring the safety of their family quarters, had to be prodded down the runway.

But at last all the cargo and the eight humans stood on the sloping mountain peak, studying the world below. And as Noah began his first tentative trek down the heights, the others lingered behind, afraid to follow.

The prophet stepped lightly upon the ground, uncertain of its consistency; but gaining courage, he walked with more confidence until he came to a little rise from which he could take in the sweep of territories before him. Trembling, he fell to his knees and buried his face in his hands, until tears spilled through his fingers and over his beard and his shoulders shook with quiet tremors. Then, without looking back, he began to pick up the loaf-sized stones which dappled the surface of the small plateau.

One by one he gathered them into a pile, and when his sons perceived his intention, they joined him on the slope.

Within an hour an altar was built, and by evening the first work of man's hands in the new world sent the musk of gray smoke and red sparks into the fresh-born sky. Of every clean animal and bird, the seventh out of seven, Yahweh's number, was offered in sacrifice, and three pair of each were left alive.

With dawn, Noah turned for the ark, the blood of his ministry caked upon his hands. His three sons, weary with the ordeal, followed until they reached the door.

But just as they were about to enter, the father stopped short and turned a furtive glance toward the open slope of the mount.

Raising a finger to his lips, he hushed his children and bid them study the landscape with him.

"Listen," he whispered. "The footsteps of Yahweh."

Shem, Ham, and Japheth looked narrowly at one another, but Noah paid them no mind. "Listen and watch!" he commanded.

The first rays of morning were just peeking over the eastern sky, filtering through the pure gray of disappearing night. Along the incline ascending from the valley floor could be seen the figure of a man walking, staff in hand, toward the Ark of Ararat.

Wafts of dissipating altar-smoke rode down the cool air toward him, and he seemed to lift his chin, inhaling the aroma deeply. When he was within earshot, he gestured a greeting and stopped, stationing himself beside his walking stick. He turned then, and with a sweep of his arm, took in the disheveled terrain.

"Never again," he cried, "will I curse the ground because of mankind! For the intent of man's heart is evil from his youth!"

The three sons shuddered, their flesh tingling, and when the Lord turned his gaze back toward them, they shrank with awe. "And I will never again destroy every living thing, as I have done," the Stranger called.

Then, trekking further up the mount, he declared, "While the earth remains, seedtime and harvest, cold and heat, summer and winter, day and night shall not cease. This is the new pattern, the new cycle and the new decree!"

The men did not fully understand such things. In the temperate, constant clime to which they were accustomed, there were no seasonal changes. But they did not question the One who now stood directly before them.

The Lord lifted his hands and placed them on the heads of the three sons. "Be fruitful and multiply, and fill the earth," he commanded.

Then, stepping to the edge of the plank, he observed the congregation of docile creatures who had spent the past year cooperating with the shipbound humans. It seemed he was pleased that the beasts stood before him in the beauty of their intended form, and he would protect their integrity at all costs, by giving them a more intense dread of man than they had known: "The fear of you and the terror of you shall be on every beast of the earth and on every bird of the sky," he pronounced. No longer would they dwell peaceably with Noah and his descendants as they had upon the ark.

And then, acknowledging that the earth would no longer yield her harvest as freely as before, and knowing that they had already violated the strict vegetarianism of Eden, Yahweh made the following concession: "With everything that creeps on the ground and all fish of the sea, into your hand they are given. Every moving thing that is alive shall be food for you. I give all to you, as I gave the green plant."

The Lord studied the faces of his four listeners and his eyes penetrated their souls. As if remembering the violence and evil which he had wiped away with the flood, he warned, "Surely I will require your lifeblood. From every beast I will require it. And from every man, from every man's brother I will require the life of a man. Whoever sheds man's blood, by man shall his blood be shed. For in the image of God was man created."

Then, his demeanor softening, he lifted his hands once again and touched the three lads.

"As for you . . . be fruitful and multiply," he repeated, a smile working at the edges of his lips. "Populate the earth abundantly and multiply in it!"

Focusing next on Noah, he spoke tenderly, "Now, behold, I myself do establish my covenant with you and with your descendants after you, and with every living creature. Never again shall all life be cut off by a deluge, neither shall there be a flood to destroy the earth."

As he said this the dawn behind him was glorious with light, and the Lord directed their attention toward the cloud-dappled sky. Across it an incredible ribbon of color, a spectrum of lavenders, blues, greens, yellows, and reds, refracted and bent through the prism of rainy vapor which lingered on the air.

"This is the sign of the covenant," he declared, "which I am making between me and you and every living creature that is with you, for all generations to come. I set my bow in the cloud, and it shall be for a sign of covenant between me and the earth. And it shall come about, when I bring a cloud over the earth, that the bow shall be in it, and I will look upon it to remember my everlasting covenant. And never again shall the water destroy all flesh that is on the earth."

P A R T V
THE SEED OF ARARAT

The sons of Noah who went forth from the ark were Shem, Ham, and Japheth. Ham was the father of Canaan. These three were the sons of Noah; and from these the whole earth was peopled.

Genesis 9:18, 19, RSV

ONE

From the summits of Ararat flowed the headwaters of the mighty river one day to be called "Euphrates," "The Fruitful." Noah and his family discovered soon after settling in their new world that the land along the river was extremely fertile, and "seedtime," as the Lord had called it, followed directly on the wake of the deluge.

It had been nearly two years since they left the ark. The days of tender shoots had passed for the second time, and harvest would shortly be upon them once again. Noah stood between two rows of maize and shielded his eyes against the glare of midday sun, something he had never needed to do in Adlandia. He studied the uppermost peaks of Ararat where an early blanket of snow had descended, a phenomenon he had only heard theorized of in the legends of Olympus, and for which he must create a name. Down the slopes from the snowline there were heavy gray clouds, and Noah could see, where the sun hit the mountainside, that they dropped sheets of rain across its face.

He remembered the first time the family had seen rain following the flood. They had watched from the plateau below the ark as it had swept in across the plain, and the women had begun to cry. Naamah, her sons, and their wives began running for the ship, until Noah called them to a halt.

"Remember the covenant!" he had shouted. "Why do

you fear? The rain will not harm us again."

But it had not been easy for them to believe. Even the prophet had felt pangs of terror at first sight of the downpour. He had allowed them all to watch from the doorway, the women clinging to their husbands, while Noah stood obstinately in the middle of the drenching cold.

Since that day, the changing seasons and alternating cycles were not so dreadful. Often, following a storm, the rainbow would appear—smaller, not so glorious as the first. But always it reminded him of the covenant, and of the day at the dolphin rock, when the Lord, through his creature, had said, "Rejoice, son of man! Rejoice!"

Noah rubbed the small of his back, sore from laboring with the hoe in his large garden plot. Though the soil was fertile, it was stony, unpredictable and more difficult to work than the ground of the old world. Down the row were the wives of Shem and Japheth, faces veiled to protect their fairer skin from the burning rays of the unveiled sun. And beyond them was Naamah, who complained these days of dry skin, and sought many cures, frequently spending her evenings mixing animal fats and oils in experimental creams.

The Sethite had chided her once over such vanity. "No woman could be more beautiful than you!" he had laughed. But even he was privately troubled by premature signs of aging which showed themselves in little splotches on his own hands and tiny creases at the corners of his eyes. Such symptoms had not shown up in Lamech until he was much, much older.

But, whatever the physical changes produced by the fallen canopy and the blaring elements, the eight of them were alive. And across the way, beyond the garden and toward the four tents which the couples had erected, was Carise, her belly swollen with the first of a new generation—a new beginning for humankind.

Yes—Ham would see one dream fulfilled: to be the first of Noah's sons to have a son.

The lively bedouin girl kept close to the small circle of shelters these days. She would have been off with her husband this morning, to seek wild game from the small herds born the first spring. But instead, she managed the growing number of cattle which the family had retained from the dispersed cargo.

She, too, rubbed the small of her back which ached from her front-heavy form. She wistfully studied the plain where only a few of the ark's animals could still be seen, gazelles and antelope who were at home in such a place. All others had wandered away to environs which would better suit them, to the heights of cold mountains or the heat of great deserts. As the world had altered, so had the needs of the creatures, and for every strange terrain, there would be proper inhabitants.

She wondered what life would be like for the stirring child within her womb. She prodded the haunches of the milk-cow, and sat down to fill her pail with the animal's frothy gift. Soon her own breasts would nurse an infant, and as she pressed her head against the cow's warm flank, she eyed her simple home and a tear rose to her lashes. She had grown up a nomad, but had always longed for a house of substance. Ham had asked his father to let him build for her a residence from the ship's wood. But the old preacher had been stubborn.

"It is the Ark of Yahweh," he had insisted. "In time the earth will give us lumber from her mountains. But we will not dismantle the memory of God's salvation. The ark must stand forever, a sign to coming generations of the faithfulness of God."

She understood. She would want her son to see the vessel. She would want to tell him of the flood and of the world as it had been.

But Ham had rebelled. It seemed his reconciliation with his father had been only tentative; and he took even this petty opportunity to be at odds with Noah. Just this morning he had stroked Carise's round belly and declared,

"I will one day build for you a mansion, my wife! We will set out on our own, to find wealth in the earth, and glory!"

And then, his quiver on his back, bow in hand, he had headed for the hunting plain.

Noah left the cornfield and came up beside Carise. "What is it, daughter?" he inquired gently. "Why do you weep?"

"The child," she whispered.

"Does the baby cause you pain?" he asked anxiously.

Carise stopped her milking, and the drops of white liquid settled to a quiet puddle in the pail.

"No—not the baby," she replied, her dark eyes wet with tears. "The baby causes me great joy. But for Ham, the child only piques his pride, and sets his mind on conquest."

TWO

The day the son of Ham was born was a day for celebration. It was harvest time, and while the earth had yielded a bounty, Carise had produced a handsome child, black and comely with a loud, earthy cry.

"His name shall be 'Canaan,'" Ham had declared, meaning "valley." Raising the wriggling babe toward heaven, he had explained, "For he shall be fertile as the Euphrates, and prosperous as the red earth!"

Several days before the birth, Naamah, Sindra, and Elsbeth had stomped grapes from the vineyard which grew alongside Noah's dwelling, and they had prepared meal-cakes and tender veal for the imminent feast. The skins of fresh grape juice they had set near the birthing tent, and the day before the party they had spread the food under linen cloths for the coming revelry.

The women had noticed, as they awaited the event, that the skins which stored the juice, though in the tent's shadow, were expanding. But they could not know that fermentation would occur more quickly under the vapor-less sky than it had in Adlandia.

When the day of the feast arrived, Noah drank deeply of the red liquid, and felt its spirit warm his throat. He was used to the taste of Lamech's wine, and had occasionally imbibed with the men at the mill, but he had never been so accustomed as to develop resistance to its effects.

He told himself that the drinks could not possibly be inebriating. The wine could not possibly have turned so soon.

But he was fooling himself. The truth was that he enjoyed the pleasant haze which fell over the spinning women as they danced to Japheth's flute, and he found the muted sense of sound and color pleasurable.

The labors of past weeks, the muscles strained from harvest and the memories of the green world which was lost forever seemed less painful with each gulp.

And he was able to laugh when he saw Ham's narrow glances; he was able to shrug off the hurt which his alienation had pricked.

"Drink with me!" he called to his dark son, patting the ground at his side. "Sit here and drink with me!"

The new father rose from his position at the head of the feast and came to Noah warily. He sat down and shared his wineskin, but handed it back with a suspicious nod.

"*You* drink, sir. And I will watch," he urged.

"So—yes. You watch," Noah slurred. "I will drink."

The women allowed the patriarch to handle the newborn infant for only a moment that day. By early evening, Naamah had ushered Noah off to his tent. "Stay with me," he had laughed, grasping for her. But she had preferred to return to the family, and bowed away gracefully.

The music, dancing, and laughter continued into the night, and as the lanterns were lit, Ham slipped quietly away from the bright circle.

Stealthily he drew near the patriarch's dwelling. A full moon shown through a flock of passing clouds in the harvest sky. Ham needed no light to illumine the tent's interior when he opened the flap. What he saw delighted his rebellious heart. In the privacy of Noah's stupor the patriarch lay exposed—naked before the one who had always scorned him.

"Ha!" Ham cried. But Noah, his eyes rolled up in his sotted head, did not stir.

"Ha!" the dark son bellowed, staggering hilariously toward the revelers. "Come see the righteous prophet!" he called, gesturing toward his father's abode. "See Yahweh's chosen one! How he serves his Creator in the fullness of natural glory!"

The music ceased, and the women stood still. Shem and Japheth, perplexed, rose and went to Ham with furrowed brows.

"See!" he repeated. "The holy one! Naked as the infant born this day!"

Shem stopped short and drew Japheth back from the tent. "Do not go in!" he commanded. "Our father has done shamefully."

Suddenly the youngest understood. "You mean. . . ."

"Yes." Shem nodded.

"Oh," Japheth stammered, a blush rising to his pale cheeks. "But Ham—how could you?"

"He could because he does not love Noah!" Shem growled, turning blazing eyes on the mocking defiler.

Ham began to mimic the supposed behavior of his father, swaying in the moonlight and stripping off his cloak. Shem, indignant, clutched the garment as it was flung to the ground and thrust a corner of it into Japheth's hands.

"We will walk backward," he ordered, carrying another corner himself. "And we will cover our father's body without a glance."

Japheth agreed and followed Shem's lead as they treaded lightly toward the door, keeping their gaze fixed outside.

They could hear Noah's heavy, sonorous breathing behind them as they gingerly draped him with the mantle. And when they had completed the task, they exited, closing the flap with respect.

Ham found this all more than he could bear, and doubling over with laughter, departed from their scowling presence, into the Ararat plain. His hilarity filled the silent valley where music had died away, and only the cries of little Canaan competed.

THREE

The patriarch sat outside his tent the next morning with his head in his hands. His brain throbbed and his tongue pushed against the sides and roof of his mouth.

He was wrapped in the mantle which his sons had spread over him—the garment of Ham. And he felt the foolishness of his condition, but had no strength to correct it. *So,* he thought to himself, as he watched the ground through a blur of regret, *this is the prophet of God!*

He struck his thigh with his fist, and reviled his own name. But in an instant, Naamah was at his shoulder.

"Your trials have been great," she spoke gently, "your integrity impeccable. Why do you expect perfection of yourself?"

But no reasoning would assuage his guilt. He peered at her with red eyes and shook his aching head. "I have tried to teach my sons the ways of God. How shall they ever listen to me again?"

Naamah's heart wrenched with her husband's agony, but she had no words to comfort him.

"I was always a sober man," he droned.

"You were, indeed, my lord," Naamah assured him. "It is sometimes true, however, that in an undefended moment our least likely enemy may overtake us."

Noah stood up, grasping the tent pole for support. A sneer of self-disgust translated itself into blaming anger. "Enemy? Do you speak of the wine or of my son Ham?"

The woman watched him painfully as he staggered away from the dwelling. "Ham has no power over you!" she cried. "Why do you let him torment you? His stony heart will only be his own demise."

The patriarch stopped short and stood silent a long while. A great heaviness settled over him, and a shudder of sorrow worked across his back. Turning to Naamah, his eyes full of remorse, he cried, "I want only the best for him! Do you think I would be happy to see him suffer?"

Naamah rose and ran to her husband, clinging to him. "Oh, my lord, I know! I know you love him."

The prophet studied the plain where Ham had last been seen and wondered when he would return. Within Carise's tent, the new mother and child were just waking. A whimper could be heard as the baby was raised to her breast, and Noah trembled at the sound, saying, "I fear the son of Ham shall be the one to suffer—the undeserving victim of his father's spurned estate."

FOUR

When Ham returned to his wife and child, it was with news of a beautiful valley to the east, the plain one day to be called "Shinar." There, he insisted, he would found his empire and establish his future descendants. "It is lush, green . . . and empty," he laughed ironically. "Strange, that I who have always longed to conquer, should be saved to triumph over an empty world. A victor, they shall call me, who had no enemies!"

Carise listened patiently as they loaded their few possessions into a small cart constructed from materials brought on the ark. "Every man has an enemy," she commented quietly, "even if it is his own soul."

Ham pretended not to hear, and lifted her to the wagon seat, handing her the swaddled baby.

Noah came out to watch the preparations and stepped up to the little ox-powered vehicle. He stroked the harness belt of the bulky creature who would take his middle son away. The other family members stood nearby in a cluster, the women crying softly as Carise turned moist eyes toward them.

"So you are determined to do this thing?" Noah asked as Ham settled onto the driver's bench.

"I am," was the cryptic reply. "There shall be a throne for me and a nation, though I must create it from my own sweat and my own loins!"

Noah grasped him by the knee and warned, "Beware,

son, lest your glory turn to dust and your freedom to slavery. One day your unforgiving heart will be your ruin, and Canaan shall bear the curse. A servant of servants shall be he to his brothers."

Ham drew away and lifted his gaze to the ark's pinnacle. "Even the troublesome raven whom you evicted went out to claim a territory. Shall I, the dark son, do any less? Curse me if you wish, Father. I flee to claim my destiny."

In a strong, shining hand, Ham raised the whip and the ox started. As the little cart rolled down the verdant plain, Noah's throat grew tight. But though his voice was strangled, he called, "Remember Yahweh! Do not forget our God!"

Ham released a cynical laugh. "I will carve a niche for him in the hills of Shinar!" he cried back. "In the treeless world which he has left me!"

Noah heaved a sigh and flung his arms wide, drawing his other sons to him. His heart was broken irreparably as he shouted one last time toward the departing wagon. "So be it, then," his words rang forth in prophecy. "If this be your chosen way, then blessed be the Lord, the God of Shem, and let Canaan be his servant! May God enlarge Japheth, and let him dwell in the tents of Shem! And let Canaan serve them both!"

E   P   I   L   O   G   U   E

By faith Noah . . . became heir of the righteousness which is by faith.

Hebrews 11:7

And Jesus was . . . the son of Joseph . . . who was the son of David . . . who was the son of Shem, who was the son of Noah.

From the genealogy of Luke 3

Though it had been not so much a curse as a prediction, it had established the foundation of history. Once spoken, it became a reference point, and from it the streams of humanity would diverge.

The ark had cradled the seed of conflict, as had Eden. And Noah wondered how long it would be before the earth would spring forth in violence and corruption once again.

He sat beside the vessel this morning, musing over the little journal which he had kept hidden in its cabin locker since the Flood. In it were the haunting promises of his God and the tale of life in the lost Adlandia. He scanned its pages reverently, and then stood up, studying the great ship which had born the remnant of creation.

Shem joined him as he paced the porch of Ararat on which the vessel rested, and the son watched as the old man ran his hands down the rugged sides of gopher wood, and as he peered up the three stories where they were burnished in the sun. Often Noah came here and Shem usually accompanied him, listening to his reminiscences or readings from the little book.

The patriarch was nearly as old as Methuselah, now, and Shem past 400 years. From the Valley of Ararat, the human race had spread beyond counting, and had dispersed to lands so distant, Noah would never journey there. Ham's dream of conquest would be fulfilled by his descendants. The plain of Shinar, to which he carried his newborn son, would spawn the first glorious civilization of the post-Flood world, and on its heels would follow yet other mighty Hamitic empires. Shinar would be challenged by Yahweh only when it would begin to trample on his chain of order, as its predecessors had done. "A tower to reach heaven!" they would declare, just as the Adlandians had cried out "to be as the gods!" And the children of Shem and Japheth would fall prey to the same error.

But all this was yet future. For now, it was enough to rebuild the world.

Few doubted the tale of the Flood. The ark was a constant reminder. Noah had defended it from marauders and souvenir seekers countless times through the years, but rarely did anyone come these days to endure his stories of its voyage. And it often saddened him to hear how distorted the tale had become, how attached to legends of strange gods and fictitious plots.

Shem sat with him beside the place where the ramp had rested, long since fallen into disrepair, and as they ate a lunch packed by Naamah's gentle hands, the son scanned the mountaintop. The resting place of the ark had once been shrouded by the sky-canopy, and was therefore one of the legendary "Olympian" heights on which, before the deluge, no human foot had ever trod. Shem smiled quietly, remembering that to the Adlandians such places had been the "home of the gods." He then turned his gaze toward the village which had grown up at the base of the Ararat range.

"Strangers often journey through town," he commented. "Dark faces, light faces. Do you ever wonder if Yahweh might be among them?"

"I suppose he might," Noah nodded. "He has appeared in the past, and must appear from time to time. After all, this is his beloved world, you know."

Shem smiled, as the prophet raised a gnarled finger

toward the mists of Shinar. "All the land you see, and all the earth beyond our sight is his handiwork. One day, I believe, he will walk among us again, and this time he will stay, to be seen of all."

"I have heard you say this many times. But what of the others—the Fallen Ones? Will they return to rule the earth again?"

Noah laughed and shook his head. "Lucifer is never far away. He is only more subtle this time around. No, son—be sure that he does still have his minions and his power."

Shem found the prospect frightening and asked, "What of the Nephilim? Will there be giants in the earth again?"

"I think that such a thing is possible," the patriarch granted. "I do not know when or how—but Satan's ways are never very new. If nothing else, we know that many kings of earth are his puppets."

The son laughed heartily, enjoying the old man's wry humor.

"Well," he said lightly, "at least we can be certain that the earth will never be destroyed again by water."

But Noah was suddenly very somber, studying the smoke of the chimneys below. "No—not by water . . . ," he conceded.

Shem was perplexed. "Is there something troubling you, Father?" he asked.

Noah shook himself and turned wistful eyes to the lad. "The world repeats itself, you know," he explained. "Winter, summer, life, death, good, evil, decency, indecency. One day he will return, and as it was in the days before the Flood, so shall it be then."

"You mean," Shem whispered, "Yahweh will show his wrath once more?"

"His wrath and his salvation. *He* is the Ark of Safety, don't you see?"

Shem raised his face to the sunlit sky and Noah thought he could read the future in his son's strong forehead and upright countenance.

"You bear his blood in your veins," he suddenly pronounced. "The Son of God shall be a son of Shem!"

The younger Sethite studied the patriarch incredulously. "I do not understand," he marveled.

"One day history will cease its continual cycle," Noah said smiling. "A new heaven and new earth there will be. And the government of God will reign forever."

Shem caressed his father's stooped shoulders and stood to leave. As Noah watched him depart, he fondled the tattered journal which rested in his lap. Lifting it tenderly, he rose and entered the ark, secreting the little book into its private sanctuary.

When he reentered the daylight, his gaze turned toward Shinar and he remembered the eastern hills of the Adlandian coast. For a moment he thought he walked there again beside his God, and his eyes twinkled with the memory of Yahweh's touch.

If you've enjoyed this book you'll want to look for other fine
BIBLICAL NOVELS
from Tyndale House Publishers

Song of Abraham by Ellen Gunderson Traylor. This richly colorful novel unfolds the tumultuous saga of one man who founded a nation. Traylor's fascinating reconstruction of the life of Abraham portrays a man of strength, will, and purpose who remains unparalleled in history. Carefully researched and superbly told. Living Books 07-6071, $4.50.

John: Son of Thunder by Ellen Gunderson Traylor. A majestic novel that takes you right into the midst of the twelve disciples. Travel with John down desert paths, through the courts of the Holy City, and to the foot of the cross. Journey with him from his luxury as a privileged son of Israel to the bitter hardship of his exile on Patmos. Here is a saga of adventure, romance, and discovery—of a man bigger than life—the disciple "whom Jesus loved." Living Books 07-1903, $4.95.

Pontius Pilate by Paul L. Maier. A brilliant novel about this famous man in Roman history—the man who declared Jesus Christ innocent but nevertheless sent him to the cross. "A magnificent job ... tremendously rewarding reading"—*Christianity Today.* Living Books 07-4852, $3.95.

Elijah by William H. Stephens. A monumental biblical novel about one of God's greatest prophets, carefully researched for eight years and powerfully written. Here's a story of the battle between God and the gods, and the conflict between the sensual religion promoted by the pagan queen Jezebel and the revolutionary teachings proclaimed by Elijah. Living Books 07-4023, $4.50.

Ruth by Ellen Gunderson Traylor. Meet Ruth, a Moabitess, as she tries to understand her husband's people and finds herself slipping away from the harsh religion of Moab's god, Chemosh. Can she ever learn to be a child of Jehovah? Though the pain of separation and poverty would come upon her, Ruth was to become part of the very fulfillment of prophecy—and find true love on her own doorstep as well. Living Books 07-5809, $3.95.

Jonah by Ellen Gunderson Traylor. The saga of two nations, two kings, and the man who reached them both. An epic story of rebellion and obedience, *Jonah* tells of God's work in one man's soul to bring his word to those who might otherwise never have heard. Discover the life and times of Jonah. Trade paper 75-1946, $6.95.

Mary Magdalene by Ellen Gunderson Traylor. This gripping novel sweeps into the psyche of the renowned follower of Jesus, a woman whose sorrows rival her beauty. Interwoven with biblical narrative, the story of Mary Magdalene promises hope and healing for all wounded hearts. Living Books 07-4176, $3.95.

Hosea and Gomer by Marion Wyse. Here's a magnificent portrait of a man and a woman caught in a war between gods, a clash between nations, and a struggle between treacherous men. Rich characterizations and intriguing themes of love and hate, faith and fear, make this an unforgettable story. Living Books 07-1496, $3.95.

Marah: The Woman at the Well by Nina Mason Bergman. If you could talk with Marah, what would you learn about her life? We know she was a Samaritan, married five times and living with a man not her husband, but little else. *Marah* is one woman's story, the fictional account of what may have led her to that encounter with Jesus at midday by a well in Sychar. Full of insight, this novel encourages the reader to search for "sweeter waters." Living Books 07-4032, $3.50.

David & Bathsheba by Roberta Dorr. This epic love story comes radiantly alive through solid biblical and historical research combined with suspenseful storytelling. "Engrossing, encouraging—so that you do not want the book to end"—Catherine Marshall. Living Books 07-0618, $4.95.

Noah by Ellen Gunderson Traylor. In this imaginative biblical novel, Traylor paints a vivid picture of the pre-Flood world in which society's tamperings with nature had turned into serious abuse of God's creation. This story of the growth, struggles, and woes of the prophet Noah is a thrilling saga of faith and courage in the face of the greatest darkness man has ever seen. Trade paper 75-4703, $6.95.

The Flames of Rome by Paul L. Maier. Decadence. Murder. Sensuality. Cruelty. This was Rome in the time of the Caesars: a volatile blend of idealism and corruption. Into this explosive setting Christianity made a quiet—then shocking—entrance. Then power and faith met head-on in a clash that would change the world. Set in the time of the apostles and the early church. Living Books 07-0903, $4.95.

Ahaz: The Possessor by Constance Head. A biblical novel exploring the chaotic life of Ahaz, the faithless king of Judah, torn between the love of his beautiful wife, Abijah, and his devotion to the high priest, Ushna. *Ahaz: The Possessor* tells the turbulent story of one man's quest for peace—with his God, his nation, his wife, and himself. Living Books 07-0044, $3.95.

These books are available at your local Christian bookstore. If you're unable to find them, send a check with your order to cover the retail price plus 75¢ per book for postage and handling to: **Tyndale DMS, P.O. Box 80, Wheaton, Illinois 60189.** Prices and availability are subject to change without notice. Allow 4-6 weeks for delivery.